Dear Reader,

Crossed is the continuation of Cassia's ... , but I a
this as Ky's book. In it, we get to hear his voice and lea   r the
first time what truly happened to him when he lived in the Outer
Provinces. The landscape of the Outer Provinces is inspired
by my own home of southern Utah, a place of red rocks and
slot canyons and enormous desert skies. It's exactly the kind of
terrain that would produce a person like Ky.

In this story, Cassia and Ky must journey to find each other—and
they also discover that love is as beautiful and complicated and
intricate as any canyon. And, of course, Xander hasn't given up
yet!

My thanks for caring about these characters and for taking your
time to turn the pages of these books. Best wishes and happy
reading to you always!

Ally Condie

Ally Condie

ALLY CONDIE

the author of the Matched Trilogy,
was born and raised in southern Utah, a beautiful part of
the world that served as the inspiration for the setting of
CROSSED. Before becoming a writer, she taught high school
English in Utah and upstate New York. She lives with her
husband and three children outside of Salt Lake City, Utah.
Visit her online at www.allycondie.com.

Books by Ally Condie

MATCHED
CROSSED

ALLY CONDIE

CROSSED

razOr
bill
PENGUIN

PUFFIN BOOKS

Published by the Penguin Group
Penguin Books Ltd, 80 Strand, London WC2R 0RL, England
Penguin Group (USA) Inc., 375 Hudson Street, New York, New York 10014, USA
Penguin Group (Canada), 90 Eglinton Avenue East, Suite 700, Toronto, Ontario, Canada M4P 2Y3
(a division of Pearson Penguin Canada Inc.)
Penguin Ireland, 25 St Stephen's Green, Dublin 2, Ireland (a division of Penguin Books Ltd)
Penguin Group (Australia), 250 Camberwell Road, Camberwell, Victoria 3124, Australia
(a division of Pearson Australia Group Pty Ltd)
Penguin Books India Pvt Ltd, 11 Community Centre, Panchsheel Park, New Delhi – 110 017, India
Penguin Group (NZ), 67 Apollo Drive, Rosedale, Auckland 0632, New Zealand
(a division of Pearson New Zealand Ltd)
Penguin Books (South Africa) (Pty) Ltd, 24 Sturdee Avenue, Rosebank, Johannesburg 2196, South Africa

Penguin Books Ltd, Registered Offices: 80 Strand, London WC2R 0RL, England

puffinbooks.com

First published in the USA by Dutton Books, a member of Penguin Group (USA) Inc., 2011
First published in Razorbill, an imprint of Penguin Books Ltd, 2011
001 – 10 9 8 7 6 5 4 3 2 1

Text copyright © Allyson Braithwaite Condie, 2011
'Crossing the Bar' by Alfred Lord Tennyson,
from The Works of Alfred Lord Tennyson, Wordsworth Editions, Ltd, 1998
'Do Not Go Gentle Into That Good Night' by Dylan Thomas,
from The Poems of Dylan Thomas, copyright © 1952 by Dylan Thomas.
Reprinted by permission of New Directions Publishing Corp.
'They Dropped Like Flakes' by Emily Dickinson,
reprinted by permission of the publishers and the Trustees of Amherst College
from The Poems of Emily Dickinson, Thomas H. Johnson, ed., Cambridge, Mass:
The Belknap Press of Harvard University Press, copyright © 1951, 1955, 1979, 1983
by the President and Fellows of Harvard College
'I Did Not Reach Thee' by Emily Dickinson,
from The Poems of Emily Dickinson, Thomas H. Johnson, ed., Cambridge, Mass:
The Belknap Press of Harvard University Press, copyright © 1951, 1955, 1979, 1983
by the President and Fellows of Harvard College.

The moral right of the author has been asserted

Set in Minister-Light
Printed in Great Britain by Clays Ltd, St Ives plc

British Library Cataloguing in Publication Data
A CIP catalogue record for this book is available from the British Library

ISBN: 978–0–141–33306–9

www.greenpenguin.co.uk

Penguin Books is committed to a sustainable
future for our business, our readers and our
planet. This book is made from paper certified
by the Forest Stewardship Council.

for Ian
who looked up
and started to climb

PLAIN

RIVER

OUTER PROVINCES

THE CARVING

BEYOND THE SOCIETY

Do Not Go Gentle Into That Good Night
by DYLAN THOMAS

Do not go gentle into that good night,
Old age should burn and rage at close of day;
Rage, rage against the dying of the light.

Though wise men at their end know dark is right,
Because their words had forked no lightning they
Do not go gentle into that good night.

Good men, the last wave by, crying how bright
Their frail deeds might have danced in a green bay,
Rage, rage against the dying of the light.

Wild men who caught and sang the sun in flight,
And learn, too late, they grieved it on its way,
Do not go gentle into that good night.

Grave men, near death, who see with blinding sight
Blind eyes could blaze like meteors and be gay,
Rage, rage against the dying of the light.

And you, my father, there on the sad height,
Curse, bless me now with your fierce tears, I pray.
Do not go gentle into that good night.
Rage, rage against the dying of the light.

Crossing the Bar

by ALFRED LORD TENNYSON

Sunset and evening star,
And one clear call for me!
And may there be no moaning of the bar,
When I put out to sea.

But such a tide as moving seems asleep,
Too full for sound and foam,
When that which drew from out the boundless deep
Turns again home.

Twilight and evening bell,
And after that the dark!
And may there be no sadness of farewell,
When I embark;

For tho' from out our bourne of Time and Place
The flood may bear me far,
I hope to see my Pilot face to face
When I have crossed the bar.

CHAPTER 1
KY

I'm standing in a river. It's blue. Dark blue. Reflecting the color of the evening sky.

I don't move. The river does. It pushes against me and hisses through the grass at the water's edge. "Get out of there," the Officer says. He shines his flashlight on us from his position on the bank.

"You said to put the body in the water," I say, choosing to misunderstand the Officer.

"I didn't say you had to get in yourself," the Officer says. "Let go and get out. And bring his coat. He doesn't need it now."

I glance up at Vick, who helps me with the body. Vick doesn't step into the water. He's not from around here, but everyone in camp knows the rumors about the poisoned rivers in the Outer Provinces.

"It's all right," I tell Vick quietly. The Officers and Officials want us to be scared of this river—of all rivers—so that we never try to drink from them and never try to cross over.

"Don't you want a tissue sample?" I call out to the Officer on the bank while Vick hesitates. The icy water reaches my knees, and the dead boy's head lolls back, his open eyes staring at the sky. The dead don't see but I do.

I see too many things. I always have. Words and pictures connect together in my mind in strange ways and I notice details wherever I am. Like now. Vick's no coward but fear films his face. The dead boy's sleeves are frayed with threads that catch the water where his arm dangles down. His thin ankles and bare feet glow pale in Vick's hands as Vick steps closer to the bank. The Officer already had us take the boots from the body. Now he swings them back and forth by the laces, a sweep of black keeping time. With his other hand he points the round beam of the flashlight right into my eyes.

I throw the coat to the Officer. He has to drop the boots to catch it. "You can let go," I tell Vick. "He's not heavy. I can take care of it."

But Vick steps in, too. Now the dead boy's legs are wet and his black plainclothes sodden. "It's not much of a Final Banquet," Vick calls out to the Officer. There's anger in Vick's voice. "Was that dinner last night something *he* chose? If it was, he deserves to be dead."

It's been so long since I've let myself feel anger that I don't *just* feel it. It covers my mouth and I swallow it down, the taste sharp and metal as though I'm gnawing through foilware. This boy died because the Officers judged wrong. They didn't give him enough water and now he's dead too soon.

We have to hide the body because we're not supposed to die in this holding camp. We're supposed to wait until they send us out to the villages so the Enemy can take care of us there. It doesn't always work that way.

The Society wants us to be afraid of dying. But I'm not. I'm only afraid of dying wrong.

"This is how Aberrations end," the Officer tells us impatiently. He takes a step in our direction. "You know that. There's no last meal. There's no last words. Let go and get out."

This is how Aberrations end. Looking down I see that the water has gone black with the sky. I don't let go yet.

Citizens end with banquets. Last words. Stored tissue samples to give them a chance at immortality.

I can't do anything about the food or the sample but I do have words. They're always there rolling through my mind with the pictures and numbers.

So I whisper some that seem to fit the river and the death:

"For tho' from out our bourne of Time and Place
  The flood may bear me far,
I hope to see my Pilot face to face
  When I have crossed the bar."

Vick looks at me, surprised.

"Let go," I tell him, and at the same time we do.

CHAPTER 2
CASSIA

The dirt is part of me. The hot water in the corner wash-basin runs over my hands, turning them red, making me think of Ky. My hands look a little like his now.

Of course, almost everything makes me think of Ky.

With a piece of soap the color of this month, of November, I scrub my fingers one last time. In some ways I like the dirt. It works into every crease of my skin, makes a map on the back of my hands. Once, when I felt very tired, I looked down at the cartography of my skin and imagined it could tell me how to get to Ky.

Ky is gone.

All of this—faraway province, work camp, dirty hands, tired body, aching mind—is because Ky is gone and because I want to find him. And it is strange that absence can feel like presence. A missing so complete that if it were to go away, I would turn around, stunned, to see that the room is empty after all, when before it at least had something, if not *him*.

I turn away from the sink and glance about our cabin. The small windows along the top of the room are dark with evening. It's the last night before a transfer; this next work assignment will be my final one. After this, I've been informed, I will go on to Central, the biggest City of the Society, for my final work position in one of the sorting centers there. A *real* work position, not this digging in the dirt, this hard labor. My three months' work detail has taken me to several camps, but so far all of them have been in Tana Province. I had hoped to find my way to the Outer Provinces somehow, but I am no closer to Ky than I was when I began.

If I'm going to run to find Ky, it has to be soon.

Indie, one of the other girls in my cabin, pushes past me on her way to the sink. "Did you leave any hot water for the rest of us?" she asks.

"Yes," I say. She mutters something under her breath as she turns on the water and picks up the soap. A few girls stand in line behind her. Others sit expectantly on the edges of the bunks that line the room.

It's the seventh day, the day the messages come.

Carefully, I untie the small sack from my belt. We each have one of these little bags and we are supposed to carry them with us at all times. The bag is full of messages; like most of the other girls, I keep the papers until they can't be read anymore. They are like the fragile petals of the newroses Xander gave me when I left the Borough, which I have also saved.

I look at the old messages while I wait. The other girls do the same.

It doesn't take long before the papers yellow around the edges and turn to decay—the words meant to be consumed and let go. My last message from Bram tells me that he works hard in the fields and is an exemplary student at school, never late to class, and it makes me laugh because I know he's stretching the truth on that last count at least. Bram's words also make tears come to my eyes—he says he viewed Grandfather's microcard, the one from the gold box at the Final Banquet.

The historian reads a summary of Grandfather's life, and at the very end is a list of Grandfather's favorite memories, Bram writes. *He had one for each of us. His favorite of me was when I said my first word and it was "more." His favorite of you was what he called "the red garden day."*

I didn't pay close attention to the viewing of the microcard on the day of the Banquet—I was too distracted by Grandfather's final moments in the present to fully note his past. I always meant to look at the card again, but I never did, and I wish now that I had. Even more than that, I wish I remembered the red garden day. I remember *many* days sitting on a bench and talking with Grandfather among the red buds in the spring or the red newroses in the summer or the red leaves in the fall. That must be what he meant. Perhaps Bram left off an *s*—Grandfather remembered the *red garden days*, plural. The days of spring and summer and autumn where we sat talking.

The message from my parents seems full of elation; they had received the word that this next work camp rotation would be my last.

I can't blame them for being glad. They believed enough

in love to give me a chance to find Ky, but they are not sorry to see that chance end. I admire them for letting me try. It is more than most parents would do.

I shuffle the papers back behind each other, thinking of cards in games, thinking of Ky. What if I could get to him with this transfer, stay hidden on the air ship and drop myself like a stone from the sky down into the Outer Provinces?

If I did, what would he think if he saw me after all this time? Would he even recognize me? I know I look different. It's not just my hands. In spite of the full meal portions, I've grown thinner from all the work. My eyes have shadows because I can't sleep now, even though the Society doesn't monitor our dreams here. Though it worries me that they don't seem to care very much about us, I like the new freedom of sleeping without tags. I lie awake thinking about old and new words and a kiss stolen from the Society when they weren't watching. But I *try* to fall asleep, I really do, because I see Ky best in my dreams.

The only time we can see people is when the Society allows it. In life, on the port, on a microcard. Once there was a time when the Society let its citizens carry around pictures of those they loved. If people were dead or had gone away, at least you remembered how they looked. But that hasn't been allowed in years. And now the Society has even stopped the tradition of giving new Matches pictures of each other after their first face-to-face meeting. I learned that from one of the messages I *didn't* keep—a notification from the Matching Department sent out to all those who had chosen to be Matched. It read, in part: *Matching procedures are being streamlined for maximum efficiency and to increase optimal results.*

I wonder if there have been other errors.

I close my eyes again, wishing I could see Ky's face flash in front of me. But every image I conjure lately seems incomplete, blurring in different places. I wonder where Ky is now, what is happening to him, if he managed to hang onto the scrap of green silk I gave him before he left.

If he managed to hold on to me.

I take out something else, spread the paper open carefully on the bunk. A newrose petal comes out along with the paper, feeling like pages to my touch, its pink yellowing around the edges, too.

The girl assigned to the bunk next to me notices what I'm doing and so I climb back down to the bunk below. The other girls gather around, as they always do when I bring out this particular page. I can't get in trouble for keeping this—after all, it's not something illegal or contraband. It was printed from a regulation port. But we can't print anything besides messages here, and so this scrap of art has become something valuable.

"I think this might be the last time we can look at it," I say. "It's falling to pieces."

"I never thought to bring any of the Hundred Paintings," Lin says, looking down.

"I didn't think of it either," I say. "Someone gave this to me."

Xander did, back in the Borough, the day we said

good-bye. It's #19 of the Hundred Paintings—*Chasm of the Colorado*, by Thomas Moran—and I gave a report on it once in school. I said then that it was my favorite painting and Xander must have remembered that all those years. The picture frightened and thrilled me in some vague way—the sky was so spectacular, the land so beautiful and dangerous, so full of heights and depths. I was afraid of the vastness of a place like that. At the same time, I felt sorrow that I would never see it: green trees clinging to red rocks, blue and gray clouds floating and streaming, gold and dark over all of it.

I wonder if some of that longing came through in my voice when I spoke of the painting, if Xander noticed and remembered. Xander still plays the game in a subtle way. This painting is one of his cards. Now, when I see the painting or touch one of the newrose petals, I remember the way he felt so familiar and knew so much, and I ache for what I've had to let go.

I was right about this being the last time we could look at the picture. When I pick it up, it falls to pieces. We all sigh, at the same time, our combined exhalation moving the fragments on its breeze.

"We could go view the painting on the port," I tell them. The one port in camp sits humming over in the main hall, large and listening.

"No," says Indie. "It's too late."

It's true; we're supposed to stay in our cabin after dinner. "Tomorrow during breakfast, then," I say.

Indie makes a dismissive gesture, turns her face away. She's right. I don't know why it's not the same, but it isn't. At first, I thought it was *having* the picture that made it special, but it's not even that. It's looking at something without being watched, without being told how to see. That's what the picture has given us.

I don't know why I didn't carry around pictures and poems all the time before I came here. All that paper in the ports, all that luxury. So many carefully selected pieces of beauty and still we didn't look at them enough. How did I not see that the color of the green near the canyon was so new you could almost feel the smoothness of the leaf, the stickiness like butterfly wings opening for the first time?

In one swift motion, Indie brushes the pieces from my bed. She didn't even look to do it. That's how I know she cared about losing the picture, because she knew exactly where the fragments lay.

I carry them to be incinerated, my eyes blurring with tears.

It's all right, I tell myself. *You have other, solid things left, hidden under the papers and petals. A tablet container. A silver box from the Match Banquet.*

Ky's compass and the blue tablets from Xander.

I don't usually keep the compass and the tablets in the bag with me. They're too valuable. I don't know if the Officers search through my things but I'm sure the other girls do.

So, on the first day in each new camp, I bring out the compass and the blue tablets, plant them deep, and come for them later. Besides being illegal, they are both valuable gifts: the compass, golden and bright, can tell me which direction I need to go. And the Society has always told us that, with water, the blue tablet can keep us alive for a day or two. Xander stole several dozen for me; I could live for a long time. Together, their gifts are the perfect combination for survival.

If I could only get to the Outer Provinces to use them.

On nights like tonight—the night before a transfer—I have to find my way back to where I planted them and hope I remember the spot. This evening I was the last one inside, my hands stained dark with dirt from a different part of the field. It's why I hurried to wash my hands; what I hope Indie didn't notice with her sharp eyes as she stood behind me. I hope that no traces of soil fall out of the bag and that no one hears the musical chime, the sound of promise, as the silver box and the compass bump into each other and against the tablet container.

In these camps, I try to conceal the fact that I'm a Citizen from the other workers. Though the Society usually keeps knowledge of status confidential, I've overheard conversations between some of the girls about having to give up their tablet containers. Which means that somehow—through their own mistakes or those of their parents—some of these girls have lost their Citizenship. They're Aberrations, like Ky.

There's only one classification lower than Aberration: Anomaly. But you almost never hear of them anymore. They seem to have vanished. And it seems to me now that, once the Anomalies were gone, the Aberrations took their place—at least in the collective mind of the Society.

No one talked about the Rules of Reclassification back in Oria, and I used to worry that I could cause the Reclassification of my family. But now I've figured out the rules from Ky's story and from listening to the other girls speak in unguarded moments.

The rules are this: If a *parent* becomes Reclassified, the whole family does, too.

But if a *child* becomes Reclassified, the family does not. The child alone bears the weight of the Infraction.

Ky was Reclassified because of his father. And then he was brought to Oria when the first Markham boy died. I realize now how truly rare Ky's situation was—how he could only come back from the Outer Provinces because someone else was killed, and how his aunt and uncle, Patrick and Aida Markham, might have been even higher up in the Society than any of us realized. I wonder what has happened to them now. The thought makes me cold.

But, I remind myself, leaving to find Ky will not destroy my family. I can cause my own Reclassification, but not theirs.

I cling to this thought—that they will still be safe, and Xander, too, no matter where I have to go.

"Messages," says the Officer as she enters the room. It's the one with the sharp voice and the kind eyes. She gives us a nod as she begins to read the names. "Mira Waring."

Mira steps forward. We all watch and count. Mira gets three messages, the same as usual. The Officer prints out and reads the pages before we see them to save the time of all of us lining up at the port.

There is nothing for Indie.

And only one message for me, a combined one from my parents and Bram. Nothing from Xander. He has never missed a week before.

What happened? I tighten my hand on my bag and I hear the crumple of paper inside.

"Cassia," the Officer says. "Please come with me to the main hall. We have a communication for you."

The other girls stare at me in surprise.

And then a chill cuts through me. I know who it must be. My Official, checking in on me from the port.

I can see *her* face clearly in my mind, every icy line of it.

I don't want to go.

"Cassia," the Officer says. Looking back at the girls, at the cabin that suddenly seems warm and cozy, I stand up to follow her. She leads me back along the path to the main hall and over to the port. I hear it humming all the way across the room.

I keep my eyes down for a moment before looking up toward the port. Compose your face, your hands, your eyes. Look out at them so they cannot see into you.

"Cassia," someone else says, a voice I know.

And then I look up, and I don't believe what I see.

15

He's here.

The port is blank, and he stands before me, real.

He's here.

Whole and healthy and unharmed.

Here.

Not alone—an Official stands behind him—but still, he's—

Here.

I put my red, mapped hands over my eyes because it's too much to see.

"Xander," I say.

CHAPTER 3
KY

It's been a month and a half since we left that boy in the water. Now I lie in the dirt and fire comes down from above.

It's a song, I tell myself, same as I always do. The bass sound of the heavy shots, the soprano of the screams, the tenor of my own fear. All part of the music.

Don't try to run. I told the others too, but new decoys never listen. They believe what the Society told them on the way out here: *Do your time in the villages and we'll bring you home in six months. We'll give you Citizen status again.*

No one lasts six months.

When I climb out, there will be black buildings and splintered gray sagebrush. Burned, fallen bodies strewn along the orange sandy earth.

And now there's a break in the song and I swear. The air ships are on the move. I know what draws their fire.

Early this morning, boots crunched in the frost behind me. I didn't look back to see who followed me to the edge of the village.

"What are you doing?" someone asked. I didn't recognize

the voice, but that didn't mean much. They're always sending new people out here to the villages from the camp. We die faster and faster these days.

I knew even before they pushed me onto that train back in Oria that the Society would never use us to fight. They have plenty of technology and trained Officers for that. People who aren't Aberrations or Anomalies.

What the Society needs—what we are for them—are bodies. Decoy villagers. They move us. Put us wherever they need more people to draw fire from the Enemy. They want the Enemy to think the Outer Provinces are still inhabited and viable, although the only people I've seen here are ones like us. Dropped down from the sky with just enough to keep us alive until the Enemy kills us.

No one goes home.

Except me. I came home. The Outer Provinces are where I once belonged.

"The snow," I told the new decoy. "I'm looking at the snow."

"It doesn't snow here," he scoffed.

I didn't answer. I kept looking up at the top of the nearest plateau. It's something worth seeing, white snow on red rocks. While it melts it turns from white to crystal clear and shot through with rainbows. I've been up high before when the snow came down. It was beautiful the way it feathered the winter-dead plants.

Behind me, I heard him turn and run back toward the

camp. "Look up on the plateau!" he yelled, and the others stirred and called back in excitement.

"We're going up to get the snow, Ky!" someone hollered at me a few moments later. "Come on."

"You won't make it," I told them. "It will melt too fast."

But no one listened to me. The Officials still keep us thirsty and what water we do have tastes like the insides of our canteens. The closest river now *is* poisoned and rain doesn't come often.

One cold swallow of fresh water. I can see why they wanted to go.

"You sure?" one of them called back to me, and I nodded again.

"You going, Vick?" someone called out.

Vick stood up, shielded his hard blue eyes with one hand, and spit down into the frosted sagebrush. "No," he said. "Ky says it'll melt before we get there. And we've got graves to dig."

"You're always making us dig," one of the decoys complained. "We're supposed to act like farmers. That's what the Society says." He was right. They want us to use the shovels and seeds from the village sheds to plant winter crops and to leave the bodies where they lie. I've heard other decoys say that that's what they do in the other villages. They leave the carcasses for the Society or the Enemy or any animals who might want them.

But Vick and I bury people. It started with the boy and the river and no one's stopped us yet.

Vick laughed, a cold sound. In the absence of any Officials or Officers he has become the unofficial leader out here and sometimes the other decoys forget that he doesn't actually have any power within the Society. They forget that he's an Aberration, too. "I don't make you do anything. Neither does Ky. You know who does, and if you want to take your chances up there, I won't stop you."

The sun climbed higher and so did they. I watched for a while. Their black plainclothes and the distance between the village and the plateau made them look like ants swarming a hill. Then I stood up and started back to work, digging holes in the graveyard for the ones who died in the firing the night before.

Vick and the others worked next to me. We had seven holes to dig. Not too many, considering the intensity of the firing and the fact that there were almost a hundred of us to lose.

I kept my back to the climbers so I didn't have to see how the snow was all gone by the time they reached the top of the plateau. Climbing up there was a waste of time.

It's also a waste of time to think about people who are gone. And judging by the way things out here are going, I don't have a lot of time to waste.

But I can't help it.

On my first night in Mapletree Borough, I looked out of the window in my new bedroom and not one thing was familiar or seemed like home. So I turned away. And then Aida came through the door, and she looked enough like my mother that I could breathe again.

She held out her hand with the compass in it. "Our parents only had one artifact, and two daughters. Your mother and I agreed that we would take turns sharing it, but then she left." She opened my hand and put the compass inside. "We had the same artifact. And now we both have the same son. It's for you."

"I can't have it," I told her. "I'm an Aberration. We're not allowed to keep things like this."

"Nevertheless," Aida said. "It is yours."

And then I gave it to Cassia to keep and she gave me the green silk. I knew they'd take it from me someday. I knew I would never get to keep it. And so that's why, when we walked down from the Hill the last time, I paused and tied it to a tree. Quickly, so she wouldn't notice.

I like to think of it out there on top of the Hill under wind and rain.

Because in the end you can't always choose what to keep. You can only choose how you let it go.

Cassia.

I was thinking of her when I first saw the snow. I thought, *We could climb up there. Even if it all melted. We'd sit and write words on the still-damp sand. We could do that, if you weren't gone.*

But then, I remembered, *you're not the one who's gone. I am.*

A boot appears now at the edge of the grave. I know whose it is by the notches carved around the edge of the sole—a method some use out here to mark time survived. No one else has as many cuts, as many days tracked. "You're not dead," Vick says.

"No," I say, pushing myself to my feet. I spit dirt out of my mouth and reach for the shovel.

Vick digs next to me. Neither of us talk about the people we won't be able to bury today. The ones who tried to climb to the snow.

Back in the village, I hear the decoys calling to each other and to us. *Three more dead here,* they cry out, and then fall silent as they look up.

Not one of the decoys who went up to the plateau will be coming back. I find myself hoping the impossible, that at least they quenched their thirst before the fire. That they had mouths full of clean, cold snow when they died.

CHAPTER 4
CASSIA

Xander, here, in front of me. Blond hair, blue eyes, smile so warm that I can't stop from reaching out to him even before the Official has given us permission to touch.

"Cassia," Xander says, and doesn't wait, either. He pulls me into his arms and we both hold on tight. I don't even try to keep myself from burying my face against his chest, against his clothes that smell like home and him.

"I've missed you," Xander tells me, his voice rumbling above my head. It sounds deeper. He seems stronger. It's such a good and glorious feeling, this being with him, that I lean back and grab his face in both my hands and pull him down and kiss him on the cheek, in a place dangerously near his mouth. When I step away we both have tears in our eyes. It is such a strange sight, Xander with tears, that I catch my breath.

"I've missed *you*," I tell him, and I wonder how much of the ache inside me comes from having lost Xander, too.

The Official behind Xander smiles. Our reunion lacks nothing. He steps away a little, discreet, giving us space, and enters something into his datapod. Probably something like: *Both subjects expressed appropriate reaction upon seeing each other.*

"How?" I ask Xander. "How are you here?" Though it's so good to see him, it's almost too good. Is this another test from my Official?

"It's been five months since our Matching," he says. "All the Matchees from our month are having their first face-to-face meetings. The Department hasn't eliminated *that* yet." He smiles down at me, something sad in his eyes. "I pointed out that we don't live near each other anymore, so we deserved a meeting, too. And it's customary to meet where the girl lives."

He didn't say *at the girl's home*. He understands. He's right. I live here. But this work camp is not home. I could call Oria home, because Xander lives there, and Em, and because I began there. Although I haven't lived there, I could also call the new place in Keya home, because my parents and Bram live there.

And there is a place where Ky lives that I think of as home, even though I cannot name it and don't know where, exactly, it is.

Xander reaches for my hand. "We're allowed to go on an outing," he says. "If you'd like."

"Of course," I say, laughing; I can't help it. Minutes ago I stood scrubbing my hands and feeling alone and now Xander is here. It's as though I have walked by the lighted windows of a house in the Borough, pretending I don't care about what I've lost and left behind, and then suddenly I'm in that golden-warm room without even having lifted my hand to open the door.

The Official gestures toward the exit, and I realize he's not the same Official who accompanied us on our outing to the dining hall back in the Borough. That was a special arrangement for Xander and me, arranged in place of our first port-to-port communication since we already knew each other. The Official who escorted us that night was young. This one is, too, but kinder looking. He notices my glance and inclines his head, a gesture formal and polite but warm somehow. "There are no longer specific Officials assigned to each Match," he tells me in an explanatory tone. "It's more efficient."

"It's too late for a meal," Xander says. "But we can go into town. Where would you like to go?"

"I don't even know what's there," I say. I have a blurry memory of coming into town on the long-distance train and walking down the street to the transport that brought us to the camp. Of almost-bare trees sparking the sky with their sparse red and gold leaves. But was that *this* town, or one near a different camp? It must have been earlier in the fall for the leaves to be so bright.

"The facilities are smaller here," Xander says. "But they have what we did in the Borough—a music hall, a game center, a showing or two."

A showing. I haven't been to one in so long. For a moment I think that's what I'll choose; I even open my mouth to say it. I picture the theater going dark and my heart pounding as

I wait for images to come rising onto the screen and music to swell through the speakers. Then I remember the firings and the tears in Ky's eyes as the lights came up, and another memory flickers inside me. "Do they have a museum?"

Something dances in Xander's eyes; I can't tell what. Amusement? Surprise? I lean closer to try to see; Xander is not usually a mystery to me. He's open, honest, a story I read again and again and love every time. But, in this moment, I can't tell what he thinks. "Yes," he says.

"I'd like to go there," I say, "if that would be all right with you."

Xander nods.

It takes some time to walk into town and the smell of farming hangs thick in the air—burning wood and cool air and apples turning to cider. I feel a wave of affection for this place that I know has to do with the boy standing near me. Xander always makes every place, every person, better. The evening air holds the bittersweet tang of what might have been, and I catch my breath as Xander turns to look at me under the warm light of the street lamp. His eyes still speak of what might be.

The museum only has one floor and my heart sinks. It's so small. What if things here are different than they are in Oria?

"We close in half an hour," the man at the front desk says. His uniform seems threadbare and tired and so does he, as though he's coming apart along the edges. He slides his hands along the top of the desk and pushes a datapod toward us. "Type in your names," he says, and we do, the Official going first. Up close, the Official seems to have the same tired look about his eyes as the older man at the desk.

"Thank you," I say, after I enter my name and slide the datapod back across the surface toward the man.

"We don't have much to see," he tells us.

"We don't mind," I say.

I wonder if our Official thinks it a strange choice to come here, but to my surprise he turns away almost immediately as we enter the museum's main display room. As though he *wants* to give us space alone to talk. He walks to a glass-fronted case and leans forward, his hands behind his back in a posture that seems almost elegant in its casualness. A kind Official. Of course they must exist. Grandfather was one.

Relief washes over me as I find what I'm looking for almost immediately—a glassed-in map of the Society. It's in the middle of the room. "There," I say to Xander. "Should we look at that one?"

Xander nods. While I read the names of the rivers and Cities and Provinces, he shifts position next to me and runs his hand through his hair. Unlike Ky, who holds still in places like this, with Xander it's always a series of confident movements, little waves of motion. It's what makes him so effective in the games—the quirking of his eyebrows, the smiling, the way his hands continually move the cards.

"That display hasn't been updated recently," a voice

behind us says, startling me. It's the man from the desk. I glance around the room, looking for another worker. He sees me doing it and smiles almost mournfully. "The others are in the back closing up for the night. If you want to know anything, I'm the only one to ask."

I look over at our Official. He still stands at the case nearest the entrance, his full interest seemingly absorbed by whatever is in the display. I look at Xander and try to send him a message without speaking. *Please.*

For a moment I think he doesn't understand or doesn't want to. I feel his fingers tighten around mine and see a hardening in his eyes and a slight clenching of his jaw. But then his expression softens and he nods. "Hurry," he says, and he lets go and walks toward the Official on the other side of the room.

I have to try, even though I don't think this tired gray man has any answers for me and the hope I had seems to be slipping away. "I want to know more about the Glorious History of Tana Province."

A pause. A beat.

The man draws in a breath and begins to speak. "Tana Province has beautiful geography and is also renowned for its farming," he says, his voice flat.

He doesn't know. My heart sinks. Back in Oria, Ky told me that the poems Grandfather gave me could be valuable, and also that asking the history of the Province was a way to let the Archivists know you wanted to trade. I'd hoped it would be the same way here. It was stupid of me. Perhaps there are no Archivists in Tana at all, and if there were, they must have better places to be than waiting for closing time in this sad little museum.

The man continues. "Floods sometimes occurred in Tana pre-Society, but that has been controlled for many years now. We are one of the most productive farming Provinces in the Society."

I don't look back at Xander. Or the Official. Just at the map in front of me. I tried to trade before and it didn't work then either. But the first time it was because I couldn't bring myself to give away the poem Ky and I shared.

Then I notice that the man has stopped speaking. He looks at me directly. "Is there anything else?" he asks.

I should give up. Should smile and turn away to Xander and forget about this, accept that the man knows nothing and move on. But for some reason I think suddenly of one of those last red leaves holding on against the sky. I breathe. It falls.

"Yes," I say softly.

Grandfather gave me two poems. Ky and I loved the Thomas one, but there were other words, too, and those are the ones that come to me now. I don't remember all of it, that poem by Tennyson, but one stanza comes back to me clear in my mind as though it were written there all along.

Perhaps it was the man's mention of flooding that brought it back:

> *"For tho' from out our bourne of Time and Place*
> *The flood may bear me far,*
> *I hope to see my Pilot face to face*
> *When I have crossed the bar."*

As I speak the words quietly, the man's face changes. He becomes clever, alert, alive. I must have remembered correctly. "That's an interesting poem," he says. "Not, I think, one of the Hundred."

"No," I say. My hands tremble and I dare to hope again. "But still worth something."

"I'm afraid not," he says. "Unless you have the original."

"No," I say. "It was destroyed." *I destroyed it.* I remember that moment at the Restoration site and how the paper fluttered up before it went down to burn.

"I'm sorry," he says, and it sounds as though he is. "What is it you were hoping to trade *for*?" he asks, a hint of curiosity in his voice.

I point to the Outer Provinces. If I can just get to them, there's a slim but real chance I can find Ky. "I know they're taking the Aberrations there," I say softly. "But I want to know *exactly* where and how I can get there. A map."

He shakes his head at me. *No.*

He can't tell me? Or he won't? "I have something else," I say.

I angle my back so that neither Xander nor the Official can see my hands; I reach into the bag. My fingers brush the foil of the tablets and the hard surface of the compass at the same time and I stop.

Which should I trade?

Suddenly I'm dizzy, confused, remembering the time I had to sort Ky. The steam in the room, the sweat, the ache of the decision pressing against me . . .

Stay clear, I tell myself. I glance over my shoulder at Xander and meet the blue of his eyes for one brief moment before he turns back to the Official. I remember Ky looking down at me from the air-train platform before they took him away and feel again the panic of time running out.

I make up my mind and reach into the bag, pulling out the item for trade. I hold it up just high enough for the man to see, trying to keep my hands from shaking and attempting to convince myself that I *can* give this up.

He smiles and nods at me. "Yes," he says. "*That* is worth something. But what you want would take days—weeks—to arrange."

"I only have tonight," I say.

Before I can say anything more, the man takes the offering and leaves my hand empty. "Where are you going next?"

"The music hall," I say.

"Check under your seat when you leave," he whispers. "I will do the best I can." Above us, the lights dim. His eyes do, too, and then, in the flat voice he first used he tells me, "We're closing. You all need to go."

Xander leans over during the music. "Did you get what you needed?" he asks, his voice deep and low and his breath brushing my neck. On his other side, the Official stares ahead. He taps his fingers on the armrest of his chair, keeping time to the music.

"I don't know yet," I tell him. The Archivist said to look under my seat when I left, not before, but I am still tempted to try earlier. "Thank you for helping me."

"It's what I do," Xander says.

"I know it is," I say. I remember the gifts he gave me: the painting, the blue tablets neatly rowed in their compartments. Even the compass, I realize, my gift from Ky, was something Xander saved for me once, on that day back in the Borough when they took the artifacts.

"But you don't know everything about me," Xander says. A mischievous grin crosses his face.

I glance down at his hand around mine, his thumb brushing across my skin, and then I look back up into his eyes. Though he still smiles there's something serious about his expression now. "No," I agree. "I don't."

We hold on to each other. The Society's music plays around and over us, but our thoughts are always our own.

When I stand up, I brush my hand underneath the chair. Something's there—a folded square of paper—and it comes away easily when I tug on it. Though I want to look *now*, I slip it into my pocket instead, wondering what I have, what I've traded for.

The Official walks us back to the main hall of the camp. When we go inside, he glances around the hall, at the long tables and the single hulking port, and when he looks back at me there's an expression in his eyes that I think might be pity. I lift my chin.

"You have ten minutes to say good-bye," the Official tells us. His voice, now that we are back in the camp, sounds sharper than it did before. He pulls out his datapod and nods to the Officer waiting to take me back to my cabin.

Xander and I both take a deep breath at the same time and then we laugh together. I like the sound of it, our laughter echoing around the almost empty hall. "What was he looking at for so long?" I ask Xander, nodding toward the Official.

"A display on the history of Matching," Xander says quietly. He looks at me as though there's some meaning there I should understand, but I don't. I wasn't paying close enough attention to the Official.

"Nine minutes," he says without looking up.

"I still can't believe they let you come," I tell Xander. "I'm so glad they did."

"The timing was optimal," Xander says. "I'm leaving Oria. I'm only passing through Tana on my way to Camas Province."

"What?" I blink in surprise. Camas is one of the Border Provinces, right along the edge of the Outer Provinces. I feel strangely untethered. Much as I love looking at the stars, I never learned to guide by them. I mark my course by people: Xander, a point on the map; my parents, another point; Ky, the final destination. When Xander moves, the geography of everything changes.

"I have my final work position," Xander says. "It's in Central. Like yours. But they want me to have experience in the Border Provinces first."

"Why?" I ask him softly.

Xander's tone is sober. "There are things I need to learn there for my work assignment that I can't learn anywhere else."

"And then to Central," I say. The idea of Xander in Central feels right and final. Of course he would belong in the capital of the Society. Of course they would see his potential and bring him there. "You're really leaving."

An expression of what looks like anger flashes momentarily across his face. "Do you have any idea what it's like being left?"

"Of course I do," I say, stung.

"No," he says. "Not the way Ky left you. He didn't want to go. Do you know what it's like for someone to *choose* to leave you?"

"I didn't choose to leave you behind. We were Relocated."

Xander exhales. "You still don't understand," he says. "You left me before you left Oria." He glances over at the Official and then back at me, his blue eyes serious. He's changed, since I've seen him, become harder. More careful.

More like Ky.

I know what he means now about my leaving. For Xander, I began to leave when I chose Ky.

Xander looks down at our hands, still clasped together.

My gaze follows his. His hand is strong, the knuckles rough. He can't write with his hands, but they are quick and sure over the cards and in the games. This physical contact, though not with Ky, is still with someone I love. I hold on as if I won't ever let go, and part of me doesn't want to.

The air in the main hall feels cool and I shiver. Would you call this season late fall? Early winter? I can't tell. The Society, with their extra crops, has blurred the line between seasons, between when you can plant and harvest and when you must let things lie. Xander takes his hands away and leans forward, looking at me deep. I catch myself gazing at his mouth, remembering our kiss back in the Borough, that sweet innocent kiss before everything changed. I think Xander and I would kiss differently now.

In a whisper that brushes along my collarbone, Xander

asks, "Are you still going to the Outer Provinces to find him?"

"*Yes,*" I whisper.

The Official calls out the time. Only a few minutes left. Xander forces a smile, tries to speak lightly. "You really want this? You want Ky, whatever the cost?" I can almost imagine the words the Official taps into the datapod as he watches us now: *Female Matchee expressed some agitation, soon after the male Matchee told her about his field assignment in Camas. Male was able to console her.*

"No," I say. "Not at any cost."

Xander draws in his breath sharply. "So where do you draw the line? What won't you give up?"

I swallow. "My family."

"But you don't mind giving *me* up," he says. His jaw tightens and he looks away. *Look back,* I think. *Don't you know that I love you, too? That you have been my friend for years? That I still feel Matched to you in some ways?*

"I'm not," I say softly. "I'm not giving you up. Look." And then I risk it. I pull open the bag and show him what's still inside, what I kept. The blue tablets. Though he gave them to me to find Ky, they are still *Xander's* gift.

Xander's eyes widen. "You traded Ky's compass?"

"Yes," I say.

Xander smiles and in the expression I see surprise and cunning and happiness all mingled there together. I've surprised Xander—and myself. I love Xander in ways that are perhaps more complicated than I first expected.

But it's Ky I have to find.

"It's time," the Official calls. The Officer looks in my direction.

"Good-bye," I tell Xander, my voice catching.

"I don't think so," he says, and he leans down to kiss me the way I kissed him earlier, right near my mouth. If either of us moved a little, everything would change.

CHAPTER 5
KY

Vick and I lift one of the bodies and carry it toward a grave. I recite the words I say over all of the dead now:

> *"For tho' from out our bourne of Time and Place*
> *The flood may bear me far,*
> *I hope to see my Pilot face to face*
> *When I have crossed the bar."*

I don't see how there can be more than this. How anything from these bodies can last when they die so easily and decay so fast. Still, part of me wants to believe that the flood of death carries us someplace after all. That there's someone to see at the end. That's the part of me that says the words over the dead when I know they don't hear a thing I say.

"Why do you say that every time?" Vick asks me.

"I like the sound."

Vick waits. He wants me to speak more but I won't. "You know what it means?" he asks, finally.

"It's about someone hoping for more," I tell him noncommittally. "It's part of a poem from before the Society."

Not from the poem that belongs to Cassia and me. I won't speak *those* words to anyone again until I can tell them to her. The poem I say now is the other one she found in her artifact when she opened it that day in the woods.

She didn't know I was there. I stood, watching her read the paper. I saw her lips forming the words of a poem I didn't know, and then of one I did. When I realized what she was saying about the Pilot, I stepped forward and a stick snapped under my foot.

"Doesn't do them any good," Vick tells me, gesturing to one of the bodies and then shoving his sandy hair back from his face in irritation. They won't give us scissors or razors for cutting our hair or shaving—too easy to turn into weapons to kill each other or ourselves. It doesn't usually matter. Only Vick and I have been out here long enough to have hair that falls into our eyes. "So that's *all* it is? Some old poem?"

I shrug.

It's a mistake.

Usually, Vick doesn't care when I don't answer him, but this time I see a challenge in his eyes. I start planning the best way to take him down. The increase in firings has affected him, too. Put him on edge. He's bigger than me but not by much, and I learned to fight out here years ago. Now that I am back I remember it, like the snow on the plateau. My muscles tense.

But Vick stops. "You never cut notches in your boot," he says, his voice back to even and his eyes back to calm.

"No," I agree.

"Why?"

"No one needs to know," I say.

"To know what? How long you've lasted?" Vick asks.

"To know anything about me," I say.

We leave the graves behind and take a break for lunch, sitting on a group of sandstone boulders outside of the village. The colors are the red orange brown of my childhood, and their texture is the same: dry and rough and—in November—cold.

I use the narrow end of the decoy gun to scratch a mark into the sandstone. I don't want anyone to know I can write, so I don't write her name.

Instead I draw a curve. A wave. Like an ocean, or a piece of green silk rolling in the wind.

Scratch, scratch. The sandstone, shaped by other forces, water and wind, is now altered by me. Which I like. I always carve myself into what others want me to be. With Cassia on the Hill—only then was I truly myself.

I'm not ready yet to draw her face. I don't even know if I can. But I scratch another curve into the rock. It looks a little like the C I first taught her to write. I make the curve again, remembering her hand.

Vick leans over to see what I'm doing. "That doesn't look like anything."

"It looks like the moon," I tell him. "When it's thin."

Vick glances up at the plateau. Earlier today some air

ships came for the bodies. That hasn't happened before. I don't know what the Society has done with them, but I wish I'd thought to climb up to the top and write something to mark the decoys' passing.

Because now there is nothing to say that they were ever there. The snow melted before they could make a footprint in it. Their lives ended before they even knew what they could be.

"You think that boy was lucky?" I ask Vick. "The one who died in camp, before we came to the villages?"

"Lucky," Vick says, as if he doesn't know what the word means. And maybe he doesn't. Luck is not a word the Society encourages. And it's not something we have much of out here.

There was a firing our first night out in the villages. We all started running to take cover. A few of the boys ran out into the street with their guns and shot at the sky. Vick and I ended up in the same house with one or two others. I don't remember their names. They're gone now.

"Why aren't you out there trying to shoot back?" Vick asked me then. We hadn't talked to each other much since we put the boy in the river.

"No reason to," I said. "The ammunition isn't real." I put my standard-issue gun on the ground next to me.

Vick puts his gun down, too. "How long have you known?"

"Since they gave them to us on our way here," I said. "What about you?"

"The same," Vick answered. "We should have told the others."

"I know," I said. "I was stupid. I thought we'd have a little more time."

"Time," Vick said, "is what we don't have."

The world shattered outside and someone else started screaming.

"I wish I had a gun that worked," Vick said. "I'd blow everyone on those air ships away. Pieces of them would come down like fireworks."

"Finished," Vick says now, folding up his foilware into a sharp silver square. "We'd better get back to work."

"I wonder why they don't just give us blue tablets," I say. "Then they wouldn't have to bother with our meals."

Vick looks at me as if I'm crazy. "You don't know?"

"Know what?" I ask.

"The blue tablets don't save you. They stop you. If you take one, you'll slow down and stay where you are until someone finds you or you die waiting. Two will finish you outright."

I shake my head and look up at the sky, but I'm not looking for anything. I only look to see the blue. I hold my hand up and block out the sun so I can see the sky around it better. No clouds.

"Sorry," Vick says, "but it's true."

I glance over at Vick. I think I see concern on his stone-hard face. It's so ludicrous, all of it, that I start to laugh, and Vick laughs too. "I should have known," I say. "If something happened to the Society, they wouldn't want anyone to live on without them."

A few hours later we hear a beep from the miniport Vick carries. He pulls it from his belt loop and checks the screen. Vick's the only decoy who has a miniport—a device roughly the same size as a datapod. Miniports, however, can be used for communication. A datapod only stores information. Vick keeps the miniport with him most of the time, but now and then—like when he tells new decoys the truth about the village and the guns—he hides the port somewhere for a little while.

We're pretty sure that the Society tracks our location by the miniport. We don't know if they can listen in on us too, the way they can on the larger ports. Vick thinks so. He thinks the Society listens all the time. I don't think they care.

"What do they want?" I ask Vick as he reads the message on his screen.

"We're moving," he says.

Others fall in line with us as we walk to meet the ships that land silently outside of the village. The Officers act hurried, as usual. They don't like to spend much time out here. I'm not sure if it's because of us or because of the Enemy. I wonder who they think is the bigger threat.

He's young, but the Officer in charge of this transfer reminds me of the one who used to be in charge of us on the Hill back in Oria. His expression says *How did I end up here? What am I supposed to do with these people?*

"So," he says, looking out at us. "Up on the plateau. What was that? What happened there? The casualties wouldn't have been nearly so bad if you'd all stayed down in the village."

"There was snow up there this morning and they went up to get it," I say. "We're always thirsty."

"You're sure that's the only reason they were up there?"

"There aren't many reasons to do anything," Vick says. "Hunger. Thirst. Not dying. That's all there is. So if you don't believe us, take your pick from the other two."

"Maybe they hiked up there for the view," the Officer suggests.

Vick laughs, and it's not a good sound. "Where are the replacements?"

"They're on the ship," the Officer says. "We're going to take you all to a new village, and we'll give you more supplies."

"And more water," Vick says. Though he's unarmed and at the mercy of the Officer he sounds like he's the one giving the orders. The Officer smiles. The Society isn't human but the people who work for it sometimes are.

"And more water," the Officer says.

Vick and I both curse under our breath when we see the replacements on the air ship. They are young, much younger than us. They look to be fourteen, thirteen. Their eyes are wide. Frightened. One of them, the youngest-looking kid, looks a little like Cassia's brother, Bram. He's darker-skinned than Bram, darker than me, even, but his eyes are bright like Bram's. Before it was cut, his hair must have been curly like Bram's.

"The Society must be running out of bodies," I say to Vick, keeping my voice low.

"Maybe that's the plan," he says.

We both know the Society wants the Aberrations dead. It explains why we're dumped out here. Why we don't get to fight. But there's another question, one I can't answer:

Why do they hate us so much?

We fly blind. The air ship is windowless except for the pilot's compartment.

So it's not until we step outside that I know where we are.

I don't know the village itself but I know the area. The field we walk is orange-sanded and black-rocked, yellow-grassed with plants that grew green this summer. There are fields like this one all over the Outer Provinces. But I still know exactly where I am because of what I see in front of me.

I'm home.

It hurts.

There it is on the horizon—the landmark of my childhood.

The Carving.

From where we are now, I can't see all of it—just pieces of red or orange sandstone jutting up here and there. But when you get closer—when you reach the edge and look into the Carving—you realize that the stones aren't small at all. They're the tips of formations as large as mountains.

The Carving isn't one canyon, one mountain, but many—a network of interlocking formations that goes on for miles. The land rises and falls like water, its high jagged peaks and deep slot canyons striped with the colors of the Outer Provinces—gradations of orange, red, white. In the faraway stretches of the Carving the fire colors of the sandstone grow shadowed with blue from distant clouds.

I know all of this because I've been to the edge several times.

But I've never been inside.

"What are you grinning about?" Vick asks me, but before I can answer, the Bram kid comes up to us and gets right in Vick's face.

"I'm Eli," the kid says.

"All right," Vick says, and then turns away in irritation, back to the row of faces who have selected him as their leader even when he never wanted to be one. Some people can't help being leaders. It's in their blood and bones and brains, and there's no getting around it.

And some people follow.

You have a better chance of surviving if you follow, I remind myself. *Your father thought he was a leader. Couldn't get enough of being a leader, and look what happened to him.* I stand one step behind Vick.

"Aren't you going to give us a speech or anything?" Eli asks. "We just got here."

"I'm not in charge of this mess," Vick says. And there it is. The anger that he spends most of his energy keeping in check shows a little. "I'm not the Society's spokesman."

"But you're the only one with one of those," Eli says, pointing at the port clipped to Vick's belt.

"You want a speech?" Vick asks, and all the new kids nod and stare at him. They'll have heard the same lecture we did when we came in on the air ships about how the Society needs us to act like villagers and civilians to draw out the Enemy. How it's only a six-month job, and once we go back to Society our Aberration status will be wiped clean.

It will take exactly one day of firing for them to realize that no one has lasted six months. Not even Vick comes close to having that many notches on his boots.

"Watch the rest of us," Vick says. "Act like a villager. That's what we're supposed to do here." He pauses. Then he pulls the port from his belt and tosses it to a decoy who has been around a couple of weeks. "Take this for a run," he says. "Make sure it still works out by the end of the town."

The kid takes off. As soon as the port is out of earshot, Vick says, "The ammunition is all blanks. So don't bother trying to defend yourselves."

Eli interrupts. "But we practiced firing with them back in training camp," he protests. I start grinning, in spite of myself and the fact that I should and do feel sick that someone so young ended up out here. This kid *is* like Bram.

"Doesn't matter," Vick says. "They're all blanks now."

Eli digests this, but then he has another question. "If this is a village, where are all the women and kids?"

"*You're* a kid," Vick says.

"Am not," Eli says. "And I'm not a girl. Where are they?"

"No girls," Vick says. "No women here."

"But the Enemy must know we're not real villagers, then," Eli says. "They must have figured it out."

"Right," Vick says. "They're killing us anyway. No one cares. And now we've got work to do. We're supposed to be a village full of farmers. So let's get farming."

We start toward the fields. The sun shines hot over-head. I can feel Eli's angry gaze even after we turn away from him.

"At least we have enough water to drink," I say to Vick, gesturing to the full canteen. "Thanks to you."

"Don't thank me," Vick says. He lowers his voice. "There's not even enough to drown in."

The crop here is cotton—nearly impossible to grow. The poor-quality wisps inside the cotton bolls come apart easily.

"No wonder we don't worry about there being no girls or kids," Eli says behind me. "The Enemy must know this isn't a real village just from looking at it. No one would be stupid enough to farm cotton out here."

At first I don't answer him. I haven't fallen into the trap of talking to anyone while we work, except for Vick. I've stayed away from all the others.

But I'm weak right now. The cotton today and the snow yesterday have made me think again of Cassia's story of the cottonwood seeds snowing in June. The Society hated the cottonwood trees, but they are exactly the kind of trees that are right in the Outer Provinces. The wood is good for carving. If I could find one, I would cover the bark with her name the way I used to cover her hand with mine on the Hill.

I start talking to Eli to keep from wanting what's too hard to have.

"It's stupid," I tell Eli, "but it's more realistic than some of the stuff the Society has done. A few of the villages around here started as farming communities for Aberrations. Cotton was one of the crops the Society had them try to grow. This was back when there was more water. So it's not *completely* impossible that someone would be farming here."

"Oh," Eli says. And then he falls silent. I don't know why I'm trying to give him hope. Maybe it was remembering the cottonwood seeds.

Or remembering her.

When I look over later, I see that Eli is crying, but it's not enough to drown in so I don't do anything yet.

On our walk back into the village from the field, I jerk my head at Vick, our signal that I want to talk without the port.

"Here," he says, tossing the port to Eli, who has stopped crying. "Take this for a run." Eli nods and takes off.

"What is it?" Vick asks.

"I used to live near here," I say, trying to keep any emotion from my voice. This part of the world used to be my home. I hate what the Society has done to it. "My village was only a few miles away. I know the area."

"So are you going to run?" Vick asks.

There it is. The real question. The one we all ask ourselves all the time. *Am I going to run?* I've thought about it every day, every hour.

"Are you thinking about going back to your village?" Vick asks. "Can someone there help you?"

"No," I say. "It's gone."

Vick shakes his head. "Then there's no point in running. We can't go far without someone seeing us."

"And the closest river is too far away," I say. "We can't escape that way."

"Then how?" Vick asks.

"We're not going to go across or down. We're going to go through."

Vick turns. "Through *what?*"

"The canyons," I tell him, pointing to the Carving near us, miles long and cut with little openings impossible to see from here. "If you hike in far enough there's fresh water."

"The Officers always tell us that the canyons in the Outer Provinces are crawling with Anomalies," Vick says.

"I've heard that, too," I admit. "But some of them have built a settlement and they help travelers. I heard that from people who'd been inside."

"Wait. You *know* people who've gone into the canyons?" Vick asks.

"I *knew* people who had been there," I say.

"People you could trust?"

"My father," I say, as if that ends the conversation and Vick nods.

We walk a few steps more. "So when do we leave?" Vick asks.

"That's the problem," I say, trying not to let him see how relieved I am that he'll come. Facing those canyons is something I'd rather not do alone. "To keep the Society from hunting us down and making an example of us, the best time to go is during a firing when there's chaos. Like a night firing. But with a full moon, so that we can see. They might think we died instead of escaped."

Vick laughs. "Both the Society and the Enemy have infrared. Whoever's above will see us run."

"I know, but they might miss three little bodies when there's plenty more right here."

"Three?" Vick asks.

"Eli's coming with us." I hadn't known until I said it.

Silence.

"You're crazy," Vick says. "There's no way that kid will last until then."

"I know," I tell Vick. He's right. It's only a matter of time before Eli goes down. He's small. He's impulsive. He asks too many questions. Then again, it's only a matter of time for all of us.

"So why keep him around? Why bring him along?"

"There's a girl I know back in Oria," I say. "He reminds me of her brother."

"That's not reason enough."

"It is for me," I say.

Silence stretches between us.

"You're getting weak," Vick says finally. "And that might kill you. Might mean you never see her again."

"If I don't look out for him," I tell Vick, "I'd be someone she didn't know, even if she *did* see me again."

CHAPTER 6
CASSIA

O nce I'm sure the others sleep, their breathing heavy in the room, I roll over onto my side and slip the Archivist's paper from my pocket.

The page feels pulpy and cheap, not like the thick cream-colored sheet with Grandfather's poems. It's old, but not as old as Grandfather's paper. My father might be able to tell me the age; but he's not here, he let me go. As I unfold the page carefully it makes small sounds that seem loud, and I hope the other girls will think it is the rustling of blankets or an insect singing its wings.

It took a long time for everyone to fall asleep tonight. When I came back from my outing they told me that none of us have received our transfer assignments yet; that the Officer said they would tell us our destinations in the morning. I understood the girls' uneasiness—I feel it, too. We've always known the night before where we'd be sent the next day. Why the change? With the Society, there's always a reason.

I slide the paper into a square of spilled-white light from the moon outside. My heart pounds quickly, a running beat though I am still. *Please let this be worth the cost,* I think to nothing and no one, and then I look at the page.

No.

I push my fist against my mouth to keep from saying the word out loud into the sleeping room.

It's not a map, or even a set of directions.

It's a story, and I know the moment I read the first line that it's not one of the Hundred:

A man pushed a rock up the hill. When he reached the top, the stone rolled down to the bottom of the hill and he began again. In the village nearby, the people took note. "A judgment," they said. They never joined him or tried to help because they feared those who issued the punishment. He pushed. They watched.

Years later, a new generation noticed that the man and his stone were sinking into the hill, like the setting of the sun and moon. They could only see part of the rock and part of the man as he rolled the stone along to the top of the hill.

One of the children became curious. So, one day, the child walked up the hill. As she drew closer, she was surprised to see that the stone was carved with names and dates and places.

"What are all these words?" the child asked.

"The sorrows of the world," the man told her. "I pilot them up the hill over and over again."

"You are using them to wear out the hill," the child said, noticing the long deep groove worn where the stone had turned.

"I am making something," the man said. "When I am finished, it will be your turn to take my place."

The child was not afraid. "What are you making?"

"A river," the man said.

The child went back down the hill, puzzling at how one could make a river. But not long after, when the rains came and the flood flashed through the long trough and washed the man somewhere far away, the child saw that the man had been right, and she took her place pushing the stone and piloting the sorrows of the world.

This is how the Pilot came to be.

The Pilot is a man who pushed a stone and washed away in the water. It is a woman who crossed the river and looked to the sky. The Pilot is old and young and has eyes of every color and hair of every shade; lives in deserts, islands, forests, mountains, and plains.

The Pilot leads the Rising—the rebellion against the Society— and the Pilot never dies. When one Pilot's time has finished, another comes to lead.

And so it goes on, over and over like a stone rolling.

Someone in the room turns and stirs and I freeze, waiting for the girl's breathing to even back into sleep. When it does, I look down at the last line on the page:

In a place past the edge of the Society's map, the Pilot will always live and move.

The hot pain of hope shoots unexpectedly through me as I realize what this truly says, what I've been given.

There's a rebellion. Something real and organized and longstanding, with a leader.

Ky and I are not alone.

The word *Pilot* was the link. Did Grandfather know this? Is that why he gave me the paper before he died? Have I been wrong all along about the poem he meant me to follow?

I can't sit still.

"Wake up," I whisper so softly that I can barely hear myself. "We're not alone." I put one foot over the edge of my bed. I could climb down and wake the other girls and tell them about the Rising. Maybe they already know. I don't think so. They seem so hopeless. Except for Indie. But, though she has more fire to her than the others, she also doesn't have purpose. I don't think she knows either.

I should tell Indie.

For a moment I think I'll do it. My feet hit the ground softly as I reach the bottom of the ladder, and I open my mouth. Then I hear the sound of an Officer on patrol walking past our door and I freeze, the dangerous paper like a small white flag in my hand.

In that moment I know that I won't tell the others. I'll do what I always do when someone trusts me with dangerous words:

I'll destroy.

"What are you doing?" Indie asks softly behind me. I didn't hear her coming across the room, and I almost jump but I catch myself in time.

"Washing my hands again," I whisper, resisting the urge to turn around. The icy water streams over my fingers, making a river sound in the dark of the cabin. "I didn't get them clean enough earlier. You know how the Officers are about getting dirt on the beds."

"You'll wake the others," she says. "They had a hard time getting to sleep."

"I'm sorry," I say, and I am. But I could think of no other way to drown the words.

It took me long agonizing moments to rip the paper into tiny bits. First I held it against my lips, breathed on it so that the tearing wouldn't be so loud. I hope I've torn the pieces small enough that they won't choke and flood the sink.

Indie reaches across and turns off the water. For a moment I think she *does* know something. Perhaps she doesn't know about the Rising, the rebellion, but I have the strangest feeling she knows something about me.

Click. Click. The heels of the patrol Officer's boots on the cement. Indie and I both dart for our beds, and I climb the rungs as fast as I can and peer out the window.

The Officer pauses by our cabin for a moment, listening, and then walks on.

I stay sitting up for a moment, watching her go back along the path. She pauses at the door of another cabin.

A rebellion. A Pilot.

Who could it be?

Does Ky know about any of this?

He might. The man in the story who pushes the stone sounds like Sisyphus, and Ky told me about him back in the

Borough. And I remember how Ky gave me his own story in pieces. I have never thought I had all of it.

Finding him has been the only thing for so long. Even without a map, even without the compass, I know I can do it. I've imagined the moment of meeting over and over again; how he'll pull me close, how I'll whisper a poem to him. The only flaw in my dream is that I haven't finished writing anything for him yet; I can never get past the first line. I've written so many beginnings over these months out here and yet the middle and the end of our kind of love are things I haven't seen yet for myself.

I pull the bag tight against my side and lie down as gently as I can, cell by cell, it feels, until the bed bears all my weight, from the light ends of my hair to the heaviness of my legs, my feet. I won't sleep tonight.

They come in the early dawn, the way they came for Ky.

I don't hear any screams but something else alerts me. Some heaviness in the air, perhaps; some change in the notes of the birds who sing the morning in as they pause in the trees while traveling south.

I sit up and look out the window. Officers bring girls from other cabins, some of whom cry and try to twist away. I press close to the glass to see more, my heart pounding, sure that I know the girls' destination.

How can I go with them? My mind sorts the numbers. How many miles, how many variables there are against my getting this close again. I couldn't seem to get to the Outer Provinces on my own, but perhaps the Society will take me there now.

Two Officers push open the door. "We need two girls from this cabin," one of them says. "Bunk 8 and Bunk 3." The girl from Bunk 8 sits up, looking startled and tired.

Bunk 3, Indie's bunk, is empty.

The Officers exclaim and I look out the window. Someone stands alone on the edge of the trees that grow near the path. It's Indie. Even in the light-leaking dawn, I know who she is by her bright hair, by the way she stands. She must have heard too and slipped out somehow. I didn't see her leave.

She's going to run.

While the Officers are distracted with pulling the girl from Bunk 8 and calling into their miniports about Indie, I move fast. I slip the three tablets from my container—green, blue, red—and wrap them up inside my packet of blue tablets. I hide the tablets under the messages in my bag and pray no one will search too deep. The container I tuck underneath my mattress. I have to get rid of as many signs of Citizenship as I can.

And then I realize.

Something is missing from my bag.

The silver box from my Match Banquet.

I rifle once more through the papers; feel my way along the blankets on the bed; look down at the floor. I haven't dropped it or lost it; it's gone.

I would have had to get rid of it anyway; that's what I planned to do; but the loss is unsettling.

Where could it be?

There's no time to worry about it now. I slip down from my bunk to follow the Officers and the crying girl. The others in the cabin pretend to sleep, just like the people in the Borough on the morning they took Ky.

"*Run, Indie,*" I whisper under my breath. I hope we both get what we want.

If you love someone, if someone loved you, if they taught you to write and made it so you could speak, how can you do nothing at all? You might as well take their words out of the dirt and try to snatch them from the wind.

Because once you love, it is gone. You love and you cannot call it back.

Ky is heavy in my mind, deep in my heart, his palms warm on my empty hands. I have to try to find him. Loving him gave me wings and all my work has given me the strength to move them.

An air ship lands in the center of the camp. The Officers, some of whom I haven't seen before, look harried, worried. The one wearing a pilot's uniform says something curt and looks at the sky. The sun will rise soon.

"We're missing one," I hear him say quietly, and then I slip into line.

"Are you sure?" the other Officer asks, running her eyes over us. Counting. Her expression changes and she looks relieved. She has long lovely brown hair and seems gentle, for an Officer.

"No," she says. "We have enough."

"We do?" asks the first Officer. He counts for himself. Do I imagine that his eyes linger on my face, remembering that I wasn't there before? Not for the first time, I wonder how much of what I do is known and predicted by my Official. Does *she* still watch? Does the Society?

Another Officer hauls Indie on board as the rest of us finish filing through the door. There are claw marks on his face. Field dirt streaks his uniform and her plainclothes, like wounds seeping soil.

"She tried to run," he says, pushing her into the seat next to me. He snaps a pair of handlocks onto Indie's wrists. She doesn't flinch at the sound of them snapping shut, but I do.

"Now we have too many," the female Officer says.

"They're Aberrations," he snaps. "Does it matter? We have to go."

"Should we search them now?" she asks.

No. They'll find the tablets in my bag.

"We'll do it in the air. Let's go."

Indie looks over at me and our eyes meet. For the first time since I've known her, I feel a strange sense of kinship with her, of familiarity that's as close to friendship as we've come. We knew each other in the work camp. Now, we're crossing into a new experience together.

Something about all of this feels strange—harried, unorganized, unlike the Society. Even though I'm grateful for the chance to slip through the crack, I still feel their walls pressing in on every side, their presence both crushing and comforting.

An Official boards the air ship. "Everything ready?" he asks, and the Officers nod. I wait for more Officials to climb on—they almost always move in threes—but the door closes. Only one Official, and three Officers, one of them the pilot. By the way the Officers react to the Official, I can tell that he is the highest-ranking of the group.

The air ship lifts into the sky. It's my first time traveling like this—I've only been in air cars and on air trains and transports before—and my stomach sinks with disappointment when I realize there are no windows.

This is not how I thought it would be to fly high. No sight of what lies below or where the stars might be when night comes. The pilot in the front compartment of the air ship looks out; but the Society keeps the rest of us from the sight of our own flight.

CHAPTER 7
KY

Everyone's watching you," Vick tells me.

I ignore him. Some of the cylinders the Enemy shot down at us last night didn't explode completely. They still had powder inside. I push some of it into the barrel of a gun. The Enemy puzzles me—their ammunition seems to become more and more primitive and less and less effective the longer we're out here. Maybe they really are losing.

"What are you doing?" Vick asks.

I don't answer. I'm trying to remember how this is done. The powder turns my hands black as I sift it through my fingers.

Vick grabs my arm. "Stop," he says in a low voice. "All the other decoys are staring."

"Why do you care what they think?"

"It's bad for morale if someone like you goes crazy."

"You said yourself that we're not their leaders," I say to Vick. Then I look over at the decoys. They all avoid my eyes except for Eli. He stares at me and I give him a quick grin to let him know that I'm not insane.

"Ky," Vick says, and then he suddenly gets it. "You figuring out a way to turn this back into ammo?"

"It won't be much good," I say. "It'll only do one big blast, and you'll have to treat it like a grenade. Throw the gun and run away."

Vick likes the possibilities. "We could put rocks, other stuff in there. Have you figured out the fuse?"

"Not yet," I say. "That's the hardest part."

"Why?" he asks, speaking low so the others can't hear. "It's a good idea, sure, but it's going to be too hard to set it off while we're running."

"It's not for us," I say, and I glance again at the others. "We'll teach them how to do it before we leave. But we're running out of time. I say we leave the dead to everyone else today."

Vick stands up, turns around to face the group. "Ky and I are taking a break from burying today," he says. "The rest of you can take a turn. Some of you new decoys haven't even done it yet."

While they leave, I look down at my hands—ash-black and covered with the stuff that rained down death on us the night before—and remember the way we used to scavenge remnants back in my real village. The Society and the Enemy thought they were the only ones with fire but we knew how to use theirs. And how to make our own. We used stones called *chert* to light small fires when we really needed them.

"I still think we should go on a night where there isn't a

firing," Vick says. "They might just think we blew ourselves up with this stuff if we can make it convincing." He gestures to the powder scattered all around us.

He has a point. I've been so sure that they'll hunt us down that I haven't thought of other possibilities. Still, it's more likely that others will try to follow if there isn't a battle to distract them and death to cover our tracks. And I don't want anyone to try to come with us. The Society will notice if more than a few decoys leave, and we might still be worth hunting.

And I have no idea what we're going to find in the Carving. I'm not trying to lead. I only want to survive.

"How about this?" I say. "We'll go tonight. Whether there's a firing or not."

"All right," Vick says after a moment.

It's settled then. We're going to run. Soon.

Vick and I work fast, trying to come up with a way to get the guns to explode. When the others come back from digging the graves and figure out what we're trying to do, they help us by gathering gunpowder and rocks. Some of the boys begin humming and singing as they work. I go cold as I recognize the tune, although I shouldn't be surprised by what they sing. It's the Anthem of the Society. The Society took music away by choosing the Hundred Songs carefully—complicated songs that only their engineered voices can navigate easily—and the Anthem is the only tune that most people can carry. Even it has a rising soprano line that no untrained person could sing.

Most people can only copy the flat, drumming bass line or the easy notes of the alto and tenor parts. That's what I hear now.

Some of those who lived in the Outer Provinces managed to hold onto their old songs. We used to sing them together while we worked. A woman once told me that it wasn't hard to remember ancient melodies with rivers and canyons and the Carving nearby.

I only wanted to remember the *how* of doing this. But the *who* and *why* from before keep coming back too.

Vick shakes his head. "Even if we figure this out, we're still leaving them to die," he says.

"I know," I say. "But at least they can fight back."

"Once," Vick says. There's a slump to his shoulders that I've never seen before. As if he's finally realizing the leader he is and always has been and the realization weighs him down.

"It's not enough," I say, turning back to my work.

"No," Vick agrees.

I've tried not to really see the other decoys but I have. One has a bruised face. Another has freckles who looks enough like the boy we put in the river that I wonder if they were brothers, but I never asked and I never will. All of them wear ill-fitting plainclothes and fancy coats to keep them warm while they wait to die.

"What's your real name?" Vick asks me suddenly.

"Ky is my real name," I tell him.

"But what's your full name?"

I pause for a minute as it flashes across my mind for the first time in years. *Ky Finnow.* That was my name then.

"Roberts," Vick says, impatient with my hesitation. "That's *my* last name. Vick Roberts."

"Markham," I tell him. "Ky Markham." Because that's the name she knows me by. That's my real name now.

Still, my other name sounded right, too, when I said it in my mind. *Finnow.* The name I shared with my father and mother.

I look over at the decoys gathering rocks. Part of me likes the sense of purpose in their movements and knowing that I helped them feel better for even a little while. But deep down I know that all I've done is throw them a scrap. They're still going to starve.

CHAPTER 8
CASSIA

The Society's first order of business, as we all sit in the well-chilled air and shiver, is to promise us coats. "Before the Society, when the Warming happened, things changed in the Outer Provinces," the Official tells us. "It gets cold, but not as cold as it once did. It's still possible to freeze at night, but if you wear the coats, you'll be fine."

The Outer Provinces, then. It's certain. The other girls, even Indie, look straight ahead; they don't blink. Some of them shake more than others.

"This is no different from any other work camp assignment," the Official says into our silence. "We need you to plant a crop. Cotton, actually. We want the Enemy to think that this part of the country is still occupied and viable. It's a strategic action on the part of the Society."

"It's true then? There's a war with the Enemy?" one of the girls asks.

The Official laughs. "Not much of one. The Society is solidly in power. But the Enemy is unpredictable. We need them to think the Outer Provinces are well-populated and thriving. And the Society doesn't want any one group to bear the burden of living out there too long. So they've implemented a six-month rotation program. As soon as your time is up, you'll come back, as Citizens."

None of this is true, I think, *even though it seems that you believe it is.*

"Now," he says, gesturing at the two Officers who aren't piloting the ship. "They will take you behind that curtain, search you, and give you your standard-issue attire. Including the coats."

They're going to search us. Now.

I'm not the first girl called back. Frantic, I try to find a place to hide the tablets, but I can't see a spot. The Society-made landscape of the air ship is all slick smooth surfaces, no nooks and crannies. Even our seats are hard and smooth, the belts strapping us in simple and tight. There's nowhere to put the tablets.

"Something to hide?" Indie whispers to me.

"Yes," I say. Why lie?

"Me too," she whispers. "I'll take yours. You take mine when it's my turn."

I open my bag and slide out the package of tablets. Before I can do anything more, Indie—quick even in her handlocks—palms it. What will she do next? What does she need to hide and how will she reach it with her hands cuffed like that?

I don't have time to see. "Next," the brown-haired Officer calls out, pointing to me.

Don't look back at Indie, I tell myself. *Don't give anything away.*

Back behind the curtain, I have to strip down to my underclothes, while the Officer searches the pockets of my old brown plainclothes. She hands me a new set of plainclothes—black.

"Let's see the bag," she says, taking it from me. She rifles through the messages, and I try not to wince as one of the older ones from Bram comes apart in pieces.

She hands the bag back to me. "You can get dressed," she says.

The moment I finish with the last button on my shirt, the Officer calls out to the head Official. "This one has nothing," she says about me. The Official nods.

Back in my seat next to Indie, I slide my arms into my newly acquired coat. "I'm ready," I say softly, barely moving my lips.

"It's already in your coat pocket," Indie says.

I want to ask her how she's done it so quickly but I don't want to be overheard. I feel almost giddy with relief at what we managed. What *Indie* managed.

When the Officer points at Indie a few moments later, she stands up and walks with her head bowed and her locked hands held obediently in front of her. *Indie does a good job pretending to be broken,* I think to myself.

Across the ship, the girl they searched after me begins to sob. I wonder if she tried to hide something and failed—which is what would have happened to me without Indie.

"You'd better cry," another girl says dully. "We're going to the Outer Provinces."

"Leave her alone," a third girl says. The Official notices the crying girl and brings her a green tablet.

Indie says nothing when she returns from the search. She doesn't glance in my direction. I feel the weight of the tablets in my coat pocket. I wish I could look and make sure they are all there, the blue ones from Xander and my own three tucked inside, but I don't. I trust Indie and she trusts me. The weight of the package is almost the same; any added heaviness imperceptible. Whatever she wanted to hide must be small and light.

I wonder what it is. Perhaps she will tell me later.

They give us minimal gear: two days' worth of food rations, an extra set of plainclothes, a canteen, a pack in which we can carry everything. No knives, nothing sharp. No guns or weapons. A flashlight, but so lightweight and full of curved edges that it wouldn't be much good for fighting.

Our coats are light but warm, made of something special, I can tell; and I wonder why they'd waste resources on people they send out here. The coats are the only sign that they might care if we live or die. More than anything else they've given us, the coats represent investment. Expenditure.

I glance up at the Official. He turns, opens the door to the pilot's compartment again. He leaves it slightly ajar, and I can see the constellation of instruments lit up on the panel inside. To me they seem as numerous and incomprehensible as the stars, but the pilot knows his way.

"This ship sounds like a river," Indie says.

"Are there many rivers where you're from?" I ask.

She nods.

"The only river I've heard of anywhere near here is the Sisyphus River," I say.

"The Sisyphus River?" Indie asks. I glance over to make sure the Officers and Official don't listen to us. They seem tired; the female Officer even closes her eyes briefly.

"The Society poisoned it," I tell her. "Nothing can live in it, or on its banks. Nothing can grow there."

Indie looks at me. "You can't ever really kill a river," she says. "You can't kill anything that's always moving and changing."

The Official moves around the air ship, talking to the pilot, speaking with the other Officers. Something about the way he moves on the ship reminds me of Ky; the way he could balance on a moving air train and anticipate small shifts in direction.

Ky did not need the compass with him to do that. I can travel without it, too.

I fly toward Ky and away from Xander and into what is Outer, different.

"Almost there," the brown-haired Officer calls out. She glances over at us and I see something there—pity. She feels sorry for all of us. For me.

She shouldn't. No one on this air ship should. I am finally going to the Outer Provinces.

I let myself imagine that Ky waits for me when we land. That I am only moments away from seeing him. Maybe even touching his hand, and later, in the dark, his lips.

"You're smiling," Indie says.

"I know," I say.

CHAPTER 9
KY

Evening falls hard while we wait for the moon. The sky turns blue and pink and blue again. A darker, deeper blue, the next thing to black.

I still haven't told Eli that we're going.

Moments ago, Vick and I showed everyone how to fire the guns. Now we're waiting to run out on the others and down into the gaping jagged mouth of the Carving.

We hear the sharp beep of an incoming message on the miniport. Vick puts it up to his ear and listens.

I wonder what the Enemy thinks of us, these people that the Society rarely bothers to defend. They gun us down and then we crawl back out in a seemingly endless supply. Do we seem like rats, mice, fleas, some kind of vermin that can't be killed? Or does the Enemy have some idea of what the Society is doing?

"Listen," Vick calls out. He's finished with the miniport. "I just got a message from an Official in charge." A murmur runs through the crowd. They stand with black-powdered hands and eyes alive with hope. It's hard to keep from looking away. Words start going through my mind, a familiar rhythm, and it's only after a few moments that I realize what I'm doing. I'm saying the words for the dead over them.

"We're getting new villagers soon," Vick says.

"How many?" someone calls out.

"I don't know," Vick says. "All I know is that the Official says they're going to be different, but we're to treat them as any other villager and we'll be accountable for anything that happens to them."

Everyone's silent. That's one of the things they told us that *has* held true—if any of us kill or hurt one of the others, the Officials come for you. Fast. We've seen it before. The Society made it clear: we're not to injure each other. That's for the Enemy to do.

"Maybe they're sending a big group," someone calls out. "Maybe we should wait until they get here to try to fight."

"No," Vick says, the ring of authority in his voice. "If the Enemy comes tonight, we fire tonight." He points to the round white moon rising along the horizon. "Let's get in position."

"What do you think he means?" Eli asks after the others have gone. "About the new villagers being different?"

Vick sets his mouth in a firm line and I know we've had the same thought. Girls. They're going to send girls.

"You're right," Vick says, looking at me. "They're getting rid of Aberrations."

"And I bet they let all the Anomalies get gunned down before us," I say, and almost before the words are out of my mouth I see Vick's hand tighten into a fist and he swings right at my face. I move just in time. He misses, and instinctively I hit him square in the stomach. He staggers back but doesn't fall.

Eli gasps. Vick and I stare at each other.

The agony in Vick's eyes didn't come from the punch I landed. Vick's been hit before, like I have. We can handle that kind of pain. I'm not sure why what I said caused such a reaction in him, but I know there's no way he'll ever tell. I keep my secrets. He keeps his.

"You think I'm an Anomaly?" Vick asks, quiet. Eli takes a step back, keeping his distance.

"No," I say.

"What if I were?"

"I'd be glad," I say. "It would mean that someone survived. Or that I'm wrong about what the Society's doing out here—"

Vick and I both look at the sky. We've heard the same thing, felt the same shift.

The Enemy.

The moon is up.

And it's full.

"They're coming!" Vick calls out.

Other voices pick up the call. They shout and yell and I hear terror and anger and something else in their voices that I recognize from long ago. The joy of fighting back.

Vick looks at me and I know we think the same thing. We're tempted to stay and fight this out. I shake my head at

Vick. *No.* He can stay, but I won't. I have to get out of here. I have to try to get back to Cassia.

Flashlights move and shift in the light. Dark figures run and scream.

"Now," Vick says.

I drop my gun and grab Eli's arm. "Come with us," I tell Eli. He looks at me, confused.

"Where?" he asks. I point in the direction of the Carving, and his eyes widen. *"There?"*

"There," I say, *"now."*

Eli hesitates for just a moment and then he nods and we run. I leave the gun behind on the ground. One more chance, maybe, for someone else, and out of the corner of my eye I see Vick put his gun down too, and the miniport next to it.

In the night, it feels like we're running fast over the back of some kind of enormous animal, sprinting over its spines and through patches of tall, thin, gold grass that now glimmers like silver fur in the moonlight. Soon enough we'll hit hard rock as we get closer to the Carving, and that's when we'll be the most exposed.

Less than half a mile later I feel Eli falling back. "Drop the gun," I tell him, and when he doesn't, I reach over and knock it out of his hands. It clatters to the ground and Eli stops.

"Eli," I say, and then the firing begins.

And the screaming.

"Run," I tell Eli. "Don't listen." I try not to hear any of it either—the screaming, the yelling, the dying.

We hit the edge of the sandstone, and Eli and I pull up next to Vick, who has stopped to get his bearings. "That way," I say, pointing.

"We have to go back and help them," Eli says.

Vick doesn't answer but takes off again, running.

"Ky?"

"Keep running, Eli," I tell him.

"Don't you care that they're dying?" Eli asks.

Pop-pop-pop.

The pathetic little sounds of the guns we rigged come from behind us. Out here, it's nothing.

"Don't you want to live?" I ask Eli, furious that he's making this so hard, that he won't let me forget what is happening behind us.

And then the animal underneath our feet shudders. Something big has hit, and Eli and I move fast, no instinct left but to live. Nothing in my mind except *run*.

I've done this before. Years ago. My father told me once, "If anything happens, run for the Carving," he said, and so I did it. As always, I wanted to survive.

But that time the Officials came down in an air ship in front of me, making short work of the miles it had taken me hours to run. They pushed me to the ground. I struggled. A rock scraped against my face. But I held on to the one thing I'd carried out of the village—my mother's paintbrush.

On the air ship I saw the only other survivor—a girl from my village. Once we were flying again, the Officials held out the red tablets for us to take. I'd heard the rumors. I thought I was going to die. So I clamped my mouth shut. I wouldn't take mine.

"Come now," said one of the Officials sympathetically, and then she shoved my mouth open and pushed a green tablet in. The false calm came over me, and I couldn't fight when she put the red one in my mouth too. But my hands knew. They gripped the paintbrush so hard that it broke.

I didn't die. They took us back behind a curtain in the air ship and washed our hands and faces and hair. They were gentle with us while we were forgetting and gave us fresh clothes and told us a new story to remember instead of what really happened.

"We're sorry," they said, arranging their faces into expressions of regret. "The Enemy made a strike on the fields where many in your village were working. Overall casualties were low, but your parents were killed."

I thought, *Why tell us this? Do you think we're going to forget? Casualties weren't low. Almost everyone died. And they weren't in the fields. I saw it all.*

The girl cried and nodded and believed, even though she should have known they were lying. And I realized that forgetting was exactly what I was supposed to do.

I pretended to forget. I nodded like the girl and tried to put the same blank look on my face that she had under her tears.

But I didn't cry like she did. I knew that if I did I would never stop. And then they would know what I'd really seen.

They took away the broken paintbrush and asked why I had it.

And for a moment I panicked. I couldn't remember. Was the red tablet working? Then I did remember. I had the paintbrush because it was my mother's. I found it in the village when I came down from the plateau after the firing.

I looked at them and said, "I don't know. I found it."

They believed me and I learned how to lie just enough to not get caught.

The Carving looms closer now. "Which one?" Vick calls out to me. Up close to the Carving you can see what you can't see from far away—the deep cracks in its surface. Each a different canyon and a different choice.

I don't know. I've never been here before, only heard my father talk about it, but I have to decide fast. I'm the leader now for a minute. "That one," I say, pointing to the closest divide in the earth. The one with a pile of boulders lying near it. Something about it seems right, like a story I have known before.

No flashlights now. The moon will have to do. We need both hands to get down into the earth. I cut my arm on a rock and the burrs of plants attach anywhere they can, like stowaways.

Behind us, I hear a boom—a sound that isn't like the Enemy's fire. And it wasn't in the village. It was close. Somewhere on the plain right behind us.

"What's that?" Eli asks.

"Go," Vick and I tell him at the same time, and we scramble fast, faster, cut and bleeding and bruised. Hunted.

After a few moments, Vick pauses and I push past him. We have to get deep inside the slot canyon *now*. "Careful," I call back. "Ground's rocky." I hear Eli and Vick breathing behind me.

"What was that?" Eli asks again as soon as we get inside.

"Someone followed us," Vick says. "And got shot down."

"We can stop for a minute," I say, climbing under a large overhang of rock. Vick and Eli scramble in with me.

Vick's breathing is raspy. I look at him. "It's fine," he says. "It happens when I run, especially where there's dust."

"Who shot them down?" Eli asks. "The Enemy?"

Vick doesn't say anything.

"*Who?*" Eli asks, voice shrill.

"I don't know," Vick says. "I really don't."

"You don't know?" Eli says.

"No one knows anything," Vick says. "Except Ky. He thinks he's found the truth in a girl."

Hate boils up in me, pure exhausted rage, but before I can do anything, Vick adds, "Who knows. He might be right." He pushes away from the rocky wall he's leaning against. "Let's go. You first."

The canyon air burns cold in my throat as I draw in my breath and wait for my eyes to adjust and the shades of darkness to turn into shapes of rocks and plants. "This way," I say. "Shine your flashlights low if you need them, but the moon should be enough."

The Society likes to keep things from us, but the wind doesn't care what we know. It brings hints of what has happened as we slip farther into the canyon—the smell of smoke and a white substance that falls on us. White ash. I don't for one moment think that it's snow.

CHAPTER 10
CASSIA

When we land I want to be the first off the air ship, to see if Ky is there. But I remember what he told me back in the Borough about blending in, so I stay in the middle of the group of girls and search for Ky in the rows and rows of black-coated boys standing before us.

He's not here.

"Remember," the Official says to the boys, "treat these new villagers as you treat the others. No violence of any kind. We'll be watching and listening."

No one responds. There doesn't seem to be a leader. Next to me, Indie shifts her weight. A girl behind us stifles a sob.

"Come forward to get your rations," the Official says, and there is no pushing. No shoving. The boys all drift into a line and file past. It must have rained last night. Their boots are thick with red clay mud.

I look at each face.

Some seem terrified; some seem cunning and dangerous. None seem kind. They have all seen too much. I watch their backs, their hands as they take the supplies, their faces as they pass the Official. They don't fight over the food; there is some for everyone. They fill their canteens from big blue barrels of water.

I'm sorting them, I realize. And then I think, *What if I had to sort myself?* I wonder. *What would I see? Would I see someone who is going to survive?*

I try to look down at myself, at the girl who watches the Official and the Officers pack up and leave in the air ship. She wears unfamiliar clothes and looks hungrily at faces she does not know. I look down on her tangled brown hair, the way she stands small and straight, even after the Officers and Official leave and one of the boys steps forward to tell the new girls that there is no crop, that the Enemy shoots every night, that the Society has stopped giving out weapons and that the weapons never worked anyway, that everyone in the camp has been sent here to die and no one knows why.

The girl stays straight and strong when others sink to their knees because she knew this all along. She can't quit, can't throw her hands in the air or cry tears into the dirt because she has someone to find. Alone out of all the girls, she smiles a little.

Yes, I tell myself. *She is going to survive.*

Indie asks me for the packet. I hand it to her and, as she slips something from inside the tablets and hands them back, I realize I still don't know what it was that she needed to hide. But now is not the time to ask. There's another, more urgent question to answer: Where is Ky?

"I am looking for someone," I say loudly. "His name is Ky." Some have already begun to leave, now that the boy has finished telling us the truth.

"He has dark hair and blue eyes," I call out, louder. "He came from a city, but he knows this land, too. He has words." I wonder if he's found a way to sell them, barter them for something out here.

People stare back with different colors of eyes—blue, brown, green, gray. But none of the colors are Ky's; none of the blues are quite right.

"You should try to rest now," the boy who told us the truth says. "It's hard to sleep at night. That's when they usually fire." He seems exhausted, and I see a miniport in his hand as he turns away. Was he the leader once? Does he keep on delivering information now out of habit?

Others turn away, too. The apathy here frightens me more than the situation itself. These people don't seem to know about any rebellion or Rising. If no one cares anymore, if everyone has given up, who will help me find Ky?

"I can't sleep," a girl from our air ship says softly. "What if it's my last day?"

At least she can talk. Some of the others seem almost catatonic with shock. I see a boy walk over to one of the girls, say something. She shrugs, looks back at us, walks away with him.

My heart beats faster. Should I stop her? What will he do?

"Have you looked at their boots?" Indie whispers to me.

I nod. I've noticed the mud on them and the boots themselves—thick-soled and made of rubber. They're like ours, except the sides of their soles are scarred with notches. I have an idea of what they must mean, what they must mark. Days survived. My heart sinks because none of the boys have very many cuts in their boots. And Ky has been gone for almost twelve weeks.

People shuffle away. They seem to be going to the places where they sleep, minding their own business, but a few boys circle our group of girls. They look hungry.

Don't sort, I tell myself. *See.*

They have very few notches carved in their soles. They aren't apathetic yet. They still want things. They are new. They likely haven't been here long enough to know Ky.

You're still sorting. See.

One has burned hands and black powder all over his boots, clear up to his knees; he stands at the back of the group. He sees me looking at his hands and locks eyes with me, makes a gesture I do not like. But I hold his gaze. I try to see.

"You know him," I say to the boy. "You know who I'm talking about."

I don't expect him to admit it, but he nods.

"Where is he?" I ask.

"Dead," the boy says.

"You lie," I say, pushing down the rush of tears and the

worry inside. "But I'll listen to you when you want to tell the truth."

"What makes you think I'd tell you anything?" he asks.

"You don't have much time left to talk," I say. "None of us do."

Indie stands next to me, her eyes on the horizon. She looks for what might come our way. Others gather near us, listening.

For a moment, it seems that the boy might speak, but then he laughs and turns away.

But I'm not worried. I know he'll be back—I saw it in his eyes. And I'll be ready.

The day passes long and short at the same time. Everyone waits. The pack of boys returns, but something keeps them at a distance from our group. Perhaps it is the threat of the old leader, who stays near us, miniport at hand to report anything untoward. Do they fear the consequences if they injure us and the Official comes back?

I'm eating my foilware dinner with the other girls when I see the burned-hand boy coming back toward me. I stand up and hold out the last of my food. The portions are so small here; anyone who's been out here for long must be starving.

"Stupid," Indie mutters next to me, but she stands up, too. After helping each other on the air ship we seem to have become allied somehow.

"You bribing me?" the boy asks, venom in his voice, as he gets closer and sees my outstretched offering of meat-and-carb casserole.

"Of course," I say. "You're the only one who was there. You're the only one who knows."

"I could just take it," he says. "I could take anything I wanted from you."

"You could," I say. "But it wouldn't be smart."

"Why not?" he says.

"Because no one else will listen the way I will," I say. "No one else wants to know. But I do. I want to know what you saw."

He hesitates.

"The others don't want to hear about it, do they?" I ask.

He leans back and brushes a hand through his hair, a gesture left over from another time, I think, because it is short now, like all the other boys'. "All right," he says. "But it was in a different camp. The one I was in before I came here. It might not be the same person. The Ky I know had words, like you said."

"What words did he have?" I ask.

The boy shrugs. "Ones to say over the dead."

"What did they sound like?" I ask.

"I don't remember much," he says. "Something about a Pilot."

I blink in surprise. Ky knew the words of the Tennyson poem, too. How? Then I remember that day in the woods

88

when I first opened the compact. Ky told me later that he saw me. Perhaps he saw that poem too, over my shoulder, or perhaps I whispered it aloud as I read it again and again there in the woods. I smile. *So we share the second poem, too.*

Indie looks back and forth between the boy and me, her eyes curious. "What did he mean about the Pilot?" she asks.

The boy shrugs. "I don't know. It was something he said whenever people died. That's all." Then the boy begins to laugh, a sound without any humor in it. "But he must have been saying those words for hours that last night."

"What happened the last night?"

"There was a firing," he says, no more laughter. "The worst one of all."

"When was it?"

He looks down at his boot. "Two nights ago," he says, as if he can hardly believe it. "Feels like it's been longer than that."

"You saw him that night?" I say, my heart racing. If this boy is to be believed, Ky was alive and near two nights ago. "Are you sure? You saw his face?"

"Not his face," the boy says, "his back. He and his friend Vick ran off and left us for dead. They left us to die so they could save themselves. Only six of us survived. I don't know where the Officers took the other five after they brought me here. I'm the only one in this camp."

Indie glances at me, her eyes questioning, asking *Is it him?* It doesn't seem like Ky, to leave people behind, and yet it *does* seem like Ky to find the one chance in a hopeless situation and take it. "So he took off the night of the firing. And left you—" I can't finish the sentence.

It's silent there under the sky.

"I don't blame them," the boy says, his bitterness turning to exhaustion. "I'd have done the same thing. If too many of us ran, we'd have been caught. They tried to help us. Showed us how to make it so our guns would fire once, so we could at least shoot back. Still, they knew what they were doing the night they left. Their timing was perfect. So many people died that night, some of them from our own guns, the Society might not know who ended up ash and who didn't. I noticed, though. I saw them go."

"Do you know where they are now?" Indie asks.

"Somewhere in there." He points toward the sandstone formations barely visible from here. "Our village was over near those rocks. He called that place the Carving. He must have been desperate. It's death in there. Anomalies, scorpions, flash floods. Still . . . " He pauses, looks up at the sky. "They took this kid with them. Eli. Only thirteen, probably, the youngest in our group, couldn't keep his mouth shut. What good was he to them? Why not take one of us?"

It *is* Ky. Hope and disappointment both wash over me.

"But if you saw him go, why didn't you follow?" I ask.

"I saw what happened to someone who did," the boy says flatly. "He was too late. The air ships gunned him down. Only the three of them made it in." He looks back at the Carving again, remembering.

"How far away is the Carving?" I ask.

"A long run from here," he says. "Twenty-five, thirty miles." He raises his eyebrows at me. "So you think you'll get there on your own? It rained last night. Their footprints will be gone."

"I'd like you to help me," I say. "Show me where exactly he went."

He grins, a grin I don't like but can understand. "And what do I get in return?"

"Something you can use to survive in the canyons," I say, "stolen from a medical center in the Society. I'll tell you more when you get us to the Carving safely." I glance over at Indie. We haven't talked about whether or not she's coming with me; but it seems like we're a team now.

"Fine," he says, looking interested. "But I don't want another leftover meal that tastes like foilware." Indie makes a small sound of surprise, but I know why he's not holding out: he *wants* to leave with us. He wants to escape, too, but he won't do it alone. Not when he was in Ky's camp. Not now. He needs us as much as we need him.

"It won't be," I say. "I promise."

"We'll have to run all night. Can you do that?"

"Yes," I say.

"I can too," Indie says, and I glance over at her. "I'm

coming," she says, and it's not a question. She does what she wants. And this is the run of a lifetime.

"Good," I say.

"I'll come get you when it's dark and everyone's asleep," the boy says. "Find somewhere to rest. There's an old store, near the edge of the village. That might be the best place. The decoys who stay there won't hurt you."

"All right," I say. "But what if there's a firing?"

"If there's a firing, I'll come find you after it's over. If you're not dead. Did they give you flashlights?"

"Yes," I tell him.

"Bring them. The moon will help, but it's not full any more."

The moon comes up white over the black ridge, and I realize that the ridge was there all along, a thing I had forgotten, although I could have noticed it by the lack of stars in the space of its shape. The stars here are like the ones in Tana, many and sharp in the clean night air. "I'll be back soon," Indie says, and before I can stop her she slips away.

"Be careful," I whisper, too late. She's gone.

"When do they usually come?" one of the girls asks. We all stand gathered at the windows, which have no glass anymore. The wind blows through, its current a river of cold air from window to window.

"You never know," a boy says. His face is full of resignation. "You *never* know." He sighs. "When they do come, the best place is the cellars. This village has them. Some don't."

"Some people take their chances up here, though," another boy says. "I don't like the cellars. I don't think right when I'm down there."

They speak as though they've been here forever, but when I shine the flashlight down I see that they each only have five or six notches on their boots.

"I'm going to stand outside," I say after a while. "There's no rule against that, is there?"

"Stay in the shadows and don't shine the light," the boy who doesn't like the cellar tells me. "Don't draw attention. What if they're flying above, waiting?"

"All right," I say.

Indie slips in through the door just as I am leaving and I breathe a sigh of relief. She didn't run away again. "It's beautiful here," she says, almost conversationally, as she falls into step next to me.

She's right. If you can look past everything that's happening, the land *is* beautiful. The moon washes white light along the cement sidewalks and I see the boy. He's careful; he stays in the shadows, but I know he's there. His whisper next to my ear doesn't surprise me, and Indie doesn't jump either.

"When do we go?" I ask him.

"Now," he says. "Or you won't make it before dawn."

We follow him to the end of the town; I see other people slipping through the shadows, too, doing different things with the little time they have left. No one seems to notice us.

"Doesn't anyone try to escape?" I ask.

"Not often," he says.

"What about a rebellion?" I ask as we reach the edge of town. "Does anyone out here ever talk about something like that?"

"No," the boy says flatly. "We don't." He stops. "Take off your coats."

We stare at him. He laughs a little as he pulls off his coat and loops it through the strap of his pack. "You won't need it for long," he tells us. "You'll get warm fast enough."

Indie and I pull off our coats, too. Our black plainclothes blend with the night.

"Follow me," he says.

Then we run.

After a mile, only my hands are still cold.

Back in the Borough I ran barefoot on the grass to try to help Ky. Out here I wear heavy boots and have to run around rocks that threaten to turn my ankle and yet I feel lighter than I did back then, and lighter by far than I ever felt running on the smooth belt of the tracker. I'm filled with adrenaline and hope; I could run forever this way, running to Ky.

We pause to drink, and I feel the icy water thread through me. I can trace its exact path down my throat to my stomach, a trail of cold that makes me shudder, once, before I twist the lid back onto the canteen.

But too soon I start to tire.

I trip on a rock, dodge a bush too late. It sinks its teeth, its prickly seeds, into my clothes and my leg. Our feet crunch in frost. We're lucky there is no snow; and the air is desert-cold, a sharp, thin cold that tricks you into thinking you aren't thirsty, because breathing is like drinking in ice.

When I reach up and touch my lips, they are dry.

I don't look back over my shoulder to see if anyone chases us or swoops through the night to hover over our shoulders. We have enough to watch out for straight ahead. The moon gives sufficient light that we can see, but we risk the flashlights now and then when we come to shadowy places.

The boy turns his on and swears. "I forgot to look up," he says. When I do, I see that, in our struggle to avoid little ravines and sharp-edged rocks, we have begun to turn around.

"You're tired," Indie says to the boy. "Let me lead."

"I can do it," I say.

"Wait," Indie tells me, her voice tight and tired. "I think you might be the only one who'll have enough left to run us in at the end."

Our clothes catch on tough spiky bushes; the sharp smell in the air is distinct, dry. *Could it be sage?* I wonder. *Ky's favorite smell from home?*

Miles on, we stop running in a line. We run side by side. It is inefficient. But we need each other too much.

We've all fallen. We all bleed. The boy's injured his shoulder; Indie's legs are scraped; I fell into a small ravine and my body feels battered. We run so slow we almost walk.

"A marathon," Indie breathes. "That's what you call a run like this. I heard a story about it."

"Can you tell it to me?" I ask her.

"You don't want to hear it."

"I do." Anything to keep my mind off how hard this is, how far we still have to go. Even though we draw closer, any steps at all begin to feel like too many. I can't believe Indie can talk. The boy and I both stopped miles ago.

"It was at the end of the world. A message had to be delivered." She breathes hard, her words grow choppy. "Someone ran to deliver it. Twenty-six miles. Like us. He made it. Gave the message."

"And then they rewarded him?" I say, my breath ragged. "Did an air ship come down and save him?"

"No," she says. "He delivered his message. Then he died."

I start to laugh, which isn't good for saving breath, and Indie laughs, too. "I told you that you wouldn't want to hear it."

"At least the message got through," I say.

"I guess," Indie answers. As she glances over at me with a smile still on her face, I see that what I have mistaken for coldness in her is actually warmth. There's a fire in Indie that keeps her alive and moving even in a place like this.

The boy coughs and spits. He's been out here longer than we have. He sounds weak.

We stop talking.

A few miles still out from the Carving, the air smells different. Not clean, like the plant smell from earlier, but dark and smoky, like burning. As I look across the land, I think I see glimmers of embers, shifts in the light, bits of amber-orange under the moon.

I notice another scent in the night—one I don't know well, but that I think might be death.

None of us say anything, but the smell keeps us running when almost nothing else would, and for a little while, we don't breathe deep.

We run forever. I say the words from the poem over and over to the beat of my feet. It almost sounds like someone else's voice. I don't know where I find the air and I keep getting the words wrong: *From out our bourne of death and space the flood will wash me far* but it doesn't even matter. I never knew that words might not matter.

"Are you saying that for us?" the boy gasps out, the first time he's spoken in hours.

"We're not dead," I say. No one dead feels this tired.

"We're here," the boy says, and he stops. I look at where he points and I see a group of boulders that will be difficult, but not impossible, to climb down.

We made it.

The boy doubles over in exhaustion. Indie and I look at

each other and I reach to touch the boy's shoulder, thinking he's ill, but then he straightens up.

"Let's go," I say, not sure why he waits.

"I'm not coming with you," he says. "I'm taking that canyon instead." He points back along the Carving.

"Why?" I ask, and Indie says, "How do we know we can trust you? How do we know this is the right canyon?"

The boy shakes his head. "That's the one," he tells us, holding out his hand for payment. "Hurry. It's almost morning." He speaks softly, without feeling, and that's what convinces me he's telling the truth. He's far too tired to lie. "The Enemy didn't end up firing tonight. People will realize we've gone. They might report it on the miniport. We have to get into the canyons."

"Come with us," I say.

"No," he says. He looks up at me and I see that he needed us for the run. It's one that would be too hard to do alone. Now, for whatever reason, he wants to take his own path. He whispers. "Please."

I reach into my pack and pull out the tablets. As I unwrap them, my hands clumsy and cold even as sweat trickles down my back, he looks behind him at where he wants to be. I want him to come with us. But it's his choice.

"Here," I say, holding out half of the tablets. He looks down at them, sealed away in their little compartments, the backing of each tablet labeled neatly. Blue. Blue. Blue. Blue.

And then he laughs.

"Blue," he says, laughing harder. "All blue." And then, as if he's brought the color into being by saying it, we all notice that the sky has turned to morning.

"Take some," I say, moving closer to him. I see sweat frozen on the ends of his too-short hair; frost on his eyelashes. He shudders. He should put on his coat. "Take some," I say again.

"No," he says, pushing my hand away. The tablets fall to the ground. I cry out, dropping to my knees to pick them up.

The boy pauses. "Maybe one or two," he says, and I see his hand dart down. He snatches the packet and breaks away two little squares. Before I can stop him, he throws the rest back at me and turns to run.

"But I have others," I call after him. He helped us get here. I could give him the green to calm. Or the red, and then he could forget that long awful run and the scent of his friends' deaths as we passed by the burned village. I should give him both. I open my mouth to call out again but we never even knew his name.

Indie has not moved.

"We have to go after him," I say, urging her. "Come on."

"Number nineteen," she says softly. What she says doesn't make sense to me until I follow her gaze and see past the boulders. What's beyond them is now visible: the Carving up close and with light for the first time.

"Oh," I whisper. "Oh."

The world changes here.

Before me is a land of canyons, of chasms, of gashes and gorges. A land of shadows and shades, of rises and falls. Of red and blue and very little green. Indie's right. As the sky lightens and I see the jagged stones and gaping canyons, the Carving does remind me a little of the painting Xander gave me.

But the Carving is real.

The world is so much bigger than I thought it was.

If we descend into that Carving with its miles of mountains and acres of valleys, with its cliffs and its coves, we will vanish almost entirely. We will become almost nothing.

I think suddenly of a time in Second School, back before we began to specialize, when they showed us diagrams of our bones and our bodies and told us how fragile we were, how easily we could break or become ill without the Society. I remember seeing in the pictures that our white bones were actually filled with red blood and marrow, and thinking *I didn't know I had this inside of me.*

I didn't know the earth had this inside of it. The Carving seems as wide as the sky it stands under.

It is the perfect place for someone like Ky to hide. An entire rebellion could take cover in a place like this. I begin to smile.

"Wait," I say as Indie moves to climb down the boulders and into the Carving. "It will be sunrise in a few minutes." I'm greedy. I want to see more.

She shakes her head. "We have to be inside before it gets light."

Indie's right. I take one final look back at the boy growing smaller, moving faster than I thought he could. I wish I had thanked him before he left.

I climb down behind Indie, scrambling into the canyon where I hope Ky went only two days ago. Away from the Society, from Xander, from my family, from the life I knew. Away from the boy who led us here, from the light that creeps across this land, turning the sky blue and the stone red, the light that could get us killed.

CHAPTER 11
KY

There should be patrols in the canyon. I thought we'd have to barter and beg our way past checkpoints like my father did the first time he came. But no one comes. At first the stillness is unsettling. Then I begin to realize that the Carving still teems with life. Black ravens wheel in the sky above and send sharp calls down into the canyons. There's scat from coyotes, jackrabbits, and deer on the ground, and a tiny gray fox slips away from the stream when we come to drink. A small bird seeks shelter in a tree that has a long dark wound down the middle. It looks as though the tree were struck once by lightning but then grew around the burn.

But still nothing human.

Has something happened to the Anomalies?

The stream grows larger the farther into the canyon we go. I keep us walking on the rounded, smoothed-out rocks next to it. If we step on them we don't leave as many footprints for someone to find. *In the summer, I use a walking stick and go right in the river itself,* my father told me.

But the water's too cold to walk in now. Sheets of ice edge the banks. I look around and wonder what my father would have seen in the summertime. Scrubby small trees that are barren now would be full-leaved, or as full-leaved as anything gets in the desert. The sun would beat down hot, and the cool water would feel good on his feet. Fish would swim away when they felt him coming.

On the third morning we find the ground covered in frost. I haven't seen any chert to start a fire with. We'd have frozen without our coats.

Eli speaks, echoing my thoughts. "At least the Society gave us these," he says. "I've never had a coat that works this well."

Vick agrees. "They're almost military grade," he says. "I wonder why the Society wasted them on us?"

Hearing them talk makes me realize what's been bothering me at the back of my mind: *Something's wrong with this, too.*

I pull my coat from my back and the wind makes me want to shudder, but I keep my hands steady as I pull out a sharp piece of agate.

"What are you doing?" Vick asks.

"Cutting up my coat."

"You going to tell me why?"

"I'll show you." I spread out the coat like the carcass of an animal and make an incision. "The Society doesn't like to waste things," I say. "So there's a reason we have these." I peel back the upper layer of material.

Waterproof wires—some blue, some red—wind like veins through the padding inside.

Vick swears and moves to rip off his coat. I put up my hand to stop him. "Wait a minute. We don't know what they do yet."

"They're probably tracking us," Vick says. "The Society could know where we are."

"That's true, but you might as well stay warm while I look." I pull the wires, remembering how my father used to do this. "There's a warming mechanism inside the coats," I say. "I recognize the wiring. *That's* why they work so well."

"And what else?" Vick asks. "Why'd they want to keep us warm?"

"So we'll keep the coats on," I say. I look at a neat web of blue wiring that traces along with the red wiring of the warming mechanism. The blue threads from the collar of the coat down the arms to the wrists. The web covers the back and front and sides and underneath the arms. In a place near the heart there's a tiny silver disk about the size of a microcard.

"Why?" Eli asks.

I start to laugh. I reach inside and unhook the blue wires from the disk, carefully weaving them in and out of the red ones. I don't want to alter the warming mechanism. It works fine as it is. "Because," I tell Eli, "they don't care about us, but they love data." Once the silver disk is free, I hold it up. "I bet this records things like our pulse rates, our hydration levels, our moment of death. And anything else they've thought up that they want to know about while we're out in the villages. They're not using these to track us constantly. But they gather our data after we die."

"The coats don't always burn," Vick says.

"And even if they do, the disks are fireproof," I say. Then I start to grin. "We've been making it hard for them," I tell Vick. "All those people we buried." My grin fades as I think of the Officers dragging the bodies back out of the dirt just to strip them of their coats.

"That first boy in the water," Vick remembers. "They made us take off his coat before we got rid of him."

"But if they don't care about us, why would they care about our data?" Eli asks.

"Death," I say. "It's the one thing they haven't fully conquered. They want to know more about it."

"We die, they learn how not to," Eli says. His voice sounds distant, as though he isn't only thinking of the coats but of something else too.

"I wonder why they didn't stop us," Vick says. "We've been burying for weeks."

"I don't know," I say. "Maybe they wondered how long we could keep it up."

None of us speak for a moment. I wind the blue wires and leave them—the Society's entrails—under a rock. "Do either of you want me to fix yours?" I ask. "It won't take long."

Vick hands his over. Now that I know where the blue

wires are, I can be more careful with my incisions. I make only a few small holes and pull the blue wires out. One of the holes is in the spot over his heart so I can extract the disk.

"How are you going to get yours back together?" Vick asks, shrugging into his coat.

"I'll have to wear it like this and find a way to fix it later," I say. One of the trees near us is pinyon pine and it weeps sap. I pull some off and use it to stick the cut edges of my coat back together in a few places. The sap's smell, sharp and earthy, makes me think of the taller pines on the Hill. "I'll probably still be warm enough as long as I'm careful about the red wires."

I reach for Eli's coat but he holds it back. "No," he says. "It's all right. I don't mind."

"All right," I say, surprised, and then I think I understand. The tiny disk is the closest any of us might come to immortality. It's not as good as the stored tissue samples that ideal Citizens get—a chance at living again someday when the Society has the technology.

I don't think they'll ever figure out how to do it. Even the Society can't bring people back. But it is true that in the Society our data lives on forever, rolling over and over to become whatever numbers the Society needs. It's like what the Rising has done with the legend of the Pilot.

I've known about the rebellion and its leader for as long as I can remember.

But I never told Cassia.

The closest I came was the day on the Hill when I told her the story of Sisyphus. Not the Rising's adaptation of it, but the version that I like best. Cassia and I stood in that dark green forest. Both of us had red flags in our hands. I finished the story and was about to say more. Then she asked me the color of my eyes. In that moment I realized that loving each other felt more dangerous—more like a rebellion—than anything else ever could.

I'd heard parts of the Tennyson poem all my life. But in Oria, after I saw Tennyson's words on Cassia's lips, I realized that the poem didn't *belong* to the Rising. The poet didn't write it for them—he wrote it long before the Society even existed. It was the same with the story of Sisyphus. It existed long before the Rising or the Society or my father claimed it as their own.

When I spent my days in the Borough doing the same tasks over and over, I changed the story too. I decided that it was the thoughts in your own mind that mattered more than anything else.

So I never talked to her about how I'd heard the other poem before, or about the rebellion. Why? We had the Society trying to find its way into our relationship. We didn't need anyone else there, too. The poems and stories we shared with each other could mean what *we* wanted them to mean. We could choose our own path together.

We finally see a sign of the Anomalies: a place where they used to climb. The ground at the base of the cliff is spotted with blue fragments. I bend down to look more closely. For a moment they look like the broken casings of some kind of beautiful insects. Blue and bruised purple underneath. Broken and mixed with red mud.

Then I realize they're the juniper fruit from the tree growing near the wall. They've fallen to the ground and been crushed by someone's boots, and the rain has blurred the footprints so that they are only vague indentations. I run my hand along the cuts in the rock and the metal bores where the Anomalies ran their climbing gear through. The ropes are gone.

CHAPTER 12
CASSIA

As we walk, I look for something to mark Ky's passage through this place. But I find nothing. We see no footprints, no signs of human life. Even the trees are small and stunted, and one of them bears a distinct dark scar right through its center. I feel stricken, too. Although the boy who ran to the Carving with us talked about the recent rains, I still hoped to find some of Ky's tracks.

And I hope to find evidence of the Rising. I open my mouth to ask Indie if she's heard of it but something holds me back and I don't. I'm not sure what I expect a sign of a rebellion to look like, anyway.

There is a tiny stream, so small that it almost disappears when Indie and I both put our canteens in at the same time. The stream dries up or sinks underground entirely by the time it reaches the edge of the Carving. In staggering through the dark I did not notice when the stream began, only that it suddenly was. Pieces of driftwood wait on small sandy beaches, bone-dry, having floated in on a bigger river in a different time. I can't stop wondering what this might look like from above: a shiny silver thread, pulled from one of the choices I saw in the Hundred Dresses, winding through the vastness of red rock that is the Carving.

From above, Indie and I would be too small to see at all.

"I think we're in the wrong canyon," I tell Indie.

Indie doesn't answer at first; she's bending to pick up something fragile and gray from the ground. She holds it carefully in her hands and shows it to me.

"An old wasp nest," I say, looking at the thin, tissue-paper circles turning within and without each other.

"It looks like a seashell." Indie opens her pack and tucks the abandoned nest safely inside. "Do you want to try and go back out?" she asks. "Go to another canyon?"

I pause. We've been moving for almost twenty-four hours now, and we are out of food. We have eaten most of our two days' ration to give us strength after our long run to the Carving. I don't want to waste tablets on going back out, especially since I don't know what might be following, or waiting.

"I guess we should keep going," I say. "Maybe we'll see some sign of him soon."

Indie nods, hoists her pack, and picks up the two knife-sharp stones she always carries while we walk. I do the same. We've seen the prints of animals here, though we haven't seen a trace of an Anomaly yet.

We haven't seen a trace of any person—alive or dead, Aberration or Anomaly, Official or rebel.

∼

In the dark that night, I sit and work on my poem. It helps me keep from thinking about all I've left behind.

I write another first line.

I couldn't find a way to fly to you so I walked every step on this stone.

So many beginnings. I tell myself that in a way it's good that I haven't found Ky yet, because I still don't know what to whisper to him when I see him, which words would be the very best ones to give.

Indie finally speaks. "I'm hungry," she says. Her voice sounds as hollow as the empty wasp's nest.

"I'll give you a blue tablet if you want," I tell her. I don't know why I'm so averse to taking them, since this is precisely the type of situation Xander wanted to help me through. Maybe it's because the boy who ran with us didn't seem to want them. Or because I hope to have something to give Ky when I see him, since I gave away the compass. Or because Grandfather's voice echoes in my mind from when he talked about a different tablet, the green one: *You are strong enough to go without.*

Indie gives me a sharp, puzzled look.

A thought comes to my mind and I pull out my flashlight. I shine it around, noticing again something I saw earlier and stored away in my memory: a plant. My mother didn't teach me specific names of many plants, but she did tell me the general signs of poison. This plant shows none of those signs, and the very presence of the spikes seem to indicate that it has something within to protect. It's fleshy and green, edged with purple. It isn't lush like the vegetation in the Borough but it's certainly better than the tired tumbles of sticks and leaves that many of the plants here have turned into for the winter. Some of them have small gray cocoons strung along their bare branches, memories of butterflies.

Indie watches for a moment as I gingerly pull off one of the broad, spiked leaves. Then she crouches next to me and does the same, and we both carefully use our rock knives to scrape away the spikes. It takes a little while, but then we each have a small, skinned-looking gray-green piece of plant in front of us.

"Do you think it's poisonous?" Indie asks me.

"I'm not sure," I say. "I don't think so. But I'll go first."

"No," Indie says. "We'll both try a little and see what happens."

For a minute we do nothing but chew, and while it's not the same as the food I've eaten all my life, Society food, it's still enough to take the edge off and dampen the hunger. Cut me open, and you might find a girl held together not by bone, but by stringy dry sinews, ones that look like the bark that hangs off the trees here in strips.

When nothing happens after a few moments, we both take another bite. I think of another word that might rhyme and write it down, then scratch it back out. It doesn't work.

"What are you doing?" Indie asks.

"I'm trying to write a poem."

"One of the Hundred Poems?"

"No. This one is new. It's my own words."

"How did you learn to write?" Indie moves a little closer, looks curiously at the letters in the sand.

"He taught me," I say. "The boy I'm looking for."

She falls silent again and I think of another line.

Your hand around mine, showing me shapes.

"Why are you an Aberration?" Indie asks. "Are you first-generation?"

I hesitate, not wanting to lie to Indie, but then I realize that I'm not lying anymore. If the Society has discovered my escape, I'll certainly earn Aberration status. "I am," I say. "First generation."

"So it was *you* who did something?" she asks.

"Yes," I say. "I caused my own Reclassification." That's true, too, or will be. When my status changes, it won't be my parents' fault.

"My mother made a boat," Indie says, and I hear her swallow another piece of the plant. "She carved it out of an old tree. She worked on it for years. And then she paddled away and the Officials found her within an hour." She sighs. "They picked her up and saved her. They told us she only wanted to try out the boat and that she was grateful they found her in time."

I hear a strange sound in the dark that I can't place, a sort of delicate movement like a whispering. It takes me a moment to realize that the sound is Indie, turning the wasp nest around and around in her hands as she speaks.

"I've never lived near the water," I say. "Not the ocean, anyway."

"It calls," Indie says softly. Before I can ask what she means, she adds, "Later, when the Officials were gone, she told my father and me what *really* happened. She said that she *meant* to go. She said the worst part was that she didn't even lose sight of the shore before they found her."

I feel that I stand at the edge of an ocean and something, some knowledge, laps at my feet. I can almost see the woman on the boat in the water, drifting farther, seeing nothing behind her but sea and sky. I can almost hear her deep breath of relief as she turns her face away from where the shore once was, and I wish she had made it far enough for that.

Indie says quietly, "When the Officials found out what she'd told us, they gave us all red tablets."

"Oh," I say. Should I act as if I know what happens next? The forgetting?

"I didn't forget," Indie says. And though it's too dark to see her eyes anymore, I can tell that she looks at me.

She must think I know what the red tablets do. She is like Ky and Xander. She is immune.

How many more are there like them? Am I one of them?

The red tablet tucked among the blue tempts me sometimes, the way it did the morning they took Ky away.

But now, it's not because I want to forget. It's because I want to *know*. Am I immune, too?

But I might not be. And now is not a time for forgetting. Besides, I might need the red tablet later.

"Were you angry that she tried to go?" I ask, thinking of Xander and what he said about how I left. The moment the words leave my mouth I wish them unsaid, but Indie doesn't take offense.

"No," she says. "She always planned to come back for us."

"Oh," I say. Neither of us speaks for a moment, and I think suddenly of a time when Bram and I stood near the little Arboretum pond waiting for my mother. Bram wanted to throw a stone into the pool but knew he'd get in trouble if someone saw him. So he waited. Watched. Just when I thought he'd lost his nerve he snapped his arm forward and the rock went in and rippled the water.

Indie throws first. "She'd heard about a rebellion on an island off the coast. She wanted to find it and come back for the family."

"I've heard of a rebellion, too," I say, unable to control my excitement. "The one I've heard of is called the Rising."

"That's the same one," Indie says, sounding eager. "It's everywhere, someone told her. This Carving is exactly the kind of place it might be."

"I think that too," I say. In my mind, I see a piece of translucent paper laid over one of the Society's maps, its markings showing places the Society doesn't know about or doesn't want us to see.

"Do you believe in a leader called the Pilot?" I ask.

"Yes," Indie says, excited. And then, to my surprise, she recites something in a gentle voice very unlike her usual brusque tone:

"Every day the sun rolls by
Across the sky and through night's door

Every night the stars light high
Above the earth and shine once more

Any day her boat might fly
Across the waves and to the shore."

"Did you write that?" I ask, a sudden flash of jealousy cutting into me. "I know it's not one of the Hundred Poems."

"I didn't write it. And it's not a poem," Indie says with certainty.

"It sounds like one," I say.

"No."

"Then what is it?" I ask. I'm learning quickly that it's useless to argue with Indie.

"Something my mother used to say every night before I went to sleep," Indie tells me. "When I was old enough to ask about it, she told me that the Pilot is the one who will lead the Rising. My mother thought it would be a woman who comes across the water."

"Oh," I say, surprised. I always thought of the Pilot as someone from the sky. But Indie might be right. I remember again the sound of the Tennyson poem. There was water in it.

Indie's thinking the same thing. "That poem *you* said when we were running," she begins. "I hadn't heard it before, but it proves that the Pilot *could* come from the water. A bar is a ridge of sand in a shallow place in the water. And a Pilot is someone who steers the ships safely in and out of the harbor."

"I don't know much about the Pilot," I say, which is true, but I do have my own hopes about the leader of the rebellion and they don't quite align with Indie's version. Still, the idea is the same, and the story the Archivist gave me says that the Pilot changes over and over. Indie and I could both be right. "But I don't think it matters. It could be either a man or a woman, coming from the sky or the water. Don't you think?"

"*Yes,*" Indie says, sounding triumphant. "I knew it. You aren't only looking for a boy. You're looking for something else, too."

I look up into the narrow river of sky above with its clear sharp stars. *Is that true? I've come a long way from the Borough,* I think, with a sudden feel of elation and surprise, *and it's not far enough yet.*

"We could climb out," Indie says softly. "Go across the top. We could try going down into another canyon. Maybe we'll find him there, or the Rising." She flicks on her flashlight and shines it up the side of the canyon. "I know how to climb. You learn it in Sonoma. My Province. We can find a good place tomorrow, somewhere the walls aren't so high and sheer."

"I haven't climbed like that before," I say. "Do you think I could do it?"

"If you're careful and don't look down," Indie says.

The silence stretches on as I look up and realize that even this limited bit of sky holds more stars than I was ever able to catch sight of in the Borough. For some reason, this gives me hope that there is much else I don't see. I hope for my parents and Bram, for Xander, for Ky. "Let's try," I say.

"We'll find a place early," Indie says. "Before it's very light. I don't want to cross in broad daylight."

"I don't either," I say, and in the sand I write a beginning line and for the first time, a second line too:

I climb into the dark for you
Are you waiting in the stars for me?

CHAPTER 13
KY

The sides of the canyon are black and orange. Like a fire caught burning and turned to rock. "It's so deep," Eli says, looking up in wonder. In this spot the walls rise higher than any building I've ever seen, higher than the Hill. "It's like someone huge made cuts in the earth and dropped us inside."

"I know," I say. In the Carving, you see rivers and caves and stones that you'd never see from above. It's as though suddenly you are down close looking at the workings of your own body, watching your own blood run and listening to the sound of your heart beating it through.

"It's nothing like this in Central," Eli says.

"You're from Central?" Vick and I ask at the same time.

"I grew up there," Eli tells us. "I've never lived anywhere else."

"It must seem lonely to you out here," I say, remembering how when I was Eli's age I moved to Oria and felt a different kind of loneliness—the loneliness of what seemed like too *many* people.

"How did the Anomalies get stuck in here, anyway?" Eli asks.

"The original Anomalies *chose* to be Anomalies, back when the Society came to be," I tell Eli. I remember something else, too. "And the ones who live in the Carving don't call themselves Anomalies. They prefer to be known as the farmers."

"But how could they choose?" Eli asks, fascinated.

"Before the Society took control, there were people who saw it coming and didn't want any part of it. They started storing things inside the Carving." I point at some of the curves and bends in the sandstone walls. "There are caves hidden everywhere in here. The farmers had enough food to see them through until some of the seeds they brought could be planted and harvested. They called their settlement a township, because they didn't want to use the Society's words for that, either."

"But didn't the Society track them down?"

"Eventually. But the farmers had the advantage because they came in first. They could cut down anyone who tried to follow. And the Society thought the farmers would all die off sooner or later. It's not an easy place to live." Part of my coat has come unsealed and I stop at a pinyon for more sap. "They also served another purpose for the Society. Many of the people in the Outer Provinces were too afraid to try to escape to the Carving because the Society started spreading rumors about how savage the farmers are."

"You think they'll really try to kill us?" Eli asks, sounding worried.

"They used to be merciless to any one Society," I say. "But

we're not Society anymore. We're Aberrations. They didn't kill Aberrations or other Anomalies outright unless attacked."

"How will they know what we are?" Eli asks.

"Look at us," I say. "We don't look like Citizens or Officials." The three of us are young and dirty and disheveled, clearly on the run.

"So why didn't your father bring your family in here to live?" Vick asks.

"The Society's right about some things," I say. "You die free out here but you die faster. The farmers don't have the medicine or technology in the canyons that the Society has outside. My mother didn't want that for me and my father respected it."

Vick nods. "So we're going to find these people and ask them to help us. Since they helped your father."

"Yes," I say. "And I'm hoping to trade with them. They have maps and old books. At least, they did before."

"And what do *you* have to trade?" Vick asks sharply.

"The same things that you and Eli have," I say. "Information about the Society. We've lived on the inside. It's been a while since there have been any real villages in the Outer Provinces, which means the people in the canyon might not have been able to trade or talk with anyone for a long time."

"So, if they *do* want to trade with us," Eli asks, sounding unconvinced, "what are we going to do with all those papers and old books once we get them?"

"You can do whatever you want," I say. "You don't even

have to trade for them. Get something else. I don't care. But I'm going to get a map and try to reach one of the Border Provinces."

"Wait," Eli says. "You want to go back into the Society? Why?"

"I wouldn't go *back*," I say. "I'd go a different way than the one we came. And I'd only go back far enough to send a message to her. So she'll know where I am."

"How can you do that?" Eli asks. "Even if you did make it to the Border Provinces, the Society watches the ports. They'd see it if you sent anything to her."

"That's why I want the papers from the township," I say. "I'll trade them with an Archivist. They have ways to send messages that don't involve the ports. But it's expensive."

"An Archivist?" Eli asks, puzzled.

"They're people who trade on the black market," I say. "They've been around since before the Society. My father used to trade with them, too."

"So this is your plan," Vick says. "There's nothing more to it than what you've told us."

"Not right now," I say.

"Do you think it will work?" Eli asks.

"I don't know," I say. Above us a bird starts to sing: a canyon wren. The notes are haunting and distinct. They descend like a waterfall down the rock canyon walls. I can identify the call because my father used to mimic it for me. He told me it was the sound of the Carving.

He loved it here.

When my father told stories, he blurred the line between truth and tale. "They're all true on some level," he'd say when my mother teased him about it.

"But the township in the canyon is real," I'd always ask, to make sure. "The stories you tell about that are true."

"Yes," he'd say. "I'll take you there someday. You'll see."

So when it appears before us around the next bend in the canyon, I stop short in disbelief. There it is, exactly as he said, *a settlement in a wider part of the gorge.*

A feeling of unreality settles over me like the light of late afternoon that spills over the canyon walls. The township looks almost exactly the way I remember my father describing his first visit:

The sun came down and made it all golden: bridge, buildings, people, even me. I couldn't believe the place was real, though I'd heard about it for years. Later when the farmers there taught me to write, I had that same feeling. Like the sun was always at my back.

The winter sunlight sets an orange-gold glow on the buildings and bridge in front of us.

"It's here," I say.

"It's real," Vick says.

Eli beams.

The buildings before us cluster together, then split apart around rockfall or river. Houses. Bigger buildings. Tiny fields carved out where the canyon opens wider.

But something is missing. The people. The stillness is absolute. Vick glances over at me. He feels it too.

"We're too late," I say. "They're gone."

It hasn't been long. I can still see their tracks here and there.

I also see signs that they prepared to leave. This wasn't a rushed departure, but one taken with care. The twisted black apple trees have been harvested; only a few golden apples still shine on the branches. Most of the farming equipment is gone—taken apart and carried away by the farmers, I'd guess. A few rusted pieces remain.

"Where did they go?" Eli asks.

"I don't know," I say.

Is anyone left outside of the Society?

We pass a stand of cottonwood trees on the bank of the stream. A small wiry tree grows alone at the edge.

"Hold on," I tell the other two. "This won't take long."

I don't cut deep—I don't want to kill the tree. I carve her name carefully on the trunk, thinking, as I always do, of when I held her hand in mine to teach her to write. Vick and Eli don't say anything while I carve. They wait.

When I finish I step back to look at the tree.

Shallow roots. Sandy soil. The bark is gray and rough. The leaves are long gone but her name still looks beautiful to me.

~

We're all drawn to the houses. It feels so long since we've seen a place built by real people with the intent to stay. The houses are weathered and made of pieced-together sandstone or worn gray wood. Eli climbs the steps to one of them. Vick and I follow.

"Ky," Eli says, once we're inside. *"Look."*

What I see inside makes me reconsider. Maybe there *was* an element of haste in their departure. Otherwise, would they have left their houses like this?

It's the walls that speak of hurry. Of not quite enough time. They are covered in pictures and if the farmers had had more time, they would have washed the walls clean. They say and show too much.

In this house there is a boat painted in the sky, marooned on a pillow of white clouds. The artist signed his name in the corner of the room. Those letters claim the painting—the ideas—as his own. And although this is the place I've been looking for all this time, I still catch my breath.

This township is where he learned.

About writing.

And painting.

"Let's stop here," Eli says. "They have bunks. We could stay forever."

"Aren't you forgetting something?" Vick asks him. "The people who used to live here left for a reason."

I nod. "We have to find a map and some food and get out. Let's check the caves."

We look in all of the caves along the sides of the canyon. Some of them have painted walls, like the houses, but we don't find a single scrap of paper.

They taught him to write. They knew how. *Where* would they have left their words? They couldn't have taken all of them. It's almost night and the colors in the paintings shift to grays in the fading light. I look up at the walls of the cave we're searching.

"This one is weird," Eli says, looking at the painting, too. "Some of it is missing." He shines his flashlight up. The walls have been damaged by water and only the top of the painting remains—part of a woman's head. All you can see are her eyes and forehead. "She looks like my mother," Eli says softly.

I turn in surprise to look at him. Because that's the word that's repeating over and over in my mind right now, even though my mother never came here. And I wonder if that word, *mother*, is as dangerous to Eli as it is to me. It might be even more dangerous than *father*. Because I feel no anger toward my mother. Only loss, and loss is a feeling you can't fight your way out of as easily.

"I know where they must have hidden the maps," Eli says suddenly. There's a glint of cunning in his eyes that I haven't seen before and I wonder if I like Eli so much not because he reminds me of Bram, but because he reminds me of myself. I was about his age when I stole the red tablets from the Carrows.

When I was new in Oria, it was strange to watch the people flood out of their houses and workplaces and air trains all at once. It made me nervous the way they moved at the same times to the same places. So I pretended the streets were dry gulches from home, and the people were the water after rain that turned the dry beds into streams. I told myself the people in their gray and blue plainclothes were nothing but another force of nature moving along.

But it didn't do me any good. I got lost in one of the Boroughs, of all places.

And Xander saw me using the compass to try to find my way home. He threatened to turn in Patrick for letting me keep it unless I stole some red tablets.

Xander must have known then that I was an Aberration. I don't know how he could tell so quickly, and we never talked about it after. But it doesn't matter. The lesson was a good one to learn. Do not pretend one place is like another or look for similarities. Only look for what *is*.

"Where, Eli?" I ask him.

He waits for a moment, still grinning, and I remember this, too—the moment of the reveal.

I held out my hand to show Xander the two red tablets I'd stolen. He didn't think I could do it. I wanted him to know that I was his equal even though I was an Aberration. Just once, I wanted someone to know that before I started a life pretending to be less than everyone around me. For a moment, I felt powerful. I felt like my father.

"Where the water can't reach," Eli says now, looking at the painting of the woman who has been washed away. "The caves aren't down here. They have to be up high."

"I should have known," I say as the three of us hurry out of the cave and look up at the cliffs. My father told me about the floods. Sometimes the farmers saw the river rising and knew it would happen. Other times, during the flash floods, they had almost no warning at all. They had to build and farm on the canyon floor where there was space, but when the water rose, they took to the higher caves.

The line of survival is thin in the Carving, my father said. *You hope you're on the right side of it.*

Now that we look for them, the signs of old floods are everywhere—marks of sediment up on the canyon walls, dead trees wedged high in crevices from the violence and speed of the flash floods. The force it would take to do these things is one that could bring even the Society to its knees.

"I always thought it was safer to bury stuff," Vick says.

"Not always," I tell him, remembering the Hill. "Sometimes it's safer to take it as high as you can."

It takes us nearly an hour to find the path we want. From below it is almost impossible to see—the farmers cut it into a cliff so that it blends perfectly into the scarred canyon walls. We follow the path higher and higher until we go around the side of the cliff along a bend that wasn't visible from below. I imagine you couldn't see it from above either. Only if you've dared to climb right to the spot and look closely.

Once we're there we see the caves.

They're the perfect place to store things—high and hidden. And dry. Vick ducks into the first one.

"Any food in there?" Eli asks as his belly grumbles. I grin. We rationed our food carefully but we've stumbled upon the township just in time.

"No," Vick says. "Ky, look at this."

I duck inside with him to find a cave that holds only a few bulky containers and cases. Near the door I spot marks and footprints where someone—recently—dragged some of the stockpile out of the cave and hauled it away.

I've seen cases like these. "Watch out," I tell Vick, and I pry one open carefully and look inside. Wires. Keypads. Explosives. All Society-issue, from the looks of it.

Could the farmers have been in league with the Society? It doesn't seem likely. But the farmers could have stolen or traded for these things on the black market. It would take years to assemble a cache that could fill a cave like this.

What happened to the rest of it?

Eli rustles behind me and I hold up my arm to keep him back. "It looks like what's in our coats," he says. "Should we take some of it with us?"

"No," I tell him. "Keep looking for some food. And don't forget the map." Eli slides out of the cave.

Vick hesitates. "It might be useful to have," he tells me, gesturing at the stockpile. "You could rig this stuff, right?"

"I could try," I say. "But I'd rather not. Better to use the space in our packs for food and papers if we find them." What I don't say is that the wires always lead to trouble. I think my father's constant fascination with them helped bring about his death. He thought he could be like Sisyphus and turn the Society's weapons back on them.

Of course, I tried the same thing with the other decoys when I rigged their guns before we ran into the Carving. And it likely didn't turn out any better for them than it did for my father's village. "It's dangerous to try to trade with this. I don't even know if the Archivists will touch it anymore."

Vick shakes his head but doesn't argue. He moves farther back into the cave and pulls at one of the rolls of thick plastic. "You know what these are?" he asks.

"Some kind of shelter?" I ask, looking more closely. I can see ropes and thin tubes rolled up inside.

"Boats," Vick says. "I've seen some like this before on the Army base where I lived."

It's the most he's said about his past and I wait to see if he'll say more.

But Eli calls out to us in a voice filled with excitement. "If you want food, I've found it!" he shouts.

We find him eating an apple in the second cave. "This must have been the stuff that was too heavy to carry," he says. "It's all kinds of apples and grain. And a lot of seeds."

"Maybe they stored this in case they had to come back," Vick says. "They thought of everything."

I nod in agreement. Standing there looking at what they've left, I feel admiration for the people who lived here. And disappointment. I would have liked to meet them.

Vick feels it too. "We've all thought about breaking away," he says. "They really did it."

The three of us fill our packs with food from the farmers' stores. We take apples and some kind of flat strong bread that seems like it will last for a long time. We also find a few tarred matches that the farmers must have made themselves. Maybe later there will be a place where it's safe to have a fire. Once we've finished filling our packs, we find a few more in the storage cave and fill them, too.

"Now for a map and something to trade," I say. I take a deep breath. The cave smells like sandstone—mud and water—and apples.

"I bet it's here," Eli says, his voice muffled at the back of the cave. "There's another room."

Vick and I follow him around a corner and into another recess of rock. As we shine our flashlights around, we see that it is clean. Well-organized. Full of boxes. I walk across the room and lift the lid to one of them. It's packed with books and papers.

I try not to think *This must be the spot where he learned. He could have sat right on that bench.*

"*They left so much,*" Eli whispers.

"They couldn't carry it all," I say. "They probably took the best of it with them."

"Maybe they had a datapod," Vick suggests. "They could have entered the information from the books into that."

"Might be," I say. Still, I wonder how hard it was to leave all of the real copies behind. The information in this cave is priceless, especially in its original form. And, their ancestors had brought it all in originally. It must have been hard to walk out without it.

In the center of the room stands a table made of small pieces of wood that had to have been carried through the entrance of the cave and pieced together. The whole room, like the township, has that sense of being assembled carefully. Every item seems filled with meaning. The Society didn't drop it into your lap. You worked for it. Found it. Made it yourself.

I shine my light across the table and onto a hollowed-out wooden bowl filled with charcoal pencils.

I reach inside and pick one up. It leaves a small black mark on my hand. The pencils remind me of the tools I made for writing back in the Borough. I gathered pieces of wood a few at a time on the hill or when a maple tree in the Borough lost a branch. I'd tie them together and lower them into the incinerator to char the ends for writing and drawing. Once, when I needed red, I stole a few petals from one of the blood-colored petunias in a flower bed and used them to color the Officials' hands and my hands and the sun.

"Look," Vick says behind me. He's found a box with maps inside. He pulls some of them out. The warm light of the flashlight changes the papers, making them seem even older than they really are. We sift through them until we find one that I recognize as the Carving.

"This one," I say, spreading it out on the table. We all gather around it. "Here's our canyon." I point to it but my eyes are drawn to the canyon next to ours on the map. A spot there has been inked with thick black ink Xs, like a row of stitches. I wonder what they mean. *I wish I could rewrite this map.* It would be much easier to mark how I want the world to be, instead of trying to figure out how it really is.

"I wish I knew how to write," Eli says, and I'm sorry I don't have the time to teach him. Maybe someday. Right now we have to keep moving.

"It's beautiful," Eli says, touching the map gently. "It's different from the way we paint on the screens back in the Society."

"I know," I say. Whoever made the map was something of an artist. The colors and scale of the whole thing fit together perfectly.

"Do you know how to paint?" Eli asks.

"A little," I say.

"How?"

"My mother taught herself, and then she taught me," I say. "My father used to come here and trade with the farmers. Once, he brought a paintbrush back for her. A real one. But he couldn't afford any paint. He always meant to get her some but he never did."

"Then she *couldn't* paint," Eli says, sounding disappointed.

"No," I say. "She could. She used water on rock." I think back to the ancient carvings in a small crevice near our house. I wonder now if that was where she got the idea for writing on stone. But she used water and her touch was always gentle. "Her paintings always vanished in the air," I tell Eli.

"Then how did you know what they looked like?" Eli asks.

"I saw them before they dried," I say. "They were beautiful."

Eli and Vick fall silent and I can tell they might not believe me. They might think I'm making this up and remembering pictures that I wish I'd seen. But I tell the truth. It was almost like her paintings lived—the way they shone and vanished and then new things appeared under her hands. The pictures were beautiful both because of the way they looked while they existed and because they could never last.

"Anyway," I say. "There's a way out." I show them how this canyon continues through to a plain on the other side from where we entered. Judging by the map, there's more vegetation out there and also another stream, bigger than the one in this canyon. The mountains on the opposite side of the plain have a small dark house marked on them, which I take to be a settlement or safe place, since it's the same marking the farmers used to denote their own township on the map. And past that, to the north of the mountains, is a place marked SOCIETY. One of the Border Provinces. "I think it will take two or three days to reach the plain. And another few days to cross it and get to the mountains."

"There's a stream on that plain," Vick says, his eyes brightening as he inspects the map. "Too bad we can't use one of the farmers' boats and go down it."

"We could try," I say, "but I think the mountains are a better option. There's a settlement there. We don't know where that stream leads." The mountains are on the top edge of the map; the stream runs down and disappears at the bottom of the paper.

"You're right," Vick says. "But we might be able to stop and fish. Smoked fish last for a long time."

I slide the map toward Eli. "What do you think?" I ask him.

"Let's do it," he says. He puts his finger on the dark house in the mountains. "I hope the farmers are there. I want to meet them."

"What else should we bring?" Vick asks, looking through some of the books.

"We can find something in the morning," I say. For some reason the neatly ordered and abandoned books make me feel sad. Tired. I wish Cassia were here with me. She'd turn each page and read every word. I can picture her in the dim light of the cave with her bright eyes and her smile and I close my eyes. That shadowy memory might be as close as I come to seeing her again. We have the map, but the distance we still have to cross looks almost insurmountable.

"We should sleep now," I say, pushing away the doubt. There's no good in it. "We need to start as soon as it's light." I turn to Eli. "What do you think? You want to go back down and sleep in the houses? They've got those beds."

"No," Eli says, curling up on the floor. "Let's stay here."

I understand why. Late at night the empty township feels exposed—to the river, to the loneliness that settled in when the farmers left—and to the ghostly eyes and hands of the paintings they made. Here in the cave where they kept things safe seems like the place where we might be safe too.

In my dreams, bats fly in and out of the cave all night long. Some fly fat and heavy and I know they're full of the blood of other living things. Others fly a little higher and I know they're light with hunger. But they all have noisy, beating wings.

At the end of the night, near dawn, I wake up. Vick and Eli still sleep and I wonder what it was that disturbed me. A sound in the township?

I walk to the outermost door of the caves and look out.

A light flickers in the window of one of the houses below us.

CHAPTER 14
CASSIA

I wait for the dawn, folded inside my coat. Down here in the Carving, I walk and sleep deep in the earth and the Society doesn't see me. I'm starting to believe they truly don't know where I am. I've escaped.

It feels strange.

All my life I've been watched. The Society saw me go to school and learn to swim and walk up the steps to attend my Match Banquet; they sorted my dreams; when they found my data interesting, as my Official did, they altered things and recorded my reaction.

And though it was a different kind of watching, my family watched me, too.

At the end of his life, Grandfather used to sit at a window as the sun went down. I wondered, then, if he stayed awake all night and saw the sun come back up again. During one of those long, wakeful nights, did he decide that he would give me the poems?

I pretend that Grandfather hasn't vanished but instead floats above it all, and that of all the things in the world to see from up high he chooses to see one small girl curled up in a canyon. He wonders if I will wake and rise when it becomes clear that dawn is on its way after all.

Did Grandfather mean for me to end up here?

"Are you awake?" Indie asks.

"I never slept," I say, but even as I say it, I can't be sure it's true. For what if my imagining Grandfather was really a dream?

"We can start in a few minutes," Indie says. In the seconds since we first spoke to each other, the light has changed. I can already see her better.

Indie chooses a good spot; even I can tell that. The walls are not nearly as high and sheer as they've been in other places and an old rockfall left piles of boulders part of the way up.

Still, the walls of the canyon are daunting, and I haven't had much practice—just the little time we had last night before we went to sleep.

Indie holds out her hand in a peremptory gesture. "Give me your pack."

"What?"

"You're not used to climbing," Indie says evenly. "I'll put your things in mine and you can carry yours empty. It'll be easier that way. I don't want the weight to make you fall."

"Are you sure?" Suddenly I feel that if Indie has the pack she has too much. I don't want to let the tablets go.

Indie looks impatient. "I know what I'm doing. Like you did with the plants." She frowns. "Come on. You trusted me on the air ship."

She's right, and that reminds me of something. "Indie," I ask, "what did you bring with you? What was it you had me hide on the ship?"

"Nothing," she says.

"Nothing?" I echo, surprised.

"I didn't think you'd trust me unless you thought I had something to lose, too," she says, grinning.

"But in the village, you pretended to take something back from me," I say.

"I know," she says, not a trace of apology in her voice. I shake my head and in spite of myself I start to laugh as I slide off my pack and hand it to her.

She opens it up and dumps the contents—flashlight, plant leaves, empty canteen, blue tablets—into her own pack.

I suddenly feel guilty. I could have taken off with all the tablets and she still trusted me. "You should keep some of the tablets after this," I say. "For yourself."

Indie's expression changes. "Oh," she says, her voice wary. "All right."

She hands me back my empty pack and I slide it over my shoulders. We climb wearing our coats, which makes us bulkier, but Indie thinks it easier than carrying them. She slides her own pack onto her back, over her long braid that burns almost as bright as these cliffs when the sun comes up. "Ready?" she asks.

"I think so," I say, looking up at the rock.

"Follow me," she says. "I'll talk you through it." She puts

her fingers in the holds and hoists herself up. In my eagerness to follow, I knock over a small pile of rocks. They scatter, and I hold tight.

"Don't look down," Indie says.

It takes much longer to climb than it does to fall.

It strikes me how much of this is holding on and waiting, deciding the next move and then committing to it. My fingers grip tightly into the rock and my toes curl as much as they can. I focus on the task at hand, and somehow that means that, even though I don't think of Ky, I'm completely immersed in thinking of him. Because I'm being like him.

The canyon walls here are reddish-orange, drizzled with black. I'm not sure where the black came from; it's almost like an ocean thick with tar lapped against the sides long ago.

"You're doing fine," Indie tells me as I come up next to her on a ledge. "Now this will be the hardest part," she says, pointing. "Let me try it out first."

I sit on the ledge, lean my back against the rock. My arms ache from holding on so tightly. I wish the rock would hold us, cradle us back as we cling to it, but it doesn't. "I think I've got it," Indie calls down softly. "When you come up here—"

I hear the sound of falling rocks, of flesh scraping stone. I'm on my feet. The ledge is small and my balance uncertain. "Indie!"

She dangles above me, holding onto the rocks. One of

her legs hangs down near me, scraped, bloody. I hear her swear softly.

"Are you all right?" I call up.

"Push," she says, her voice ragged. "Push me up."

I put my palms under the tread of her boot, worn from the run across the plain and dusty-soled from the canyon and the rocks.

There is a terrible moment when she rests there on my hands, so heavy, and I know she can't find anything to grab above. Then she is gone; the weight of her boot leaves my hand; the imprint of it is left on my palm.

"I'm up," she calls down. "Come around to your left. I can talk you up from here."

"Is it safe? Are you sure you're all right?"

"It's my own fault. These rocks are softer than the ones I'm used to climbing. I put too much weight on that piece and it broke off."

The scrapes on her leg belie her statement that the rock is soft, but I know what she means. Things here are so different. Poisoned rivers, softened stone. You never know exactly what you're getting into. What will hold and what will give way.

The second half of the climb goes more smoothly. Indie was right; the sheer part was the hardest to navigate. I clutch thin edges of rock using only the pads of my fingers, willing my knuckles to stay bent and my feet not to slip. I wedge my arms and knees into slots running vertically up the face of the rock, using my clothes and skin the way Indie taught me—as friction to keep my body close to the wall.

"We're almost there," she says above me. "Give me a minute and climb on up. It's not bad."

I try to catch my breath, pausing for a rest in a crevice. The rock does hold me here, I realize, and I smile, exhilarated by how high we are.

Ky would love this. Maybe he's climbing, too.

Time for the last push to the top.

I will not look down or back or anywhere but up and forward. My empty pack shifts a little and I waver, my fingernails digging into the stone. *Hold on. Wait.* Something light and winged flies past me, startling me. To calm myself, I think of the poem Ky gave me for my birthday, the one about the water:

High tide and the heron dived when I took the road
Over the border

Here on this stony shore, I feel like a creature left behind after the water has pulled back to the sea. Trying to climb over into someplace where Ky might be. *And even if he's not there, I'll find him. I'll go over again and again until I've finally crossed to where he is.*

I pause for a moment to get my balance back, and then, in spite of myself, I look over my shoulder.

The view is completely different from what Ky and I saw together at the top of the Hill. No houses, no City Hall, no buildings. It is sand and rock and scrubby tree; but it is still something I have climbed, and once again, it feels like Ky has climbed it with me somehow.

"I'm almost there," I whisper to him, to Indie.

I pull myself over the edge of the cliff, a smile on my face, and then I look up.

We are not alone.

I know now why they call this a firing. Ash, everywhere. A wind sails across the Carving, blowing the debris into my eyes and making them blur and water.

It's just the last of a big fire, I try to tell myself. Sticks laid end to end, smoke gone to the sky.

But the look on Indie's face tells me that she sees the truth and in my mind I know it too. The blackened figures strewn across the ground are not sticks. They are real, these dozens of bodies on the top of the Carving.

Indie bends down and then straightens up, holding something. A charred length of rope, most of it good. "Let's go," she says, the ash on the rope blackening her hands. She reaches up to brush back a piece of her red hair floating loose in the breeze and accidentally marks her face.

I glance at the people. They have markings on their skin, too, blue ones, twisting lines. I wonder what they mean.

Why did you come up here? How did you make this rope? What else have you learned out here while the rest of us forgot about you? Or never knew you existed at all?

"How long have they been dead?" I ask.

"Long enough," Indie says. "A week, maybe more. I'm not sure." There's a hard edge to her voice. "Whoever did this might come back. We have to leave."

Out of the corner of my eye, I see movement and turn. Tall red flags set along the ridge whip furiously in the wind. Though staked into the ground instead of tied to trees, they remind me of the red scraps Ky and I left on the Hill.

Who marked the land up here? Who killed all thsee people? The Society? The Enemy?

Where is the Rising?

"We have to leave now, Cassia," Indie says behind me.

"No," I say. "We can't leave them here."

Were they *the Rising?*

"This is how Anomalies die," Indie says, her voice cold. "The two of us alone can't change it. We have to find someone else."

"Maybe these are the people we were trying to find," I say. *Please. Don't let the Rising be gone before we've even had a chance to find it.*

Oh, Ky, I think. *I never knew. So this is the kind of death you've seen.*

Indie and I run across the top of the Carving and leave the bodies behind. *Ky's still alive*, I tell myself. *He has to be.*

Only the sun is in the sky. Nothing flies. There are no angels here.

CHAPTER 15
KY

We don't stop moving until we've put distance between us and whoever's in the township. None of us speak much; we go fast and follow the main canyon. After a few hours I get out the map to check our position.

"We seem to be climbing up all of the time," Eli says, a little out of breath.

"We are," I say.

"Then why don't we seem to be getting any higher?" Eli asks.

"The canyon walls are rising too," I say. "Look." I show him how the farmers marked elevation on the map.

Eli shakes his head in confusion. "Think of the Carving and all its canyons like a big boat," Vick tells Eli. "The part where we entered was low in the water. The part where we're coming out is high. See? When we climb out, we'll be *above* that huge plain."

"You know about boats?" Eli asks.

"A little," Vick says. "Not much."

"We can rest for a minute," I tell Eli, reaching for my canteen. I take a drink.

Vick and Eli do too. "Remember that poem you say for the dead?" Vick begins. "The one I asked you about before?"

"Yes." I look at the mountain settlement marked on the map. *There's where we need to be.*

"*How* did you know it?"

"I came across it," I say. "Back in Oria."

"Not in the Outer Provinces?" Vick asks.

He knows I know more than I'm saying. I look up. He and Eli stand on the opposite side of the map, watching. The last time Vick challenged me was out in the village when I talked about the way the Society killed Anomalies. I see the same flint-hard look in his eyes now. He thinks it's time to talk about this.

He's right.

"There, too," I say. "I've heard about the Pilot all my life." And I have. In the Border Provinces, in the Outer Provinces, in Oria, and now here in the Carving.

"So who do *you* think it is?" Vick asks.

"Some think the Pilot is the leader of a rebellion against the Society," I say, and Eli's eyes light up with excitement.

"The Rising," Vick agrees. "I've heard that, too."

"There's a rebellion?" Eli asks eagerly. "And the Pilot's the leader?"

"Maybe," I say. "But it doesn't have anything to do with us."

"Of course it does," Eli says, sounding angry. "Why didn't you tell the rest of the decoys? Maybe we could have done something!"

"What?" I ask Eli wearily. "Vick and I have both heard of

the Pilot. We don't know where he or she is. And even if we did, I don't believe the Pilot can do anything but die and take too many people with him."

Vick shakes his head but doesn't say anything out loud.

"It could have given them some hope," Eli says.

"What good is that if it there isn't anything to back it up?" I ask Eli.

He sets his jaw stubbornly. "It's not any different than what you tried to do with rigging the guns."

He's right. I sigh. "I know. But telling them about the Pilot wouldn't have done any good either. It's just a story my father used to tell." Suddenly I remember how my mother would paint illustrations while he talked. When he finished telling the story of Sisyphus and the paintings dried up, I always felt like he finally had some rest.

"I heard about the Pilot from someone back home," Vick says. He pauses. "What happened to them? Your parents?"

"They died in a firing," I tell him. At first I think that's all I'll say. But I keep talking. I have to tell Eli and Vick what happened so they'll see why I don't believe. "My father used to gather all the villagers together for meetings."

I think of how exciting it always was, everyone sliding in along the benches and talking with one another. Their faces would light up when they saw my father come into the room. "My father figured out a way to disconnect the village port without the Society knowing. That's what he thought, anyway.

I don't know if the port still worked or if someone told the Society about the meetings. But they were gathered together when the firing started. Almost everyone died."

"So was your *father* the Pilot?" Eli asks, sounding awed.

"If he was, he's dead now," I say. "And he took our whole village with him."

"*He* didn't kill them," Vick says. "You can't blame him."

I can and do. But I also see Vick's point.

"Was it Society or Enemy who killed them?" Vick asks after a moment.

"The ships looked like the Enemy," I say. "But the Society didn't come until it was all over. That was new. Back then, they usually pretended to fight for us, at least."

"Where were you when this happened?" Vick asks.

"Up on a plateau," I say. "I went to see the rain come down."

"Like the decoys who tried to get the snow," Vick says. "But you didn't die."

"No," I say. "The ships didn't see me."

"You were lucky," Vick says.

"The Society doesn't believe in luck," Eli says.

"I've decided it's the only thing I do believe in," Vick says. "Good luck and bad luck, and ours always seems to be bad."

"That's not true," Eli says. "We got away from the Society and made it into the canyon. We found the cave with the maps and we escaped the township before anyone found us."

I admit nothing. I don't believe in the Society or the Rising or any Pilot or good and bad luck. I do believe in Cassia. If I had to say I believed in anything more than that, I'd say I believe in *it is,* or *it isn't.*

Right now *I am,* and I intend to keep it that way.

"Let's go," I tell the other two, and I roll up the map.

At dusk, we decide to camp in a cave marked on the map. When we duck through the opening, our flashlights illuminate a series of paintings and carvings on the walls inside.

Eli stops in his tracks. I know how he feels.

I remember the first time I saw carvings like these. In that little rocky crevice near our village. My mother and father took me there when I was small. We tried to guess what the symbols might mean. My father practiced copying the figures in the dirt. It was before he could write. He always did want to learn, and he wanted to find the meaning in everything. Every symbol and word and circumstance. When he couldn't find the meaning, he made it for himself.

But this cave is amazing. The paintings are lush with color and the carvings etched along the surface are rich in detail. Unlike the dirt on the ground, when you carve into this stone it becomes lighter instead of darker.

"Who did this?" Eli asks, breaking the silence.

"A lot of people," I say. "The paintings look more recent. They look like the farmers' work. The carvings are older."

"How much older?" Eli asks.

"Thousands of years," I say.

The oldest carvings show people with splayed fingers and broad shoulders. They look strong. One seems to reach up to the sky. I look at the figure for a long time, at that reaching hand, and remember the last time I saw Cassia.

The Society found me in the early morning. There was no sun yet and the stars were almost gone. It was that nothing time when taking things is easiest.

I woke right when they leaned down for me in the dark with their mouths open to say the things they always said: *There's nothing to fear. Come with us.* But I hit them before they could speak. I drew their blood before they could take me away to make me spill mine. Every instinct said to fight and so I did. For once.

I fought because I had found peace in Cassia. Because I knew I could find rest in her touch that somehow both burned me up and washed me clean.

The fight didn't last long. There were six of them and only one of me. Patrick and Aida weren't awake yet. "Come quietly," the Officials and Officers said. "It will make it easier for everyone. Do we have to gag you?"

I shook my head.

"Classification always tells in the end," one of them said to the others. "This one was supposed to be easy; he's been compliant for years. But an Aberration is still an Aberration."

We were almost out the door when Aida saw us.

And then we went along the dark streets with Aida screaming and Patrick talking low and urgent and calm.

No. I don't want to think about Patrick and Aida and what happened next. I love them more than anyone in the world besides Cassia, and if I ever find her, we will look for them. But I can't think about them for long—the parents who took me in and received nothing in exchange but more loss. It was brave of them to love again. It made me think I could do it too.

Blood in my mouth and under my skin in bruises waiting to show. Head down, hands locked behind me.

And then.

My name.

She cried out my name in front of everyone. She didn't care who knew that she loved me. I called her name, too. I saw her tumbled hair, her bare feet, her eyes looking only at me, and then she pointed to the sky.

I know you meant that you would always remember me, Cassia, but I'm afraid you might forget.

We clear away pieces of brush and smaller stones so we have a place to rest. Some of the stones are chert, likely cached here by the farmers for fires. I also find a piece of sandstone, almost perfectly round, and I think instantly of my compass.

"Do you think some of the farmers camped in here on their way out of the Carving?" Eli asks.

"I don't know," I say. "Probably. It looks like a place they used often." Charry circles of old fires mark the floor, as do sandy, blurred footprints and, here and there, bones from animals cooked and eaten.

Eli falls asleep quickly, as usual. He's rolled up right under the feet of a carved figure who has both arms raised high.

"So what did you bring?" I ask Vick as I pull out the bag where I stashed things from the library cave. In our hurry to leave the township, the three of us grabbed books and papers without having much of a chance to look at them.

Vick begins to laugh.

"What is it?"

"I hope you chose better than I did," he says, showing me what he brought. In his hurry he grabbed a stack of plain little brown pamphlets. "These looked like something I saw once back in Tana. It turns out they're all the same thing."

"What are they?" I ask.

"Some kind of history," he says.

"That still might prove to be valuable," I say. "If not, I can give you some of mine." I've done a little better. I have some poetry and two books full of stories that are not among the Hundred. I glance over at Eli's pack. "We'll have to ask Eli what he brought when he wakes up."

Vick turns some pages. "Wait. This is interesting." He hands me one of the pamphlets, opened to the first page.

The paper is pulpy. Cheap, mass-produced somewhere on the edges of Society with old equipment, likely scavenged from a Restoration site. I open the pamphlet and read it by the light of the flashlight:

THE RISING:

A Brief History of Our Rebellion against the Society.

The Rising began in earnest at the time of the Hundred Committees.

In the year before the Hundred Selections began, the Cancer Eradication Rate remained stagnant at 85.1 percent. It was the first occurrence of a failure to improve since the Cancer Eradication Initiative took effect. The Society did not take this lightly. Though they knew total perfection in all areas was impossible, they decided that closing the gap on 100 percent in certain areas was of utmost importance. They knew this would require complete focus and dedication.

They decided to center all their efforts on increasing productivity and physical health. Those at the highest level of Official voted to eliminate distractions such as excess poetry and music while retaining an optimal amount to enhance culture and satiate the desire for experiencing art. The Hundred Committees, one for each area of the arts, were formed to oversee the choices.

This was the beginning of the Society's abuse of power. They also ceased to have each generation vote on whether or not they wanted to live under Society's rule. The Society began to remove Anomalies and Aberrations from the general population and isolate or eliminate those who caused the most trouble.

One of the poems that the Society did not approve for the Hundred Poems was Tennyson's "Crossing the Bar." It has become an informal password between members of our rebellion. The poem references two important aspects of the Rising:

1. A leader called the Pilot directs the Rising and

2. Those who belong to the Rising believe it is possible to cross back into the better days of the Society—the time before the Hundred Selections.

Some of the Anomalies who escaped the Society in its early years have joined the Rising. Though the Rising now exists in all parts of the Society, it remains strongest in the Border and Outer Provinces, particularly where Aberrations have been sent in increasing numbers since the advent of the Hundreds.

"Did you already know all of that?" Vick asks.

"Some," I say. "I knew the part about the Pilot and the Rising. And I knew about the Hundred Committees, of course."

"And about destroying Aberrations and Anomalies," Vick says.

"Right," I agree. My voice is bitter.

"When I heard you saying the poem over the first boy in

the water," Vick says, "I thought you might be telling me you were part of the Rising."

"No," I say.

"Not even when your father was leading?"

"No." I don't say more. I don't agree with what my father did but I don't betray him either. That's another fine line I don't like to get caught on the wrong side of.

"None of the other decoys recognized the words," Vick says. "You'd think more Aberrations would have known about the Rising and told their children."

"Maybe all of the ones who did figured out how to get away before the Society starting sending us to the villages," I say.

"And the farmers didn't belong to the Rising," Vick says. "I thought that might be why you were leading us to them— so we could join up."

"I wasn't leading you anywhere," I say. "The farmers knew about the Rising. But I don't think they were part of it."

"You don't know much," Vick says with a grin.

I have to laugh. "No," I say. "I don't."

"I thought you had some kind of greater purpose," Vick says thoughtfully. "Gathering people to bring to the Rising. But you came into the Carving to save yourself and get back to the girl you're in love with. That's all."

"That's all," I agree. It's the truth. He can think less of me if he wants.

"Good enough," Vick says. "Good night."

When I scratch into the stone with my piece of agate, it leaves clean white marks. This compass won't work, of course. It can't open. The arrow will never spin, but I carve anyway. I need to find another piece of agate. I'm wearing down this one with carving instead of killing.

While the other two sleep, I finish the compass. When I'm done, I turn it in my hand so that its arrow points in the direction I believe to be north and I lie down to rest. Does Cassia still have the real compass, the one that my aunt and uncle saved for me?

She stands on top of the hill again. A small round piece of gold in her hands: the compass. A disk of brighter gold on the horizon: the sun rising.

She opens the compass and looks at the arrow.

Tears on her face, wind in her hair.

She wears a green dress.

Her skirt brushes the grass when she bends down to put the com-pass on the ground. When she stands up again her hands are empty.

Xander waits behind her. He holds out his hand.

"He's gone," he tells her. "I'm here." His voice sounds sad. Hopeful.

No, I start to say, but Xander tells the truth. I'm not there, not really. I'm only a shadow watching in the sky. They're real. I'm not anymore.

~

"Ky," Eli says, shaking me. "Ky, wake up. What's wrong?"

Vick flicks on the flashlight and shines it in my eyes. "You were having a nightmare," he says. "What about?"

I shake my head. "Nothing," I say, looking down at the stone in my hand.

The arrow of this compass is locked into place. No spinning. No alteration. Like me with Cassia. Locked on one idea, one thing in the sky. One truth to hold to when everything else falls to dust around me.

CHAPTER 16
CASSIA

In my dream he stands in front of the sun, so he looks dark when I know that he is light. "Cassia," he says, and the tenderness in his voice brings tears to my eyes. "Cassia, it's me."

I can't speak; I reach out my arms, smiling, crying, so glad not to be alone.

"I'm going to step away now," he says. "It will be bright. But you have to open your eyes."

"They're open," I say, confused. How else could I see him?

"No," he says. "You're asleep. You need to wake up. It's time."

"You're not leaving, are you?" That is all I can think of. That he might go.

"Yes," he says.

"Don't," I tell him. "Please."

"You have to open your eyes," he says again, and so I do, I wake up to a sky full of light.

But Xander is not here.

It's a waste of water to cry, I tell myself, but I can't seem to stop. The tears stream down my face, making paths in the dust. I try not to sob; I don't want to wake Indie, who still sleeps in spite of the sun. After seeing the blue-marked bodies yesterday, we walked all day along the dry streambed of this second canyon. We saw nothing and no one.

I put my hands up to my face and leave them there, feeling the warmth of my own tears.

I'm so afraid, I think. *For me, for Ky. I thought that we were in the wrong canyon because I couldn't see any trace of him. But if they turned him into ash, I would never know where he had been.*

I always hoped I would find him—through all those months planting seeds, when I rode in that windowless air ship piloted through the night, during that long run over to the Carving.

But now there might not be anything left to find, a voice in my head nags at me. *Ky might be gone and the Rising, too. What if the Pilot died and no one took his or her place?*

I glance over at Indie and find myself wondering if she is really my friend. *Maybe she's a spy,* I think, *sent by my Official to watch me fail and die in the Carving so that the Official knows how her experiment played out all the way to the end.*

Where are these thoughts coming from? I wonder, and then it hits me. *I'm sick.*

Illness rarely happens in the Society, but of course I'm not in the Society. My mind sorts through all the variables at play: exhaustion, dehydration, excess mental strain, insufficient food. This was bound to happen.

The realization makes me feel better. If I'm sick, then

I'm not myself. I don't truly believe these thoughts about Ky and Indie and the Rising. And my mind is so muddled I'm forgetting that my Official wasn't the one who started this experiment. I remember that flicker in her eyes as she lied to me outside the Museum in Oria. She *didn't* know who put Ky's name in the Matching pool.

I take a deep breath. For a moment, the feeling from my dream of Xander comes back to me and I am comforted. "Open your eyes," he told me. What was it Xander would expect me to see? I look around the cave where we camped for the night. I see Indie, the rocks, my pack with the tablets inside.

The blue ones, at least in some way, were given to me not by the Society, but by Xander, whom I trust. I've waited long enough.

It takes me a long time to open up the compartment because I can't seem to get my fingers to work. Finally, I pop out the first blue tablet in the package, shove it in my mouth, and swallow, hard. It's the first time I've ever taken a tablet—to my knowledge, anyway. For a moment I picture Grandfather's face in my mind, and he looks disappointed.

I look back down at the hollow where the blue tablet was, expecting to see empty space. But there's something there—a small strip of paper.

Port paper. I unfold it, hands still trembling. Sealed in its compartment, the paper stayed safe, but it will disintegrate soon now that it's reached the air.

Occupation: Medic. Chance of permanent assignment and promotion to physic: 97.3%.

"Oh, Xander," I whisper.

This is a piece of Xander's official Matching information. The information I never did view on the microcard; all of the things I thought I already knew. I look at the sealed tablets in my hand. How did he do this? How did he get the scrap inside? Are there more?

I picture him now, printing out a copy of his information from the port, tearing each line carefully into strips and finding a way to put them inside the packaging. He must have guessed that I never looked at the microcard; he knew I turned away and chose to see Ky.

It's like Ky and the papers he gave me back in the Borough. Two boys, two stories written on scraps and passed on to me. My eyes burn with tears because Xander's story is one I should have already known.

Look at me again, he seems to say.

I break open another tablet from its compartment. The next paper says: *Full name: Xander Thomas Carrow.*

A memory comes back to me, of myself as a child in the Borough waiting for Xander to come out and play.

"Xander. Thomas. Carrow!" I called, hopping from one stone on his walk to the next. I was small and often forgot to hush when approaching someone else's house. Xander's name, I thought, was nice to say. It sounded exactly right.

Each word had two syllables, a perfect rhythm for marching.

"You don't have to yell," Xander said. He opened the door and smiled at me. "I'm right here."

I miss Xander, and I can't seem to stop myself from tearing into more of the tablets—not to swallow down any more blue, but to see what the scraps say:

Has lived in Mapletree Borough since birth.

Favorite leisure activity: swimming.

Favorite recreation activity: games.

Peers listed Xander Carrow's name as the student they most admired 87.6% of the time.

Favorite color: red.

That's a surprise. I always thought Xander's favorite color was green. What else don't I know about him?

I smile, feeling stronger already. When I glance over at Indie I see that she still sleeps. I feel the strongest urge to keep moving, so I decide to step outside and see better this place that we came into in the dark.

At first glance it seems like just a wide open spot in the canyon, like many others, honeycombed with caves and tumbled with rocks and smoothed with undulating stone walls. But then, as I look around again, I see that one of the walls appears strange.

I walk across the dry streambed and put my hand against the rock. The feel of it is rough under my hand. But it's not quite right. It's too perfect.

That's how I know it's Society.

In its perfection I see the cracks. I remember the metered breath of the woman in one of the Hundred Songs and how Ky told me that the Society knows that we like to hear them breathe. We like to know they're human, but even the humanity they present is careful and calculated.

My heart sinks. If the Society is here then the Rising cannot be.

I walk along the wall, running my hand along it, looking for the crack where the Society meets the Carving, and as I come closer to a clump of tangled dark bushes I see something lying on the ground.

It's the boy. The one who ran with us to the Carving and then came into this canyon instead.

He's curled up on his side. His eyes are closed. A small sprinkling of dust kicked up by the wind covers his skin and hair and clothes. His hands are discolored and red with blood and so is the place on the canyon wall where he clawed and clawed and couldn't enter. I close my eyes. The sight of that dried red blood, those crystals of canyon dirt, makes me think of the sugar and red-bled berries on Grandfather's pie plate and it makes me sick.

I open my eyes again and look at the boy. Can I do anything for him? I lean closer and see that his lips are stained blue. Since I never trained as a medic, I know almost nothing about helping people. He doesn't breathe. I check the spot on his wrist where I've learned a pulse can be taken, but it doesn't beat.

"*Cassia,*" someone whispers, and I whirl around.

It's Indie. I breathe out in relief. "It's that boy," I say.

Indie crouches next to me. "He's dead," she says. She looks at his hands. "What was he doing?"

"I think he was trying to get inside," I say, pointing. "They've made this look like rock, but I think it's a door." Indie stands up next to me and we both look at the bloody rock and the boy's hands. "He couldn't get in," I say. "And then he took the blue tablet, but it was too late."

Indie looks at me, her eyes darting and searching.

"We have to get out of this canyon," I say. "The Society's in it. I can tell."

Indie pauses. "You're right," she says after a moment. "We should go back to the other canyon. At least it had water."

"Do you think we'll have to walk back and cross where we came over earlier?" I say, shuddering involuntarily as I think of all those bodies on top of the Carving.

"We can go over here," Indie says. "We have a rope now." She points to the roots of the trees clinging to the side of the canyon and growing where no trees should be able to grow. "It will save us time." She opens her pack and reaches inside for the rope. As I watch her, she takes it out and slings it over her shoulder and then carefully rearranges something left in her pack.

The wasp's nest, I think. "You've kept it safe," I say.

"What?" Indie asks, startled.

"Your wasp nest," I tell her. "It's not broken."

Indie nods, looking wary. I must have said something wrong, but I can't think of what it might be. A deep weariness seems to have come over me and I have the strangest desire to simply curl up like the boy and rest there on the ground.

On the top of the Carving, we don't look in the direction where the bodies would be. We're too far away to see anything anyway.

I don't speak. Neither does Indie. We move fast across the Carving under the cold wind and sky. The running wakes me up and reminds me that I'm still alive, that I cannot lie down to rest yet, no matter how much I want to.

It seems like Indie and I might be the only two living people in the Outer Provinces.

Indie secures the rope on the other side. "Come on," she says, and we move back down into the first canyon, where we began. We might not have found signs of Ky here, but at least there is water, and nothing of the Society that we've noticed. Yet.

Hope looks like a footprint, a half footprint where someone grew careless and stepped into soft mud that later hardened too thick to blow away in the evening and morning winds.

I try not to think of other prints I've seen in these canyons, fossil remains of times so long past that nothing is left but imprints or bones of what was, what once lived. This mark is recent. I have to believe that. I have to believe that someone else is alive here. And I have to believe that it might be Ky.

CHAPTER 17
KY

We climb out of the Carving. Behind us lie the canyons and the farmers' township. Below us, the plain stretches out long and wide, brown and gold-grassed. Clumps of trees cluster along a stream and on the other side of the plain the blue mountains rise beyond with snow on their peaks. Snow that stays.

It is a long way to go in any season—and especially now at the very edge of winter. I know our odds aren't good, but I'm still glad to have made it this far.

"It's so far," Eli says next to me, his voice shaky.

"It might not be as far as it looks on the map," I say.

"Let's move to that first group of trees," Vick suggests.

"Is it safe?" Eli asks, looking up at the sky.

"If we're careful," Vick says, already moving, his eyes on the stream. "That stream's different from the one in the canyon. I bet the fish here are big ones."

We make our way out to the first clump of trees. "How much do you know about fishing?" Vick asks me.

"Nothing," I say. I don't even know much about water. There wasn't much of it near our village except what the Society piped in. And the streams back in the canyons aren't wide and slow in places like this one. They're smaller, quicker. "Aren't the fish dead by now? Isn't the water too cold?"

"Moving water rarely freezes," Vick tells me. He crouches down and looks into the river, where things move. "We could catch these," he says excitedly. "I bet they're brown trout. They're so good for eating."

I'm already crouched next to him, trying to figure it out too. "How can we do it?"

"They're finishing spawning," Vick tells us. "They're sluggish. We can reach in and scoop them up if we get close enough. There's not much sport it in," he says regretfully. "We'd never have done this back home. But there we had line."

"Where is back home?" I ask Vick.

He looks at me, considering, but maybe he figures that since he knows now where I'm from he can tell me where he started, too. "I'm from Camas," he says. "You should see it. The mountains are bigger than the ones over there." He gestures across the plain. "The streams are full of fish." Then he stops. Looks back at the water where things move in the deep.

Eli still crouches down, keeping low like I told him he should. Still, I don't like the way this plain sits out bare under the sky in between the Carving and the mountains.

"Look for a riffle," Vick says now to Eli. "It's a place in the stream where the water gets shallow and moves faster. Like here. And then do this."

Vick crouches down slowly and quietly by the stream's edge. He waits. Then he slides his hand into the water, behind the fish, little by little moving his fingers upstream until they're under the fish's belly. Then, quick, he flips the fish out onto the bank. It flops and gasps for air, its body slick.

We all watch the fish die.

That night, we go back inside the Carving where we can hide the smoke of a fire. I strike chert to light it, saving the farmers' matches for another time. It's the first real fire we've made and Eli loves holding his hands to the licking flames. It's one thing to be fired upon and another to be warmed. "Don't get too close," I warn Eli. He nods. The light flickers on the canyon walls and sends the colors of the sunset back. Orange fire. Orange stone.

We cook our fish slowly in the embers so it will last longer in our journey across the plain. I watch the smoke and hope it dissipates before it rises above the canyon walls.

It will take hours for all of the fish to be ready, Vick says, because we need all the water to be removed from the flesh. But they last longer this way and we'll need the food. We've balanced the odds of whoever was in the township following us all this way against that of needing more stores for the plain, and food won out. Now that we've seen how much ground we have to cross we all feel hungry.

"There's a kind of fish called rainbow," Vick says, his face reflective. "Most of them died out long ago in the Warming, but I caught one once up in Camas."

"Did it taste as good as this?" Eli asks.

"Oh, sure," Vick says.

"You threw it back, didn't you?" I ask.

Vick grins. "Couldn't stand to eat it," he says. "It was the only one I've ever seen. I thought it might be the last one left."

I sit back on my heels. My belly is full and I feel free, away from both the Society and the farmers' township. Everything isn't poisoned. Moving water rarely freezes. Those two things are good to know.

I am the happiest I've been since the Hill. I think there's a chance I might make it back to her after all.

"Were your parents Officers before they were Reclassified?" Vick asks me.

I laugh. My father, an Officer? Or my mother? For different reasons, the suggestion is ridiculous. "No," I say. "Why?"

"You know about the guns," he says. "And the wiring in the coats. I wondered if one of them had taught you."

"My father did teach me that," I say. "But he wasn't an Officer."

"Did he learn that from the farmers, too? Or the Rising?"

"No," I say. "Some of it he learned from the Society for his work." Most of it he taught himself. "What about *your* parents?"

"My father was an Officer," he says, and I'm not at all surprised. It makes sense: Vick's bearing, his ability to command, the way he said the coats were military-grade, the fact that he once lived by the Army bases. What could have happened to cause the Reclassification of someone in such good standing—a member of a family of Officers?

"My family's dead," Eli says, when it's clear that Vick doesn't intend to say anything more.

Though I'd guessed that must be the case, I still hate to hear him say it.

"How?" Vick asks.

"My parents got sick. They died in a medical center in Central. And then I got sent away. If I'd been a Citizen, someone could have adopted me. But I wasn't. I've been an Aberration for as long as I can remember."

His parents got sick? And died? That wasn't supposed to happen—didn't happen, as far as I knew—to people as young as Eli's parents must have been, not even Aberrations. Dying *that* early doesn't happen unless you live in the Outer Provinces. And it especially doesn't happen in Central. I'd assumed they'd died like Eli was meant to, out in the villages somehow.

But Vick doesn't seem surprised. I don't know if that's for Eli's benefit or if Vick has heard something like this before.

"Eli, I'm sorry," I say. I was lucky. If Patrick and Aida's

son hadn't died and Patrick hadn't pushed so hard, I never would have been brought to Oria. I might be dead right now.

"I'm sorry too," Vick says.

Eli doesn't answer. He scoots closer to the fire and closes his eyes as if talking has exhausted him. "I don't want to talk about it anymore," he says quietly. "I just wanted to tell you."

After a pause, I change the subject. "Eli," I ask, "what did you bring from the farmers' cave?"

Eli opens his eyes and pulls his pack across the ground toward him. "They're heavy, so I couldn't bring many," he says. "Only two. But look. They're books. With words *and* pictures." He opens one up to show us. A painting of an enormous winged creature with colors all along its back curls through the sky above an enormous stone house.

"I think my father told me about one of these books," I say. "The stories were for children. They could look at the pictures while their parents read them the words. Then when the kids got older they could do it all themselves."

"*These* have to be worth something," Vick says.

What Eli's chosen are hard to trade, I'd imagine. The stories can be replicated but the pictures cannot. But at the moment he grabbed them, Eli wasn't thinking of trading.

We sit by the embers of the fire and read the stories over Eli's shoulder. There are words we don't know, but we puzzle out the meanings by looking at the pictures.

Eli yawns and closes the books. "We can look at them

again tomorrow," he says decisively, and I grin to myself as he packs them into his bag. He seems to be telling us *I brought these here and you can see them on my terms.*

I pick up a stick from the ground and start writing Cassia's name in the dirt. Eli's breathing slows as he falls asleep.

"I loved someone too," Vick says to me a few minutes later. "Back in Camas." He clears his throat.

Vick's story. I never thought he'd tell it. But there's something about the fire tonight that makes us all talk. I wait a moment to make sure I ask the right question. A bright spot in the coals flares and goes dark. "What was her name?" I ask.

A pause. "Laney," Vick says. "She worked at the base where we lived. She told me about the Pilot." He clears his throat. "I'd heard it before, of course. And on the base people used to wonder if one of the Officers could be the Pilot. But for Laney and her family it was different. When they talked about the Pilot it meant more to them."

He glances at the spot where I wrote Cassia's name over and over in the dirt. "I wish I could do that," he says. "We never had anything but scribes and ports in Camas."

"I can teach you how."

"You do it," he says. "On this." He shoves a piece of wood toward me. Cottonwood, probably from the stand of trees where we fished. I start in on it with my sharp piece of stone, not looking up at Vick. Near us, Eli sleeps on.

"She used to fish, too," Vick says. "I'd go to meet her at the stream. She—" Vick stops for a moment. "My father was so angry when he found out. I'd seen him get angry before. I knew what would happen but I did it anyway."

"People fall in love," I say, my voice hoarse. "It happens."

"Not Anomalies and Citizens," Vick says. "And most people don't celebrate their Contract."

I draw in my breath. She was an *Anomaly*? They celebrated their Contract?

"It wasn't sanctioned by the Society," he says. "But when the time came I chose not to be Matched. And I asked her parents if I could Contract with her. They said yes. The Anomalies have their own ceremony. No one recognizes it but them."

"I didn't know that," I say, and I dig the agate deeper into the wood. I wasn't sure Anomalies other than the ones in the Carving still existed so recently or so close to Society. In Oria no one had seen or heard of any in years, except for the one who killed my cousin, the first Markham boy.

"I asked her parents on the day I saw the rainbow," Vick says. "I pulled it out of the river and saw the colors flash in the sun. I put it back right away when I saw what it was. When I told her parents about it, they said it was a good omen. A sign. You know what that is?"

I nod. My father talked about signs sometimes.

"I haven't seen one since," Vick says. "A rainbow trout, I mean. And it wasn't a good omen after all." He takes a deep breath. "Only two weeks later I heard that the Officials were coming for us. I went to find her, but she was gone. So was her family."

Vick reaches for the cottonwood. I hand it back to him although I haven't finished. He turns the piece and studies the way her name looks right now—LAN—almost all straight lines. Like notches in a boot. And suddenly I know what he has been marking all along. Not time survived in the Outer Provinces—time lived without her.

"The Society found me before I got home," Vick says. "They took me to the Outer Provinces right away." He hands the carving back to me and I start working on it again. The firelight plays on the agate like the sun might have on the scales of the rainbow when Vick pulled it from the water.

"What happened to your family?" I ask Vick.

"Nothing, I hope," he says. "The Society Reclassified me automatically, of course. But I wasn't the parent. My family should be fine." I hear the uncertainty in his voice.

"I'm sure they are," I tell him.

Vick looks at me. "Really?"

"If the Society gets rid of Aberrations and Anomalies, that's one thing. If they get rid of *everyone* connected to them, there won't be anyone left." This is what I hope—then Patrick and Aida might be all right, too.

Vick nods, lets out his breath. "You know what I thought?"

"What?" I ask.

"You'll laugh," Vick says. "But when you said that poem the first time, I didn't just wonder if you were part of the

Rising. I also hoped that you'd come to get me out of there. My own personal Pilot."

"Why would you think that?" I ask.

"My father was high up in the Army," Vick says. "*Very* high up. I thought for sure he'd send someone out to save me. I thought it was you."

"Sorry to have disappointed you," I say. My voice sounds cold.

"You didn't disappoint," Vick says. "You got us out of there, didn't you?"

In spite of myself I have a small feeling of satisfaction when Vick says that. I smile in the darkness.

"What do you think happened to her?" I ask after a few moments.

"I think her family ran away," Vick says. "The Anomalies and Aberrations around us were disappearing, but I don't think the Society got them all. Maybe her family left to try to find the Pilot."

"Do you think they did?" I wish now that I hadn't said so much about the Pilot not being real.

"I hope so," Vick says. His voice sounds hollow now that the story is told.

I give him the piece of cottonwood carved with her name. He looks at it for a moment and then puts it in his pocket.

"So," Vick says. "Now. Let's think about getting across

this plain and back to whoever we can find. I'm going to keep following you for a while."

"You have to stop saying that," I tell Vick. "I'm not leading. We're working together." I look up at the sky with all its stars. How they shine and burn I don't know.

My father wanted to be the person who changed everything and saved everyone. It was dangerous. But they all believed in him. The villagers. My mother. Me. Then I grew older and realized he could never win. I stopped believing. I didn't die with him because I no longer went to any of the meetings.

"All right," Vick says. "But thank you for getting us this far."

"You too," I say.

Vick nods. Before he falls asleep, he takes out his own piece of stone and carves another notch in his boot. One more day lived without her.

CHAPTER 18
CASSIA

Y ou don't look right," Indie says. "Do you think we should slow down?"

"No," I say. "We can't." If I stop I'll never start again.

"It doesn't do anyone any good if you die on the way," she says, sounding angry.

I laugh. "I won't." Though I'm exhausted, hollow and dry and aching, the idea of dying is ridiculous. I can't die now when I might draw closer to Ky with every step I take. And besides, I have the blue tablets. I smile, imagining what the other scraps inside might say.

I search and search for another sign from Ky. Though I'm not dying, I may be more ill than I first thought, because I find signs in *everything*. I think I see a message from Ky in the pattern of cracked mud on the canyon floor, where it rained once and then hardened into something that I think could be interpreted as letters. I crouch down to look at it. "What does this look like to you?" I ask Indie.

"Mud," she tells me.

"No," I say. "Look more closely."

"Skin, or scales," she says, and for a moment I am so

taken with her idea I pause. Skin, or scales. Maybe this whole canyon is one long winding serpent that we walk along, and when we reach the end, we can step right off the tail. Or we'll get to the mouth and it will swallow us whole.

I finally see a true sign when the sky above the canyon shifts from blue into blue-and-pink, and the air begins to change.

It's my name: *Cassia*, carved into a young cottonwood that grows in a patch of soil near a thread of a stream.

The tree won't have a long life; its roots already grow too shallow from trying to soak up the water. He carved my name so carefully into the bark that it almost looks as if it is part of the tree.

"Do you see *this*?" I ask Indie.

After a moment, she says, "Yes."

I knew it.

Near the stream I see a small settlement, a little black orchard of twisted trunks and golden fruit hanging low on the trees. Seeing the apples on the branches like that makes me want to bring some to Ky as proof that I followed him every step of the way. I'll have to find something else to give him besides the poem—I won't have time to finish it, to think of the right words.

Then I look back at the ground near the cottonwood and see footprints leading farther into the canyon. I didn't notice them at first; they are mingled with the tracks of other creatures that came to the stream to drink. But there among the clawed and padded prints are the distinct marks of boots.

Indie climbs over the fence into the orchard.

"Come on," I say to her. "There's no reason to stop here. We can see where they went. We have water and the tablets."

"The tablets won't help us," Indie says, and she tears an apple from a tree and takes a bite. "We should at least bring these."

"The tablets *do* help," I say. "I've taken one."

Indie stops chewing. "You've taken one? *Why?*"

"Of course I've taken one," I say. "They're as good as food for survival."

Indie hurries over to me and hands me an apple. "Eat this. Now." She shakes her head. "When did you take the tablet?"

"In the other canyon," I say, surprised at her expression of concern.

"That's why you've been sick," Indie says. "You really don't know, do you?"

"Know what?"

"The blue tablets are poisoned," she says.

"Of course they're not poisoned," I say. How ridiculous. Xander would never give me something poisoned.

Indie sets her mouth in a thin line. "The tablets *are* poisoned," she says. "Don't take any more." She opens my pack and puts a few of the apples inside. "What makes you think you know where we should go?"

"I just do," I say, making an impatient gesture at the footprints. "I'm sorting the signs."

Indie looks at me. She can't decide whether or not to believe me. She thinks I'm sick from the tablet, that I'm losing my mind.

But she saw my name on the tree and she knows that I didn't carve it there.

"I still think you should rest," Indie says, one last time.

"I can't," I say, and she can see that it's true.

I hear it not long after we leave the settlement. A sound of footsteps behind us. We're near the water and I stop.

"Someone's here," I say, turning to face Indie. "Someone is following us."

Indie looks at me, her expression wary. "I think you're hearing things that aren't there. Just like you were seeing things that don't exist."

"No," I say. "Listen."

We both stand still, listening to the canyon. It's quiet except for the rustling of leaves as the wind moves through them. The wind stops and the rattling ceases, but still I hear something. Feet on sand? A hand brushing against stone for support? Something. "There," I say to Indie. "You must have heard that."

"I don't hear anything," Indie says, but she looks unnerved. "You're not well. Maybe we should rest a little."

I answer her by walking again. I listen for the sound of someone behind us, but all I hear are the leaves, skittering and moving again on the canyon breeze.

We walk until dark, and then we use our flashlights and we keep on. Indie was right; I don't feel anyone following us now. I only hear my own breath, feel my own self, the weakness in each vein of my body, each bend of my muscle, every tired step of my feet. I will not let anything stop me when I am this close to Ky. I will take more tablets. I don't think Indie's right about them.

When she isn't looking, I open another tablet but my hands tremble too much. It falls to the ground and so does a tiny whisper of paper. And then I remember. *Xander's notes. I wanted to read them.*

The paper slips away on the wind, and it seems like far too much work to chase it down or to try to find blue in the dark.

CHAPTER 19
KY

I wake to the sound of something big in the sky.

When did they start firing so early in the morning? I think frantically. It's lighter and later than I thought. I must have been tired.

"Eli!" I call out.

"I'm right here!"

"Where's Vick?"

"He wanted to get in a couple of hours of fishing before we left," Eli says. "He told me to stay behind and to let you sleep."

"No, no, no," I say, and then neither of us says anything more, because the sound of the machines overhead is too loud. The firing sounds different, too. Heavy and ponderous. Precise. Not the scatter of rain we are used to. This sounds like hailstones as big as boulders pounding from the sky.

When it stops, I don't wait even though I should. "Stay here," I tell Eli, and I run out to the plain, start crawling through the grass, heading for that damn stream, that damn marsh.

But Eli follows me, and I let him. I crawl to that place on the bank and then I don't look.

I believe what I see. So if I don't see Vick dead it won't be true.

Instead I look at the stream where something has exploded. Brown and green marsh grasses are partly hidden beneath the dirt like the long tangled hair of bodies pulled under.

The force of the explosion has thrown earth into the stream and dammed it. Turned it into pools. Little pieces of river with nowhere to run.

I walk a few strides downstream, far enough to see that they've done it again and again and again all along the length of the river.

I hear the sound of Eli sobbing.

Then I turn and look at Vick.

"Ky," Eli says. "Can you help him?"

"No," I say.

Whatever fell hit with such impact that it looks like it sent Vick flying; his neck was broken. He must have died instantly. I know I should be glad for that. But I'm not. I look at those empty eyes that reflect back the blue of the sky because there is nothing left of Vick himself.

What drew him out here? Why didn't he fish under the cover of the trees instead of in this open place?

I see the reason in the pool near him, trapped in the

newly stilled water. I know instantly what kind of fish it is though I've never seen one before.

A rainbow. Its colors flash in the light as it struggles.

Did Vick see it? Is that why he came out into the open?

The pool grows darker. Something, a large round sphere, sits at the bottom of the water. As I look closer, I see that the sphere lets off a slow release of toxin.

They didn't mean to kill Vick. They do mean to kill this stream.

As I watch the rainbow turns over, its white belly up. It rises to the surface.

Dead like Vick.

I want to laugh and scream at the same time.

"He had something in his hand," Eli says. I look at him. He has the piece of wood carved with Laney's name. "It fell when he did." Eli reaches for Vick's hand and holds it for a moment. Then he crosses Vick's arms across his chest. "Do something," Eli tells me with tears streaming down his face.

I turn away and tear off my coat.

"What are you doing?" Eli asks in horror. "You can't leave him like this."

I don't have time to answer. I throw my coat to the ground and plunge my hands into the nearest pool of water— the one with the dead rainbow. The cold hurts. *Moving water rarely freezes, but this water isn't moving anymore.* Using both hands, I hoist the sphere out while it keeps spewing poison.

It's heavy, but I run it over to the side, put it near a rock, and start looking for the next one. I can't clear all the dirt that has exploded, blocking the river in many places, but I can take the poison out of some of the pools. I know this is as futile as everything I've done. Like trying to get back to Cassia in a Society that wants me dead.

But I can't stop.

Eli comes over and reaches into the water too.

"It's too dangerous," I tell him. "Get back in the trees."

He doesn't answer but instead helps me lift out the next sphere. I remember Vick helping me with the bodies and I let Eli stay.

All day long, Vick talks to me. I know it means I'm crazy but I can't help hearing him.

He talks to me while Eli and I pull spheres from the stream. Over and over Vick tells me his story about Laney. I picture it in my mind—him falling in love with an Anomaly. Telling Laney how he felt. Watching the rainbow and going to speak with her parents. Standing up to celebrate a Contract. Smiling as he reached for her hand to claim happiness in spite of the Society. Coming back to find her gone.

"Stop it," I say to Vick. I ignore Eli's look of surprise. I'm turning into my father. He always heard voices in his head, telling him to talk to the people, to try to change the world.

When we've cleared as many spheres as we can, Eli and I dig Vick's grave together. It's hard going, even with the loose ground, and my muscles scream in exhaustion and the grave isn't as deep as I would like. Eli works doggedly next to me, his small hands scooping out earth.

When we finish, we put Vick inside.

He'd emptied out one of his packs at our camp and brought it with him to carry his catch. I find one silver-scaled fish dead inside and I put it in the grave too. We leave Vick's coat on him. The hole over his heart where the silver disk once was looks like a small wound. If the Society digs him up, they won't know anything about him. Even the notches in his boots mean something that they won't understand.

Vick keeps talking to me while I carve a piece of sandstone into a fish to leave on his shallow grave. The fish's scales are dull and orange. A rainbow without all the colors. Not real like the one Vick saw. But the best I can do. I want it to mark not only that he died but that he loved someone and she loved him back.

"*They didn't kill me,*" Vick says to me.

"No?" I say, but I say it quiet so that Eli can't hear me.

"No," he says with a grin. "*Not as long as the fish are still around, still swimming, spawning, laying eggs.*"

"*Can't you see this place?*" I ask Vick. "*We tried. But they're going to die, too.*"

And then he stops talking to me and I know that he's really gone and I wish for a voice in my head again. I finally understand that as long as my father had that, he never had to be alone.

CHAPTER 20
CASSIA

My breathing sounds wrong. Like little waves of a stream lapping up against rock and making small tired sounds, hoping to wear away at the stone.

"Talk to me," I say to Indie. I notice she carries two packs, two canteens. How did that happen? Are they mine? I'm too tired to care.

"What do you want me to say?" she asks.

"Anything." I need to hear something besides my own breath, my own tired heart.

Somewhere, before Indie's words turn into nothing sounds in my ears, I realize that she's telling me things, many things; that she can't stop herself from talking now that she thinks I'm too far gone to really listen. I wish that I could pay better attention to the words, that I could remember this. I only catch a few phrases

Always at night before I slept
and
I thought everything would be different after

and

I don't know how much longer I can believe

It almost sounds like poetry, and I wonder again if I will ever be able to finish that poem for Ky. If I will know the right words to say when I finally see him. If he and I will ever have time for more than beginnings.

I want to ask Indie for another blue tablet from my pack, but before I can say anything I remember once again how Grandfather told me that I was strong enough not to take the tablets.

But, Grandfather, I think, *I didn't understand you as well as I thought I did. The poems. I thought I knew what you intended. But which one did you want me to believe?*

I remember the words Grandfather said when I took the paper from him that last time. "Cassia," he whispered, "I am giving you something you won't understand, yet. But I think you will someday. You, more than the rest."

A thought flitters into my mind like one of the mourning cloaks, the butterflies that string their cocoons along the twigs both here and back in Oria. It's a thought I've almost had before but I haven't let myself finish it until now.

Grandfather, were you once the Pilot?

And then another thought comes, one light and fast and that I don't grasp completely, leaving me with another impression of gently moving wings.

"I don't need them anymore," I say to myself. The tablets, the Society. I don't know if it's true. But it seems that it should be.

And then I see it. A compass, made of stone, sitting on a ledge exactly at eye level.

I pick it up, although I've dropped everything else.

I hold it in my hand as we walk even though it weighs more than many of the things I have let fall to the ground. I think, *This is good, even though it's heavy.* I think, *This is good, because it will hold me to the earth.*

CHAPTER 21
KY

Say the words," Eli tells me.

My hands shake with exhaustion from the hours of work. The sky grows dark beyond us. "I can't, Eli. They don't mean anything."

"Say them," Eli commands, tears coming again. "Do it."

"I can't," I tell him, and I put the sandstone fish down on top of Vick's grave.

"You have to say them," Eli says. "You have to do this for Vick."

"I already did what I could for Vick," I say. "We both did. We tried to save the stream. Now it's time to go. He would do the same."

"We can't cross the plain now," Eli says.

"We'll stay by the trees," I say. "It's not night yet. Let's get as far as we can."

We go back and gather our things at the camp near the mouth of the canyon. As we wrap up the smoked fish, they leave silver scales on our hands and clothes. Eli and I divide up the food from Vick's pack. "Do you want any of these?" I ask Eli when I find the pamphlets Vick brought.

"No," he says. "I like what I chose better."

I slide one into my pack and leave the rest. It's not worth carrying them all.

Eli and I start across the plain walking side by side in the dusk.

Then Eli stops and looks back. A mistake.

"We have to keep going, Eli."

"Wait," he says. "Stop."

"I'm not going to stop," I tell him.

"*Ky,*" he says. "Look back."

I turn and in the last of the evening light I see her.

Cassia.

Even far away, I know it's her by the way her dark hair tangles with the wind and how she stands on the red rocks of the Carving. She's more beautiful than snow.

Is this real?

She points to the sky.

CHAPTER 22
CASSIA

We're almost to the top; we can almost look out over the plain.

"Cassia, stop," Indie says as I start to climb an outcropping of rocks.

"We're almost there," I say. "I have to see." Over the last few hours I've felt strong again, clearheaded. I want to stand on the highest point so I can try to see Ky. The wind is cold and clean. It feels good rushing over me.

I climb on top of the highest rock.

"Don't," Indie says from below. "You're going to fall."

"*Oh,*" I say. There is so much to see. Orange rocks and a brown-grassed plain and water and blue mountains. Darkening sky, deep clouds, red sun, and a few small cold flakes of white snow coming down.

Two little dark figures, looking up.

Are they looking at me?

Is it him?

This far away, there's only one way to know.

I point to the sky.

For a moment, nothing happens. The figure stands still and I stand cold and alive and—

He starts to run.

I make my way down the rocks, slipping, sliding, trying to get to the plain. *I wish*, I think, my feet clumsy, moving too fast, not fast enough, *I wish I could run, I wish I'd written a whole poem, I wish I kept the compass*—

And then I reach the plain and wish for nothing but what I have.

Ky. Running toward me.

I have never seen him run like this, fast, free, strong, wild. He looks so beautiful, his body moves so right.

He stops just close enough for me to see the blue of his eyes and forget the red on my hands and the green I wish I wore.

"You're here," he says, breathing hard and hungry. Sweat and dirt cover his face, and he looks at me as though I'm the only thing he ever needed to see.

I open my mouth to say yes. But I only have time to breathe in before he closes the last of the distance. All I know is the kiss.

CHAPTER 23
KY

O ur poem," she whispers. "Will you say it to me?"

I put my face close to her ear. My lips brush against her neck. Her hair smells like sage. Her skin smells like home.

But I can't speak.

She is the first to remember that we are not alone. *"Ky,"* she whispers.

We both pull back a little. In the fading light I see the tangles in her hair and the tan on her skin. Her beauty always makes me ache. "Cassia," I say, my voice hoarse, "this is Eli." When she turns to him and her face lights up I know that I didn't imagine his resemblance to Bram.

"This is Indie," she says, gesturing to the girl who came with her. Indie folds her arms across her chest.

A pause. Eli and I glance at each other. I know we both think of Vick. This should be the moment we introduce him to them but he's gone.

Just last night Vick was alive. This morning he stood next to the stream, watching the trout as it swam. He thought of Laney while the colors flashed and the sun shone down.

Then he died.

I gesture at Eli, who stands very straight. "There were three of us this morning," I say.

"What happened?" Cassia asks. Her hand tightens on mine and I squeeze back gently, trying to be careful of the cuts I feel carved into her skin. *What has she been through to find me?*

"Someone came," I tell her. "They killed our friend Vick. The river, too."

Suddenly I'm aware of how we must look from above. We're standing here on the plain out in the open for anyone to see. "Let's get inside the Carving," I say. In the west beyond the mountains the sun slides low—almost gone—on a day of dark and light. Vick gone. Cassia here.

"How did you do it?" I ask, drawing closer to her as we slip into the Carving. She turns to answer me, her breath hot on my cheek. We come together to kiss again, our hands and lips gentle and greedy with each other. Against her warm skin I whisper, "How did you find us?"

"The compass," she says, and she presses it into my hand. To my surprise it's the one I made of stone.

"So where do we go now?" Eli asks, his voice wavering, when we reach the spot where we camped with Vick. It still smells like smoke. The beams of our flashlights catch the silver of fallen fish scales. "Are we still going to cross the plain?"

"We can't," Indie says. "Not for a day or two, anyway. Cassia's been sick."

"I'm fine now," Cassia tells us. Her voice sounds strong.

I reach for the chert in my pack to start another small fire. "I think we stay here tonight," I tell Eli. "We can decide more in the morning." Eli nods and without my asking begins to gather brush for the fire.

"He's so young," Cassia says softly. "Did the Society send him out here?"

"Yes," I say. I strike the chert. Nothing.

She puts her hand on mine and I close my eyes. The next time I strike, the sparks snap and fly and she catches her breath.

Eli brings an armful of stringy, tough brush. When he adds it to the fire, it crackles and the smell of sage rises into the night—sharp and wild.

Cassia and I sit as near to each other as we can. She leans into me and I keep my arms around her. I don't fool myself that I hold her together—she does that on her own— but holding her keeps me from flying apart.

"Thank you," Cassia tells Eli. I can tell from her voice that she smiles at him and he smiles back, barely. He sits in the spot where Vick sat last night. Indie moves to give Eli more space and leans in to see the fire dance. She glances at me and I see a flash of something in her eyes.

I shift position a little, blocking her view of us with my back and angling my flashlight so that it shines on Cassia's hands. "What happened?" I ask her.

She looks down. "I cut them on a rope," she says. "We

climbed into another canyon looking for you before we came back to this one." She glances at the other two and smiles at them before she leans in more closely. "Ky," she says, "we're together again."

I have always loved the way she says my name. "I can't believe it either."

"I had to find you," she says. She slips her arms around me, underneath my coat, and I feel her fingers on my back. I do the same. She's so slight and small. And strong. No one else could do what she's done. I pull her even closer, the ache and release of touching her a feeling I remember from the Hill. It is even stronger now.

"There's something I need to tell you," Cassia whispers in my ear.

"I'm listening," I say.

She takes a deep breath. "I don't have the compass any-more. The one you gave me back in Oria." She hurries on and I hear the sound of tears in her voice. "I traded it to an Archivist."

"That's all right," I tell her, meaning it. She's here. After all of this the compass isn't much to have lost along the way. And I didn't give it to her to keep for me. I gave it to her to have for her own. Still, I'm curious. "What did you get in the trade?"

"Not what I expected," she says. "I asked for information about where they were taking Aberrations and how to get there."

"*Cassia,*" I say, and stop. That was dangerous. But she knew that when she tried it. She doesn't need me to tell her.

"The Archivist gave me a story instead," she tells me. "At

first I thought he'd cheated me and I was so angry—all I had left to get me to you were the blue tablets."

"Wait," I say. "Blue tablets?"

"From Xander," she says. "I kept them because I knew we'd need them in the canyon to survive." She looks at me and misreads the look on my face. "I'm sorry. I had to decide so quickly—"

"It's not that," I tell her, grabbing her arm. "The blue tablets are poison. Did you take any?"

"Only one," she says. "And I don't believe they're poisoned."

"I tried to tell her," Indie says. "I wasn't there when she took it."

I breathe out. "How did you keep moving?" I ask Cassia. "Have you eaten?" She nods. I pull out some of the flat bread from my bag. "Eat this now," I say. Eli reaches into his bag and holds out a piece of bread too.

Cassia takes the food from both of us. "How do you know the tablets are poisoned?" she asks, her voice still doubtful.

"Vick told me," I say, trying not to panic. "The Society always told us that if there was some kind of disaster the blue tablet would save us. But it's not true. It stops you instead. And then you die if they don't come to save you."

"I still don't believe it," Cassia says. "Xander wouldn't give me something that could hurt me."

"He must not have known," I say. "Maybe he meant for you to use the tablets for trade."

"If it was going to work, it would have by now," Indie says to Cassia. "You must have walked through it somehow. I've never heard of anyone doing that. But you wouldn't stop until we found Ky."

We all look at Cassia. She's thinking something through, her eyes thoughtful. Sorting information. She's looking for facts to explain what happened, but the only one she needs I already know: She is strong in ways even the Society can't predict.

"I only took one," she says softly. "I dropped the other. And the paper that came with it."

"The paper?" I ask.

Cassia looks up, as if she's just remembered that we're there. "Xander hid little pieces of paper with notes printed on them inside the tablets. They're little scraps of information from his microcard."

"How?" I ask. Indie leans forward.

"I don't know how he managed to do any of it—steal the tablets *or* put the messages inside," Cassia says. "But he did."

Xander. I shake my head. Always playing the game. Of course Cassia didn't leave him behind completely. He's her best friend. He's still her Match. But he made a mistake in giving her the tablets.

"Will you give them back to me?" Cassia asks Indie. "Not the tablets. Only the scraps."

For a moment I see something flash in Indie's eyes. A challenge. I don't know if she really wants the papers or if she just doesn't want to be told what to do. But then she reaches into her pack and pulls out the foil-backed packet. "Here," she says. "I don't need any of it anyway."

"Can you tell me what they said?" I ask, trying not to sound jealous. Indie darts a look at me and I know I haven't fooled her.

"Just things like his favorite color and his favorite activity," Cassia says gently. I know she heard the false note in my voice, too. "I think he must have known that I never looked at the microcard."

And just like that, my worry is gone—swallowed back up—and I'm ashamed of myself. She came all this way to find me.

"That boy in the other canyon," Indie says. "When you said he'd waited too long, I thought you meant that he'd waited too long to kill himself."

Cassia covers her mouth with her hand. *"No,"* she says. "I thought he'd waited too long to take the tablet and it didn't save him." Her voice falls to a whisper. "I didn't know." She looks at Indie, horrified. "Do you think *he* knew? Did he mean to die?"

"What boy?" I ask Cassia. So much has happened to us while we were apart.

"A boy who ran with us into the Carving," Cassia says. "He's the one who showed us where you went."

"How did he know?" I ask.

"He was one of the ones you left," Indie says bluntly.

She moves back from the dying fire. The light barely reaches her face. She gestures at the canyon around us. "*This* is the painting, isn't it?" she asks. "Number nineteen?"

It takes me a moment to realize what she means. "No," I say. "The land looks alike, but that carving is even bigger than this one. It's farther to the south. I've never seen it but my father knew people who had."

I wait for her to say something else, but she doesn't.

"That boy," Cassia says again.

Indie curls up to rest. "We have to forget about him," she tells Cassia. "He's gone."

"How are you feeling?" I whisper to Cassia. I sit with my back against the rock. Her head rests on my shoulder. I can't sleep. What Indie said about the tablet wearing off could be true, and Cassia seems strong, but I need to watch her all the way through the night to make sure she's all right.

Eli stirs in his sleep. Indie stays silent. I can't tell if she sleeps or listens, so I speak quietly.

Cassia doesn't answer me. "Cassia?"

"I wanted to find you," she says softly. "When I traded for the compass, I was trying to get to *you*."

"I know," I say. "And you did. Even if they cheated you."

"They didn't," she says. "Not completely, anyway. They gave me a story that was more than a story."

"What story?" I ask.

"It sounded like the one you told me about Sisyphus,"

she says. "But they called him the Pilot, and it talked about a rebellion." She leans in close. "We're not the only ones. There's something called a Rising out there. Have you heard of it before?"

"Yes," I say, but nothing more. I don't want to talk about the Rising. She said *we're not the only ones* as though that were a good thing, but all I want right now is to feel like we *are* the only ones in the camp. The Carving. The world.

I put my hand along her face, against the curve of her cheek that I tried before to carve in stone. "Don't worry about the compass. I don't have the green silk anymore either."

"Did they take that, too?"

"No," I say. "It's still up on the Hill."

"You left it there?" she asks, surprised.

"I tied it to a branch on one of the trees," I say. "I didn't want anyone to take it away."

"The Hill," Cassia says. For a moment we are both silent, remembering. And then she says, with a teasing note in her voice, "You never said the words of our poem to me earlier."

I lean closer to her and this time I can speak. I whisper, though part of me wants to shout. "Do not go gentle."

"No," she agrees, her voice, her skin soft in that good night. And then she kisses me hard.

CHAPTER 24
CASSIA

Watching Ky wake is better than a sunrise. One moment, he's still and down deep, and the next moment I can see him returning out of the dark, coming to the surface. His face shifts, his lips move, his eyes open. And then his smile, the sun. At the same time that he bends down to me, I reach up and am warmed as our lips meet.

We talk about the Tennyson poem, and how we both remembered it, and how he saw me reading it in the woods back in Oria. He's heard that it was a password before; out here when he was young, and, more recently from Vick.

Vick. Ky talks in a soft voice about his friend who helped him bury and about the girl Vick loved named Laney. Then, in a voice hard and cold, Ky relates the story of his escape and how he left the other villagers. He shines a merciless light on himself and his own actions. But what I see is not who he left but who he brought with him. Eli. Ky did what he could.

I tell him about Indie's version of the Pilot and more about the boy who vanished into a different canyon in the Carving. "He was looking for something," I say, and I wonder if the boy knew what was behind the Society's wall in the other canyon. "And he died."

Last of all, I tell Ky about the blue-marked Anomalies on top of the Carving and how I wonder if they could have been part of the Rising.

Then we fall silent. Because we do not know what happens next.

"So the Society's in these canyons," Ky says.

Eli's eyes widen. "They're in our coats, too."

"What do you mean?" I ask, and Ky and Eli tell us about the wires that keep us warm and take our data.

"I ripped mine out," Ky says, and I realize that explains the tears in the fabric of his coat.

I glance at Eli, who looks defensive and folds his arms over his chest. "I left mine like it is," he says.

"Nothing wrong with that," Ky says. "It's your choice to make." He glances at me, asking what I will do.

I smile at him as I pull off my coat and hold it out. He takes it in his hands and looks at me standing in front of him as if he still can't believe what he sees. I don't look away. A smile crosses his lips, and then he puts the coat out on the ground in front of him and slits the fabric with swift, sure movements.

When he finishes, he gives me a tangle of blue wires and a small silver disc.

"What did you do with yours?" I ask him.

"We buried them," he says.

I nod, and begin to dig in the dirt to leave mine, too. When I finish I stand up. Ky holds out my coat and I slip back inside of it. "You should still be warm," he says. "I didn't move any of the red wires."

"What about you?" Eli asks Indie.

She shakes her head. "I'll stay like you," she says, and Eli smiles a little.

Ky nods. He doesn't seem surprised.

"What happens now?" Indie asks. "I don't think we should try to cross the plain after what happened to your friend."

Eli flinches at her bluntness, and Ky's voice, when he speaks, sounds tight. "That's true. They might come back, and even if they don't, the water out there is poisoned now."

"We pulled out some of the poison, though," Eli says.

"Why?" Indie asks.

"To try to save the stream," Ky says. "It was stupid."

"It wasn't," Eli says.

"We didn't get enough of them out to make much of a difference."

"We *did*," Eli says stubbornly.

Ky reaches inside his pack and rolls out a map, a beautiful thing with colors and markings. "We're here now," he says, pointing to a spot at the edge of the Carving.

I can't help but smile. We *are* here, together. In this wide, wild world, we've managed to meet again. I reach out my hand and trace my finger along the path I took to get to him until my hand meets his on the map.

"I was trying to find a way to you," Ky says. "I wanted to cross the plain and get back to the Society somehow. We took some things from the farmers' township for trade."

"That old abandoned settlement," Indie says. "We came through it too."

"It's not abandoned," Eli says. "Ky saw a light there. Someone didn't leave."

I shiver, remembering that feeling of being followed. "What did you take?" I ask Ky.

"This map," he says. "And these." He reaches inside his pack again and hands me something else—books.

"Oh," I say, breathing in their smell, running my fingers along their edges. "Do they have more?"

"They have everything," Ky says. "Stories, histories, anything you can imagine. They've saved them for years inside a cave in the canyon wall."

"Then let's go back," Indie says decisively. "It's not safe on the plain yet. And Cassia and I need something to trade."

"We could get more food, too," Eli says. Then he frowns. "But that light—"

"We'll be careful," Indie says. "It has to be better than trying to cross to the mountains right now."

"What do you think?" Ky asks me.

I remember that day back in Oria at the Restoration site, and how the workers gutted the books and the pages fell out. And I imagine the papers lifting, flying, winging their way for miles until they settled somewhere safe and hidden. Another thought darts into my mind: there might even be information about the Rising among the things the farmers saved. "I want to see all the words," I tell Ky, and he nods.

At night, Ky and Eli show us a place to camp that Indie and I did not notice on our way out of the Carving. It's a cave, spacious and large once you're inside; and when Ky shines his flashlight around it I catch my breath. It's painted.

I've never seen pictures like this—they're real, not on a port or printed out on a scrap of paper. So much color. So much scale—the paintings cover the walls, wash up on the ceiling. I turn to Ky. "How?" I ask him.

"The farmers must have done it," he says. "They knew how to make their own supplies with plants and minerals."

"Are there more?" I ask.

"Many of the houses back in the township are painted," he says.

"What about these?" Indie asks. She points to another set of art farther along the cave wall—carved pictures showing wild, primitive figures in motion.

"Those are older," Ky says. "But the theme is the same."

He's right. The farmers' work is less crude, more refined: a whole wall of girls in beautiful dresses and men with colorful shirts and bare feet. But the motions of the people seem to echo those of the earlier etchings.

"Oh," I whisper. "Do you think they painted a Match

Banquet?" As soon as I've said it, I feel stupid. They don't have Match Banquets here.

But Indie doesn't laugh at me. Her expression as she runs her fingers over the walls and along the pictures is a complex one, longing and anger and hope all together in her eyes.

"What are they doing?" I ask Ky. "Both of the sets of figures are . . . moving." One of the girls has her hands lifted over her head. I put mine up, too, trying to figure out what she is doing.

Ky watches me with that look in his eyes, the one sad and full of love at the same time, the one he gives me when he knows something I don't, something he thinks has been stolen from me.

"They're dancing," he says.

"What?" I ask.

"I'll show you sometime," he says, and his voice, tender and deep, sends a shiver through me.

CHAPTER 25
KY

My mother could dance and sing and she went out to watch the sunset every night. "They didn't have sunsets like these in the main Provinces," she'd say. She always found the one good part of everything and then turned her face toward it every chance she had.

She believed in my father and went to his meetings. He walked out with her in the desert after the storms and kept her company while she found hollows filled with rain and painted with water. He wanted to make things—changes—that would last. She always understood that what she did would fade away.

When I see Cassia dancing without knowing she's doing it—turning and turning in delight as she looks at the paintings and carvings in the cave—I understand why my parents both believed as they did.

It's beautiful and it's real, but our time together could be as fleeting as snow on the plateau. We can either try to change everything or just make the most of whatever time we have.

CHAPTER 26
CASSIA

Ky leaves one flashlight on so that we can see each other while we talk. When Eli and Indie fall asleep, and Ky and I are the only two left, he switches off the light to save it. The girls on the cave walls dance back into darkness and we are truly alone.

The air in the cave feels heavy between us.

"One night," Ky says. In his voice, I hear the Hill. I hear the wind on the Hill, and the brush of branches against our sleeves, and the way he sounded when he first told me he loved me. We have stolen time from the Society before. We can do it again. It will not be as much as we want.

I close my eyes and wait.

But he doesn't go on. "Come with me outside," he says, and I feel his hand on mine. "We won't go far." I can't see him; but I hear a complicated mix of emotion in his voice and feel it in the way he touches me. Love, concern, and something unusual, something bittersweet.

Outside, Ky and I walk down the path a little way. I lean back against the rock and he stands before me, reaching up to put his hand along my neck, under my hair and the collar of my coat. His hand feels rough, cut from carving and climbing, but his touch is gentle and warm. The night wind sings through the canyon and Ky's body shields me from the cold.

"One night . . ." I prompt him again. "What's the rest of the story?"

"It wasn't a story," Ky says softly. "I was about to ask you something."

"What?" The two of us draw together under the sky, our breath white and our voices hushed.

"One night," Ky says, "doesn't seem like too much to ask."

I don't speak. He moves closer and I feel his cheek against mine and breathe in the scent of sage and pine, of old dust and fresh water and of him.

"For one night, can we just think of each other? Not the Society or the Rising or even our families?"

"No," I say.

"No what?" He tangles one of his hands in my hair, the other draws me closer still.

"No, I don't think we can," I say. "And no, it isn't too much to ask."

CHAPTER 27
KY

I never named anything I've written before
no reason to
since
it would all have the same title anyway
—for you—
but I would call this one
one night
that night
when we let the world be only you
and only me
we stood on it while it spun
green and blue and red
the music ended
but we
were still
singing

CHAPTER 28
CASSIA

When the sun comes into the Carving, we are already on the move again. The path is so narrow that we usually have to walk single file, but Ky stays near me, his hand on the small of my back, our fingers brushing and clinging every chance we get.

We have never had such a thing before—a whole night to talk, to kiss and hold on—and the thought *and we never will again* keeps coming back to me, will not stay buried where it should, even in the beautiful light of the Carving morning.

When the others woke, Ky told us what he thought our plan should be: get back to the township by evenfall and try to slip into one of the houses farthest from where he saw the light. Then we'll keep watch. If there's still only one light, we can try to approach in the morning. There are four of us and, Ky thinks, only one or two of them.

Of course, Eli is so young.

I glance back at him. He doesn't notice. He walks on with his head down. Though I've seen him smile, I know the loss of

Vick weighs heavily on both of them. "Eli wanted me to say the Tennyson poem over Vick," Ky told me. "I couldn't do it."

In the lead, Indie shifts her pack and looks back at us to make sure we still follow. I wonder what would have happened to her if I had died. Would she have cried for me, or would she have gone through my things, taken what she needed, and moved on?

We steal into the township at dusk, Ky in the lead.

I didn't look closely when we came through before, and now the homes intrigue me as we move quickly down the street. People must have built their own, each house different in some way from the one next to it. And they could walk into each other's residences, cross each other's thresholds whenever they wanted. The dirt paths speak of this; unlike the ones in the Borough, the paths here do not go straight from front door to sidewalk. They wind, they web, they interconnect. The people have not been gone long enough for their comings and goings to have been completely erased. I see them there in the dirt. I almost hear their echo in the canyon, the callings-out: *hello, good-bye. How are you?*

The four of us crowd inside a tiny weathered house with a watermarked door. "I don't think anyone saw us," Ky says.

I barely hear him. I'm staring at the pictures painted on the walls. The figures were painted with a different hand than the ones in the cave, but again they are beautiful. They have no wings on their backs. They do not look surprised at flight. Their eyes are not turned up to the sky, but instead look down toward the ground, as though they will keep that sight of earth as a memory for higher days.

But still I think I recognize them.

"Angels," I say.

"Yes," Ky says. "Some of the farmers still believed in them. In my father's time, anyway."

The dark falls a little deeper and the angels turn into shadows behind us. Then Ky sees it, in the small house across the way. He points out the light to us. "It's in the same house as the night before."

"I wonder what's happening inside," Eli says. "Who do you think is in there? A thief? Do you think they're robbing the homes?"

"No," Ky says. He glances over at me in the shadowy night. "I think they *are* home."

Ky and I are both at the window at first light, watching, so we are the ones who see the man first.

He comes out of the house, alone, carrying something, and walks through the dust, along the path closer to us, down to a little stand of trees that I noticed when we first came in. Ky motions to all of us to be quiet. Indie and Eli go to the other window in the front of the house and look out, too. We all watch carefully over the edge of the windowsills.

The man stands tall and strong; he's dark and tanned. He reminds me of Ky in some ways: his coloring, that quiet movement. But there's a tiredness in him and he seems unaware of anything except what he carries, and in that moment I realize it's a child.

Her dark hair streams over his arms and her dress is white. An Official color, but of course she's no Official. The dress is lovely, as though she's going to a Banquet, but she's much too young.

And much too still.

I put my hand to my mouth.

Ky glances over at me and nods. His eyes are sad and weary and kind.

She's dead.

I glance over at Eli. Is he all right? Then I remember that he's seen much more death than this. Maybe he's even seen a child dead before.

But I never have. Tears fill my eyes. Someone so young, so tiny. *How?*

The man puts her gently on the ground, in the dead grass under the trees. Something, a sound carried on the canyon wind, reaches our ears. Singing.

It takes a long time to bury someone.

While the man digs the hole, slowly and steadily, it begins to rain again. It's not a heavy rain, but a sustained spatter of water against dirt and mud, and I wonder why he brought her out with him. Maybe he wanted her to have rain on her face, one last time.

Maybe he just didn't want to be alone.

I can't stand it anymore. "We have to go help him," I whisper to Ky, but Ky shakes his head.

"No," he says. "Not yet."

The man climbs back out of the hole and walks over to the girl. But he doesn't put her in the grave; he brings her near it and puts her body down.

And then I notice the blue lines all over his arms.

He reaches down and lifts up the girl's arm.

He pulls out something. Blue. He marks it on her skin. The rain keeps washing it off and yet he keeps drawing, over and over and over. I can't tell if he still sings. Finally the rain stops and the blue stays.

Eli's not watching anymore. He sits with his back to the wall underneath his window and I crawl over across the floor to sit next to him, not wanting my movement to catch the eye of the man outside. I put my arm around Eli and he slides closer.

Indie and Ky keep watching.

So young, I keep thinking. I hear a *thump, thump* sound and for a moment I can't tell if it is the beating of my heart or the sound of the dirt as it falls on the little girl in her grave.

"I'm going now," Ky whispers finally. "The rest of you, wait here."

I turn and look at him, surprised. I raise my head so I can see out the window again. The man has finished burying. He lifts a flat gray stone and puts it over the spot now filled in with dirt. I don't hear singing. "No," I whisper.

Ky looks at me, raises his eyebrows.

"You can't," I say. "Let's wait until tomorrow. Look at what he's had to do."

Ky's voice is gentle but firm. "We gave him all the time we could. We have to find out more now."

"*And* he's alone," Indie says. "Vulnerable."

I look at Ky, shocked, but he doesn't discount what Indie says. "It's the right time," he says.

Before I can say more, he opens the door and leaves.

CHAPTER 29
KY

D o what you want," the man calls out when I reach the edge of the graveyard. "It doesn't matter. I am the last."

If I hadn't already known he was a farmer, his accent and the formality of his speech would have given him away. My father sometimes had a hint of their inflection in his voice when he came back from the canyons.

I told the others to stay behind but of course Indie didn't listen. I hear her coming up behind me and hope that Cassia and Eli had the sense to stay in the house.

"Who are you?" the man asks.

Indie answers behind me. I don't turn around. "Aberrations," she says. "People the Society wants dead."

"We came into the canyons to find the farmers because we thought you might help us," I say.

"We're done with that," the man says. "Finished."

Footsteps. Behind us. I want to turn around and call to Cassia and Eli to return to the house but I can't turn my back on the man.

"So there are four of you," he says. "Any more?"

I shake my head.

"I'm Eli," Eli says behind me.

For a minute, the man doesn't answer. Then he says, "My name is Hunter." He looks at us closely. I do the same. He's not much older than we are, I realize, but wind and weather have marked his face.

"Did any of you live in the Society?" he asks.

"We all did," I say. "At one time or another."

"Good," Hunter says. "I might need something from you."

"In exchange for what?" I ask.

"If you can help me," Hunter says, "you can have access to whatever you want. We have food. Papers." He waves his hand wearily in the direction of the storage caves. Then he looks at me. "Though it appears you might have already helped yourselves."

"We thought this place was empty," Eli says. "We'll give it all back."

Hunter makes an impatient gesture. "It doesn't matter. What is it you want? Things for trade?"

"Yes," I say.

Out of the corner of my eye I see Cassia and Indie exchange glances. Hunter notices it too. "What else?" he asks.

Indie speaks up. "We'd like to know more about the Rising," she says. "If it's somewhere near here, how we can find it."

"And who the Pilot might be," Cassia says eagerly. Of course she wants to know about the rebellion, since it seems to be mentioned in a poem from her grandfather. I wish I'd told her everything back on the Hill. She might have understood then. But now, after she's begun to hope—I don't know what to do.

"I might have some answers for you," Hunter says. "You help me and then I'll tell you what I know."

"Let's get started," Indie says. "What do you want us to do?"

"It's not that easy," Hunter says. "We have to go somewhere, and it's getting too dark. Come back here tomorrow when it's light." He reaches for the shovel he used for the grave and I motion for the others to step back.

"How do we know we can trust you?" I ask.

He laughs again, that same humorless laugh. A faint echo of it bounces back from the walls of the canyon and among the empty houses. "Tell me," Hunter says. "In the Society, do people really live to be eighty?"

"Yes," Cassia says. "But that's only for Citizens."

"Eighty," Hunter says. "We almost never reach eighty in the Carving. Do you think it's worth it?" he asks us. "To have no choice, but to live so long?"

"Some people think it is," Cassia says quietly.

Hunter passes his blue-marked hand across his face and what he said earlier is suddenly true. He's done. Finished. "Tomorrow," he says. He turns around and walks away.

～

Everyone sleeps in the little house. Eli, Cassia, Indie. I stay awake and listen. Their breathing makes it sound as though the house itself breathes in and out but of course the walls hold still. I know Hunter won't harm us but I can't rest. I have to keep watch.

Sometime near the approach of dawn, when I'm standing in the doorway looking out, I hear a sound from the other side of the room. Someone's awake.

Indie. She comes toward me.

"What do you want?" I ask, trying to keep my tone even. I recognized Indie the moment I saw her. She is like me—a survivor. I don't trust her.

"Nothing," Indie says. In the silence I hear her shift the pack. She never lets it out of sight.

"What are you hiding in there?" I ask.

"There's nothing to hide," she says, an edge to her voice. "Everything in here belongs to me." She pauses. "Why don't you want to join the Rising?"

I don't answer. We stand in silence for a little while. Indie pulls her pack over her shoulder and holds it tightly against her chest. She seems far away. I am too. Part of me is back with Cassia under the stars in the Carving. On the Hill with the wind. Back in the Borough when I was young, I never would have believed any of this could happen. I never dreamed I could steal so much from the Society.

I hear someone stirring. Cassia.

"She dreams about Xander," Indie whispers behind me. "I've heard her call his name."

I tell myself that the scraps Xander hid in the tablets don't matter. Cassia knew Xander and she still chose me. And the scraps won't last. The port paper deteriorates so quickly. They'll turn to flakes as delicate as snow. As spent and silent as ash.

I can't lose her now.

Lived in the Outer Provinces for much of his life.

Peers listed Ky Markham's name as the student they most admired 0.00% of the time.

No one was ever going to get a list about me.

And no one who loves someone else would want that person to have a Match like me.

Does loving someone mean you want them to be safe? Or that you want them to be able to choose?

"What do you want?" I ask Indie.

"I want to know Xander's secret," Indie says.

"What do you mean?"

In answer she holds out a scrap of paper. "Cassia dropped this," Indie says. "I didn't give it back."

I know I shouldn't take the scrap but I do. Careful to keep the light away from Cassia and Eli, I switch on my flashlight to read the paper:

Has a secret to tell his Match when he sees her again.

A line like that would never be included on Xander's official microcard. He added something new. "How did he do it?" I ask in spite of myself, as though Indie would know. The Society carefully monitors all typing and printing. Did he risk using a port at school? At home?

"He must be very smart," Indie says.

"He is," I say.

"So what's the secret?" Indie asks, leaning closer.

I shake my head. "What makes you think I'd know?" I do know and I'm not telling.

"You and Xander were friends," Indie says. "Cassia told me so. And I think you know a lot more than you say."

"About what?" I ask.

"Everything," she says.

"I think the same about you," I say. "You're hiding something."

I shine the flashlight full on her and she blinks. In the light she looks almost blindingly beautiful. Her hair is a color that isn't seen very often, a fire color of red and gold. And she's tall and fine-featured and strong. Wild. She wants to survive, but there's an element of unpredictability about how she'll do it that keeps me on edge. "I want to know the secret," she says. "And how to find the Rising. I think you know the answers. You won't tell Cassia, and I think I know why."

I shake my head but don't speak. I let the silence hang between us. She can fill it if she chooses.

For an instant I think she will. Then she turns away and walks back to the spot where she slept. She doesn't look at me again.

After a moment I walk back to the door and steal outside. I open my hand to the wind and let the scrap blow away into the last of the night.

CHAPTER 30
CASSIA

On the wall across from the angels, there is a very different painting. I did not notice it before, so intent was I on the picture of the angels. The others all sleep; even Ky has slumped over near the door where he insisted on keeping watch.

I climb out of the bed and try to decide what the painting represents. It has curves, angles, and shapes, but I don't know what it could be. None of the Hundred look like this. They are all clearly people, places, things. After a few moments, I hear Ky move at the other end of the room. Our eyes meet across the gray expanse of floor and the huddled dark shapes of Indie and Eli. Silently, Ky rises to his feet and comes to stand next to me. "Did you sleep enough?" I whisper.

"No," he says, leaning in and closing his eyes.

When he opens them again neither of us have words or breath left.

We both look at the painting. After a few moments, I ask, "Is it a canyon?" but even as I name the picture, I realize it could be something else. Someone's flesh cut open, a sunset striping above a river.

"Love," he says, finally.

"Love?" I ask.

"Yes," he says.

"Love," I repeat softly, still puzzled.

"I think 'love' when I look at it," Ky says, trying to explain. "You might think something else. It's like the Pilot in your poem—everyone thinks something different when they hear that name."

"What do you think of when you hear *my* name?" I ask him.

"Many things," Ky whispers, sending rivers of chills along the length of my skin. "This. The Hill. The Carving. Places we've been together." He pulls back and I feel him looking at me and I hold my breath because I know there is so much he sees. "Places we haven't been together," he says, "*yet.*" His voice sounds fierce as he speaks of the future.

We both want to move, to be outside. Indie and Eli still sleep and we don't disturb them; they'll be able to see us from the window when they awake.

This canyon that I earlier thought so barren and dry has surprising amounts of green, especially near the stream. Watercress laces the edges of the marshy banks; moss jewels the red rocks along the river; swamp grass tangles green blades with gray. I step against the ice at the edge of the stream and it breaks, reminding me of the time I shattered the glass that protected my dress fragment back in the Borough. Looking down at where I've pressed my foot, I see that even the ice I've broken is green under the white. It is exactly the color of my dress at the Match Banquet. I noticed none of this green the first time through the canyon; I was so fixed on finding a sign of Ky.

I look up at him walking along the stream and notice the ease of his walk, even when he steps in places where shifting sands have drifted across the path. He looks back at me and stops and smiles.

You belong here, I think. *You move differently than you did in the Society.* Everything about the township seems right for him—the beautiful, unusual paintings, the stark independence of the town.

All that's missing are people for him to help lead. He only has the few of us.

"Ky," I say as we reach the edge of the stand of trees.

He stops. His eyes are all for me, and his lips have touched mine, and brushed my neck, my hands, the insides of my wrists, each finger. While we stood kissing that night under the cold burning stars and held on tight, it did not feel that we were stealing time. It felt that it was all our own.

"I know," he says.

We hold each other's eyes for another long moment before we duck under the branches of the trees. They have weathered gray bark and drifts of brown leaves underneath that move and sigh with the canyon wind.

As the leaves shift, I see other flat gray stones on the ground like the one Hunter put down yesterday. I touch Ky's arm. "Are these all—"

"Places where people are buried," he says. "Yes. It's called a graveyard."

"Why didn't they bury them higher?"

"They needed that land for the living."

"But the books," I say. "They stored those high and books aren't living."

"The living still have use for books," Ky says softly. "Not for bodies. If a graveyard floods, nothing is ruined that wasn't already gone. It's different with the library."

I crouch down to look at the stones. The places where people lie are marked in different ways. Names, dates, sometimes a line of verse. "What is this writing?" I ask.

"It's called an epitaph," he says.

"Who chooses it?"

"It depends. Sometimes if the person knows they are dying, they choose it. Often it's those left behind who have to choose something that fits the person's life."

"That's sad," I say. "But beautiful."

Ky raises his eyebrows at me and I hurry to explain. "The deaths aren't beautiful," I say. "I mean the idea of the epitaph. The Society chooses what's left of us when we die there. They say what goes on your history." Still, I wish again that I had taken the time to view Grandfather's microcard more closely before I left. But Grandfather *did* decide what was left of him as far as preservation goes: nothing.

"Did they make stones like this in your family's village?"

I ask Ky, and as soon as I do I wish I hadn't done it, wish I hadn't asked for that part of the story yet.

Ky looks at me. "Not for my parents," he says. "There wasn't time."

"Ky," I say, but he turns away and walks down another row of stones. My hand feels cold now without his around it.

I shouldn't have said anything. Except for Grandfather, the people I have seen dead were not people I loved. It is as though I have peered down into a long dark canyon where I have not had to walk.

As I move between the stones, careful not to step on them, I see that the Society and Hunter are right about the life expectancy out here. Most of the life spans don't reach eighty years. And other children lie in the ground, too, besides the one Hunter buried.

"So many children died here," I say out loud. I'd hoped the girl yesterday was an exception.

"Young people die in the Society too," Ky says. "Remember Matthew."

"Matthew," I repeat, and as I hear his name, I suddenly *remember* Matthew, really remember him, think of him by name for the first time in years instead of as just *the first Markham boy*, the one who died in a rare tragedy at the hands of an Anomaly.

Matthew. Four years older than Xander and me; so much older as to be untouchable, unreachable. He was a nice boy who said hello to us in the street but was years ahead of us. He carried tablets and went to Second School. The boy I remember, now that his name has been given back to me, was enough like Ky to be his cousin; but taller, bigger, less quick and smooth.

Matthew. It was almost as though his name died with him, as though naming the loss would have made it more real.

"But not as many," I say. "Just him."

"He's the only one you remember."

"Were there others?" I ask, shocked.

A sound from behind makes me turn; it's Eli and Indie closing the door to our borrowed house. Eli lifts a hand to wave and I wave back. The light is full in the sky now; Hunter will be here soon.

I look down at the stone he placed yesterday and reach out and put my hand on the name carved there. SARAH. She had few years; she died at five. Under the dates is a line of writing, and with a chill I realize that it sounds like a line from a poem:

SUDDENLY ACROSS THE JUNE A WIND WITH FINGERS GOES

I reach for Ky's hand and hold on as tight as I can. So that the cold wind around us won't try to steal him from me with its greedy fingers, its hands that take things from times that should be spring.

CHAPTER 31
KY

When Hunter comes to meet us he has a canteen of water and a pile of ropes slung over his shoulder. I wonder what he intends. Before I can ask, Eli speaks.

"Was she your sister?" Eli points to the newly placed stone.

Hunter doesn't glance back down at the grave. The smallest flicker of emotion crosses his face. "You saw her? How long were you watching?"

"A long time," Eli says. "We wanted to talk to you but we waited until you were finished."

"That's very kind of you," Hunter says flatly.

"I'm sorry," Eli says. "Whoever she was, I'm sorry."

"She was my daughter," Hunter says. Cassia's eyes widen. I know what she's thinking: *His daughter? But he's so young, only twenty-two or twenty-three. Certainly not twenty-nine, which is the youngest someone with a five-year-old child can be in the Society.* But this is not the Society.

Indie's the first to break the silence. "Where are we going?" she asks Hunter.

"To another canyon," Hunter says. "Can all of you climb?"

〜

When I was small my mother tried to teach me the colors. "Blue," she said, pointing to the sky. And "blue" again, the second time pointing to the water. She told me I shook my head because I could see that sky blue was not always the same as water blue.

It took me a long time—until I lived in Oria—to use the same word for all the shades of a color.

I remember this as we walk through the canyon. The Carving is orange and red, but you'd never see this kind of orange and red back in the Society.

Love has different shades. Like the way I loved Cassia when I thought she'd never love me. The way I loved her on the Hill. The way I love her now that she came into the canyon for me. It's different. Deeper. I thought I loved her and wanted her before, but as we walk through the canyon together I realize this could be more than a new shade. A whole new color.

Hunter stops ahead of us and gestures up at the cliff. "Here," he says. "This is the best place." He begins testing the rock and looking around.

I put up my hand to block the sun so I can better see the climb above us. Cassia glances at me and does the same. "This is where Indie and I came back over," she says in recognition.

Hunter nods. "It's the best place to climb."

"There's a cave in that other canyon," Indie tells Hunter.

"I know," Hunter says. "It's called the Cavern. The question I need you to answer is about what's inside."

"We didn't go in," Cassia says. "It's sealed tight."

Hunter shakes his head. "It looks like that. But my people have used it since we first came to the Carving. After the Society took it we found a way to get back in."

Cassia looks puzzled. "But then you know—"

Hunter interrupts her. "We know *what's* there. We don't know *why*." He looks at Cassia, his gaze unnerving in its assessment. "I think *you* might know why."

"Me?" she asks, sounding startled.

"You've been part of the Society longer than the others," Hunter says. "I can tell." Cassia flushes and brushes her hand down her arm, as if she wants to remove some taint of the Society.

Hunter glances over at Eli. "Do you think you can do this?"

Eli stares up at the cliff. "Yes," he says.

"Good," Hunter says. "It's not a particularly technical climb. Even the Society could do it if they tried."

"Why didn't they?" Indie asks.

"They did," Hunter says. "But this was one of our best-guarded areas. Anyone trying to climb in we cut down. And you can't fly an air ship into the canyon. It's too narrow.

They had to come in on foot and we had the advantage." He finishes another knot and hooks the rope through one of the metal bores on the wall. "It worked for a long time."

But now the farmers are gone across the plain. Or dead on top of the Carving. It's only a matter of time before the Society realizes that and decides to come in.

No one knows that better than Hunter. We have to hurry.

"We used to climb everywhere," Hunter says. "The Carving was all ours." He looks down at the rope in his hands. I think he's remembering again that everyone is gone. You wouldn't think you can forget but sometimes you can—for a moment or two. I've never been able to decide if I think that's a good thing or a bad thing. Forgetting lets you live without the pain for a moment but remembering hits hard.

It all hurts. Sometimes—when I'm weak—I wish that the red tablet *did* work on me.

"We saw bodies on top of the Carving," Indie says. She looks up at the climb, assessing it. "They had blue marks like you. Were they farmers, too? And why did they go up if it was better to wait for the Society down below?" In spite of myself I admire her. She's bold to ask Hunter those questions. I've been wanting to know the answers too.

"That place on top is the only area wide and flat enough for the Society to land their ships," Hunter says. "Lately, for whatever reason, they'd become more agressive about entering the Carving, and we couldn't guard all of the canyons. Only the one where our township is." He makes another knot, tightens the rope. "For the first time in the history of the farmers, we had a split we couldn't resolve. Some of us wanted to go up and fight so the Society would leave the canyons alone. Others wanted to escape."

"Which did you want?" Indie says.

Hunter doesn't answer.

"So those who crossed the plain," Indie says, pushing for more information, "did they go to join the Rising?"

"I think that's enough," Hunter says. The expression on his face keeps even Indie from asking more. She closes her mouth and Hunter hands her a rope. "You have the most climbing experience," he says. It's not a question. He can tell somehow.

She nods and almost smiles as she looks up at the rocks. "I used to sneak away sometimes. There was a good spot near our house."

"The Society let you climb?" Hunter asks.

She looks at him with an expression of contempt. "They didn't *let* me climb. I found a way to do it without them knowing."

"You and I will each take someone up," Hunter tells her. "It'll be faster that way. Can you do that?"

Indie laughs in response.

"Be careful," Hunter warns her. "The stone here is different."

"I know," she says.

"Can you climb up alone?" Hunter asks me.

I nod. I don't tell him that I prefer it this way. If I fall, at least I won't take anyone with me. "I'll watch you first."

Indie turns to look at Cassia and Eli. "Which one of you wants to come with me?"

"Eli," Cassia says. "You choose."

"Ky," Eli says immediately.

"No," Hunter tells him. "Ky hasn't climbed as much as we have."

Eli opens his mouth to protest but I shake my head at him. He glares at me and then walks over to stand by Indie. I think I see a small, pleased smile on Indie's face before she turns back to the rock.

I watch Cassia as she clips onto Hunter's line. Then I check Eli to make sure he's hooked up right. When I look up, Hunter is ready to begin. Cassia's jaw is set.

I'm not worried about the ascent. Hunter's the best climber. And he needs Cassia safe to help him in the cave. I believe Hunter when he says he needs to know why the Society did what they did. He still thinks that knowing why might help. He doesn't yet know that the reason will never be good enough.

Once we all reach the top of the Carving, we run. I hold on to Eli with one hand and Cassia with the other and we all move, our breath quiet and fast and our feet flying along the stone.

We're exposed and bare out on the rock under the sky for several long seconds.

It's not nearly long enough. I feel like I could run out here forever.

Look! I want to call out. *I'm still alive. Still here. Though your data and your Officials want it otherwise.*

Feet fast.

Lungs full of air.

Holding on to people I love.

I love.

The most reckless thing of all.

When we get closer to the edge we let go of each other. We need our hands for the ropes.

The second canyon is a true slot canyon—tiny and narrow— smaller than the farmers' canyon. After we've all arrived at the bottom of the cliff, Cassia points to a long smooth surface. It looks like sandstone but there is something odd about it. "That's where we noticed the entrance," she says. Her lips tighten. "The boy's body is over there, under those bushes."

The freedom I felt earlier is gone now. The feeling of Society hangs in this canyon like the torn and streaming clouds that linger after a thunderstorm.

The others notice it too. Hunter's face turns grim and I know it's the worst for him because he feels the Society in a place that used to be his.

Hunter leads us to a tiny cave in a spot where the canyon wall folds back in on itself. All five of us can barely crouch inside. The back of the cave ends in a pile of rocks. "We made a way in through here," he says.

"And the Society never found it?" Indie asks, sounding skeptical.

"They didn't even know how to look," Hunter says. He lifts up one of the rocks. "There's a crevice behind all these stones," he tells us. "Once we're inside, we can go through to a corner of the Cavern."

"How do we do it?" Eli asks.

"Move the earth," Hunter says. "And hold your breath in the tight spots." He reaches for one of the boulders. "I'll go first when it's time," he says over his shoulder. "Then Cassia. We'll talk each other through the turns. Go slowly. There's a place where you need to lie on your back and push yourself through with your feet. If you get stuck, call out. You'll be close enough to hear me. I can talk you through. It's the tightest just before the end."

I hesitate for a moment, wondering if this is a trap. Could the Society have set it? Or Indie? I don't trust her. I watch her help Hunter with the rocks, her long hair flying wildly around her in her eagerness. What does she want? What's she hiding?

I glance over at Cassia. She's in a new place where everything is different. She's seen people who died in terrible ways and she's been hungry and lost and come into the desert to find me. All things a Society girl should never have had to experience. I see a glint in her eye as she looks at me and it makes me smile. *Hold our breath?* she seems to say. *Move the earth? We've been doing that all along.*

CHAPTER 32
CASSIA

The crevice is barely wide enough for Hunter to climb into. He disappears without looking back. I'm next.

I glance over at Eli, whose eyes have gone wide. "Maybe you should wait for us here," I say.

Eli nods. "I don't mind the cave," he says. "But that is a *tunnel*."

I don't point out that he's the smallest of all of us and the least likely to get stuck because I know what he means. It seems counterintuitive, wrong, to worm our way into the earth like this. "It's all right," I say. "You don't have to come." I put my arm around him and squeeze his shoulders. "I don't think it will take long."

Eli nods again. He already looks better, less white. "We'll be back," I say again. "*I'll* be back."

Eli makes me think of Bram and how I left him behind, too.

I'm all right until I think too much, until I start calculating how many tons of rock must be above me. I don't even know how much one cubic foot of sandstone weighs, but the total amount must be enormous. And the ratio of air to stone must be small. Is that why Hunter told us to hold our breath? Does he know that there's not enough air? That I might breathe out and find nothing left to breathe back in?

I can't move.

The stone, so close around me. The passage, so dark. There are only inches between the earth and me; I'm pressed tight and lying on my back with blackness ahead and behind and the immovability of rock above and below and on every side. The mass of the Carving presses all over me; I've been afraid of its vastness and now I'm afraid of its closeness.

My face is turned to a sky that I cannot see, one blue above the stone.

I try to calm myself, tell myself it's all right. Living things have flown from tighter spaces than this. I'm just a butterfly, a mourning cloak, sealed inside a cocoon with blind eyes and sticky wings. And suddenly, I wonder if the cocoons sometimes do not open, if the butterfly inside is ever simply not strong enough to break through.

A sob escapes my throat.

"Help," I say.

To my surprise, it's not Hunter who speaks from ahead. It's Ky's voice from behind.

"It will be all right," he says. "Push along a little more."

And even in my panic, I hear the music in his deep voice, the sounds of singing. I close my eyes, imagining my breath is his own, that he is with me.

"Wait a moment if you need to," he says.

I picture myself smaller even than I am now. Climbing into the cocoon, pulling it tight around me like a real cloak, a blanket. And then I don't imagine myself bursting out. I just stay tucked inside, trying to see what I can.

At first, nothing at all.

But then I feel it. Even hidden away in the dark, I can tell that it is there. Some small part of me is always, always free.

"But I will," I say out loud.

"You will," Ky says behind me, and I move, and then I can feel space above me, air to breathe, a place to stand.

Where are we?

Shapes and figures form in the darkness, lit by tiny blue lights along the floor of the cave that shine like small raindrops. But, of course, they are too orderly to have fallen.

Other lights illuminate tall clear cases and machines that hum and moderate the temperature within the stone walls. What I see before me is Society: calibration, organization, calculation.

Someone moves and I almost gasp before I remember. Hunter.

"It's so huge," I say to him, and he nods.

"We used to meet here," he says softly. "We weren't the first. The Cavern is an old place."

I shudder when I look up. The walls of the vast space are embedded with shells of dead animals and bones of beasts, all caught in stone that was once mud. This place existed before the Society. Perhaps before people lived at all.

Ky comes into the cave then, brushing dust from his hair, and I walk over to him, and touch his hands, which feel cold and rough but nothing like stone. "Thank you for helping me," I say into the warmth of his neck. Then I pull away so he can see what's here.

"It *is* Society," Ky says, his voice as quiet as the Cavern. He strides across the floor of the cave and Hunter and I follow. Ky puts his hand on the door at the other side of the room. "Steel," he says.

"They're not supposed to be here," Hunter says, his voice tight.

It feels wrong: this overlay of the sterile and the Society over the earthy and the organic. *The Society wasn't supposed to be in my relationship with Ky, either,* I think, remembering how my Official told me that they'd known all along. The Society slides in everywhere, snakes in a crack, water dripping against a rock until even the stone has no choice but to hollow and change shape.

"I have to know what they killed us for," Hunter says to me, gesturing to the cases. They are filled with tubes. Rows and rows of them, glittering in the blue light. *Beautiful as the sea,* I imagine.

Indie comes into the cave next. She looks around and her eyes widen. "So what *are* they?" she asks.

"Let me look more closely," I say, and I walk between two of the rows of tubes. Ky comes with me. I run my hand along the cases made of smooth, clear plastic. To my surprise, there are no locks on the doors, and I open one to get a better look. It makes a soft hiss as it opens and I gaze at the tubes in front of me, overwhelmed all at once by both the amount of sameness and the amount of choice.

I don't want to disturb the tubes in case the Society has an alarm system, so I crane my neck until I can see the information on the tube in the center of the middle row. HANOVER, MARCUS. KA. The first notation is a name, clearly, and the second is the abbreviation for Keya Province. Beneath the Province, two dates and a bar code have been engraved.

These are samples of people, buried in the earth with the bones of creatures long dead and with the sediment of seas long stone, rows and rows of glass tubes similar to the one Grandfather had, the one containing his tissue preservation sample.

Behind the exhaustion and fatigue, I feel my sorting mind grind its gears, whir into action. Trying to make sense of what I see and the numbers in front of me. The cave is a place of preservation, accidental and intentional, in the mudded fossils above us and the tissues stored in tubes.

Why here? I wonder. *Why so far on the edge of the Society? Surely there are better places, dozens of them.* It is the opposite of a graveyard. It is the reverse of saying good-bye. And I understand this. Though I wish it didn't, in some ways this makes more sense to me than putting people forever into the earth and letting them go the way the farmers do.

"They're tissue samples," I tell Ky. "But why would the Society store them here?" I shiver and Ky puts his arm around me.

"I know," he says.

But he doesn't.

The Carving doesn't care.

We live, we die, we turn to rock or lie in earth or drift out to sea or burn to ash, and the Carving doesn't care about any of it. We will come and go. The Society will come and go. The canyons will live on.

"You know what they are," Hunter says. I look over at him. What must someone who has never lived in the Society think of something like this?

"Yes," I say. "But I don't know why. Wait a moment. Let me think."

"How many are in here?" Ky asks.

I do a quick estimation based on the rows in front of me. "There are thousands," I say. "Hundreds of thousands." The tubes are small, row upon row, case upon case, aisle upon aisle, in the vast space of the Cavern. "But not enough to account for all the samples that must have been taken over the years. This can't be the only facility."

"Could they be moving them out of the Society?" Ky asks.

I shake my head, confused. Why would they do that? "They're arranged by Province," I say, noting that all the tubes in the case before me say *KA*.

"Find Oria," Ky says.

"It should be on the next row," I say, calculating, walking fast.

Indie and Hunter stand together watching us. I turn the corner and find tubes marked OR for Oria. Seeing the familiar abbreviation in such a strange place gives me an odd feeling that is both intimate and distant.

I hear a sound at the secret entrance to the Cavern. We all turn. Eli comes through just like Ky did, grinning and brushing dirt from his hair. I rush over to him and grab Eli tight, my heart hammering in my chest at what he went through all alone.

"*Eli,*" I say, "I thought you were going to wait."

"I'm fine," he tells me. He glances over my shoulder, looking for Ky.

"You did it," Ky calls out to Eli, and Eli seems to stand a little straighter. I shake my head at Eli. Promising one thing, then choosing his own way when he changed his mind. Bram would have done the same thing.

Eli looks around, wide-eyed. "They're storing tubes here," he says.

"We think they're organized by Province," I tell him, and then I see Ky signaling to me.

"Cassia. I found something."

I hurry back over to where Ky is while Indie and Eli wander up and down other rows, looking for their own Provinces. "If the first date is the birthdate," Ky says, "then the second date is likely . . ." He pauses, waiting to see if I draw the same conclusion.

"The death date. The date the sample was taken," I say. And then I realize what he means. "They're too close. They're not eighty years apart."

"They weren't just storing the old," Ky says. "These people—they can't all be dead."

"They don't only take the samples when we die," I say, my mind racing. I think back—so many chances. Our forks. Our spoons. The clothes we wear. Or maybe we even give the samples ourselves, nod and scrape our own tissue away, hand it over and then take a red tablet. "The sample at the end means nothing. The Society already has tubes for everyone they want to keep. Maybe younger tissue works better. And this way, if we don't know about the other samples, they can keep us compliant until the very end." My heart leaps within me, perversely, in gratitude to the Society.

Grandfather might have a sample in here. It might not matter that my father destroyed the one taken at the Final Banquet.

"Cassia," Ky says softly. "Xander's here."

"What?" Where? Has he come to find us? How did he know?

"Here," Ky says quietly, pointing to one of the blue-lit tubes.

Of course. I avoid Ky's eyes and look at the tube. CARROW, XANDER. OR. His birthdate is correct. This is Xander's sample; but Xander is not dead.

As far as I know.

And then Ky and I both stand by the case, our eyes

running over the numbers, our fingers interlocking. Who is here? Who is saved?

"You're here," Ky says, pointing. There it is, the date of my birth. And my name: REYES, CASSIA. I draw my breath in sharply. *My name.* Seeing it here reminds me of the way it felt when they said my name at the Match Banquet. It reminds me that I belong. That my future has been secured by the Society with great care.

"I'm not here," Ky says, watching me.

"You might be in another Province," I say. "You could be—"

"I'm not here," Ky says. And for a moment, in the dim lighting of the cave, with the way he knows how to blend with the shadows, it seems that he is not. Only the feel of his hand holding tightly to mine tells me differently.

Hunter comes over to stand next to me and I try to explain. "They're tissues," I tell Hunter, "a little bit of skin or hair or fingernail. The Society takes them from its Citizens so that, someday, the Society can bring us back to life." I wince at my use of the word *us*—for all I know, I might be the only one in this cave with a tube stored here. And even that might only be because they haven't had time to change my status yet. I glance up at the walls of the cave again, at the bones and teeth and shells left behind. If what we are isn't in our bones, it must be in our tissues. It must be *somewhere.*

Hunter looks at me and then at the tubes. He looks for

so long that I open my mouth to try to explain again, but then he reaches inside a case and takes out a tube before I can stop him.

No alarm sounds.

Its absence unnerves me. Does a light flash somewhere back in the Society to tell an Official of the breach?

Hunter holds the tube up and shines a flashlight through it. The samples are so small they can't even be seen amid the solution swishing inside.

Snap. The tube breaks and blood runs red down Hunter's hand. "They killed us to store themselves," he says.

Everyone looks at Hunter. For a wild, impulsive moment, I am tempted to join Hunter in breaking—I'd open all the doors to all the cases and grab something, a stick perhaps. I'd sprint down aisles of tubes shining blue, silvery, light. I'd run the stick along them to see if they would sound like chimes. I wonder if the tune of other lives would be sour, wrong; or strong, clear, soft, and truly musical. But I don't break. I do something else instead, quickly, while they all stare at Hunter.

He opens his hand, looks at the blood and liquid in his palm. In spite of myself, I note the name on the label: THURSTON, MORGAN. I look back up at Hunter. Breaking a tube like that must require a lot of strength, but he seems not to notice the effort. "Why?" he asks. "How? *Have* they discovered a way to bring people back?"

Everyone stares, waiting for me to explain all of this. Anger and embarrassment rise up within me. Why do they think I have the answers? Because I'm the most Society of us all?

But there are things I do not understand, parts of the Society, parts of myself.

Ky puts his hand on my arm. "Cassia," he says softly.

"I'm not Xander!" I say, too loud in the echoing cave. Ky blinks as the sound of my voice calls all around him. "I don't know about medicine. Or tablets. Or sample storage. Or what the Society can or can't do in the medical field. I don't know."

For a moment, everyone is silent. Then Indie speaks. "Xander's secret," she says, turning to Ky. "Does it have anything to do with this?"

Ky opens his mouth to say something, but before he can, we all see it—a little red light flashing now on the top of the case Hunter opened.

Fear sings through me again, and I don't know which frightens me more—the Society, or the Cavern that has us caught.

CHAPTER 33
KY

Hunter reaches for another tube and snaps that one in his hand too.

"Get out of here," I say to Cassia and the others. "Go."

Indie doesn't hesitate. She turns and runs for the entrance to the cave and slides into the rocks.

"We can't leave him here," Cassia says, looking at Hunter, who sees nothing and hears nothing but the tubes he breaks in his hands.

"I'll try to get him to come with us," I promise. "But you have to go. Now."

"We need him for the climb," she says.

"Indie can help you. Go. I won't stay long."

"We'll wait at the crossing," Cassia promises. "The Society might take a long time to get here."

Unless they're in the area already, I think. *Then it could be a matter of minutes.*

Once they're gone I turn to Hunter. "You have to stop," I say. "Come back with us."

He shakes his head and breaks another tube.

"We could try to catch up with the farmers who went across the plain," I say.

"They could all be dead by now," he says.

"*Did* they leave to join the Rising?" I ask him.

He doesn't answer.

I don't try to stop him. One tube, a thousand—what's the difference? The Society will know of this either way. And part of me wants to join him. When you've lost everything, why not take what you can before they come down on you? I remember that feeling. Another, darker part of me thinks, *And if he doesn't come with us, then he can't tell Cassia about the Rising and how to find them. I'm sure he knows.*

I go back to the entrance of the crevice and find a stone. I carry it back over to him. "Try this," I say. "It will go faster."

Hunter doesn't say anything but he takes the rock from me and holds it over his head. Then he brings the stone down fast over a row of tubes. I hear them break as I slide into the crevice to get out.

Once I'm outside I listen for the sound of the air ships above us.

Nothing.

Yet.

They waited for me. "You should have gone on ahead," I say to Cassia, but that's all I have time to say before we're all clipped in and climbing. Up. Across. For a moment on the top on that bare plain of rock I wonder if I should run behind or ahead—which is the best way to protect her—and then I find us just running side by side.

"Are they going to find us?" Eli gasps once we reach the other canyon.

"We'll run on the cobble when we can," I say.

"But sometimes it's all sand," Eli says, panicked.

"It's all right," I tell him. "There's always rain."

We all look up. The sky above us is a delicate early-winter blue. Gray clouds hang in the distance but they are miles away.

Cassia hasn't forgotten what Indie said in the cave. She comes up next to me and puts her hand on my arm. "What did Indie mean?" she asks, out of breath. "About Xander's secret?"

"I don't know what she's talking about," I lie.

I don't look back at Indie. Her boots sound on the rocks behind us but she doesn't contradict me and I know why.

Indie wants to find the Rising and for some reason she thinks I'm the most likely to know how to get there. She's decided to cast her lot with mine even though she doesn't like me any more than I like her.

I reach for Cassia's hand and listen for the beats of the Society's ships above us, but for now they do not come.

Neither does the rain.

~

When Xander and I took the red tablets that day long ago, we counted to three and swallowed them at the same time. I watched his face. I couldn't wait for him to forget.

It didn't take long to realize that it didn't work and that he was immune, too. Until then I'd thought I was the only one.

"You're supposed to forget," I told Xander.

"I didn't," he said.

Cassia told me what happened that day in the Borough after I left—how she learned that Xander was immune to the red tablets. But she doesn't know his other secret. *And I'm keeping that one because it's the fair thing to do,* I tell myself. *Because it's his right to tell her. Not mine.*

I try not to think about the other reasons I don't tell Cassia Xander's secret.

If she knows it, she might change her mind about him. And about me.

CHAPTER 34
CASSIA

Indie carries her pack even more carefully than before and I wonder if something happened to her wasp nest during our crawl into the Cavern. She brought the bag with her and, though she's thin, I don't know how she managed to protect it either coming or going in a space so tight. I don't know how she could have kept the fragile shell of the nest from being crushed.

Something about the story of Indie's mother and the boat seems strange, like an echo coming off a canyon wall and leaving part of the original words behind. I wonder how well I really know Indie. But then she shifts her pack again and I have a sudden image of the fragile, papery nest inside, and a memory of a picture fallen to pieces and rose petals dry and light. I've known Indie since the work camps and she hasn't let me down yet.

Ky turns around and calls to us to hurry. Indie looks at him, and I see an expression very like hunger cross her face.

You smell the rain here before you see it or feel it. If Ky's favorite smell from the Outer Provinces is sage, I think mine is this rain that smells ancient and new, like rock and sky, river and desert. The clouds we saw earlier sail in the wind, and the sky turns purple, gray, blue as the sun goes down and we reach the township.

"We can't stay here for very long, can we?" Eli asks as we climb the path to the storage caves. A strip of lightning runs hot-white between earth and sky and thunder cracks through the canyon.

"No," Ky says. I agree, too. The danger of the Society coming in the canyons now seems to outweigh what we face out in the plain. We'll have to move.

"But we have to stop in the cave," I say. "We need more food, and Indie and I don't have any books or papers." *And there might be something to find about the Rising.*

"The storm should buy us a little time," Ky says.

"How long?" I ask Ky.

"A few hours," Ky says. "The Society's not our only danger. A storm like this could cause a flash flood in the canyon and then we couldn't cross the stream. We'd be trapped. We'll stay here just until the lightning stops."

Such a long journey, and whether or not we find the Rising could all come down to a matter of hours. *But I didn't come to find the Rising,* I remind myself, *I came to find Ky, and I have. Whatever happens next, we'll be together.*

Ky and I hurry through to the library cave and its piles of boxes. Indie follows us.

"There's so much," I say, overwhelmed, as I open the lid of

one of the boxes and see the pile of papers and books inside. This is an entirely different kind of sorting—so many pages, so much history. This is what happens when the Society does not edit and cut and prune for us.

Some pages are printed; many are written by different people. Each handwriting is distinct, different, like the people who wrote them. *They could* all *write.* I suddenly feel panic. "How will I know what matters?" I ask Ky.

"Think of some words," he says, "and look for them. What do we need to know?"

Together, we make a list. The Rising. The Society. The Enemy. The Pilot. We need to know about *water* and *river* and *escape* and *food* and *survival.*

"You too," Ky says to Indie. "Anything that has those words in it, put here." He points to the middle of the table.

"I will," Indie says. She holds his gaze for a moment. He doesn't turn away first; she does, flipping open a book and scanning its pages.

I find something that looks promising—a printed pamphlet. "We already have one of those," Eli says. "Vick found a whole pile of them."

I put down the brochure. Then I open a book and am instantly distracted by a poem.

They dropped like Flakes -
They dropped like Stars -
Like Petals from a Rose -

When suddenly across the June
A wind with fingers - goes -

It's the poem where Hunter found the line for Sarah's grave.

The page has been torn out and shoved back in—in fact, the whole book is out of order and falling apart, almost as though it were headed for a fire on a Restoration site and then someone found it and put all its little bones back in. Parts of it are still missing—the front cover seems to have been improvised after the first one was lost. It's now a plain square of heavy paper sewn over the pages, and I can't find the name of the author anywhere.

I turn over the pages to another poem:

I did not reach Thee
But my feet slip nearer every day
Three Rivers and a Hill to cross
One Desert and a Sea
I shall not count the journey one
When I am telling thee.

The Hill. And then the desert, and the journey—it sounds like my story with Ky. Though I know I should be looking for other things, I keep reading to see how it might end:

Two deserts, but the Year is cold
So that will help the sand

259

One desert crossed -
The second one
Will feel as cool as land
Sahara is too little price
To pay for thy Right hand.

I would pay almost any price to be with Ky. I think I know what the poet means, though I don't know anything about a Sahara. It sounds a little like Sarah, the name of Hunter's daughter, but a child would be too high a price to pay for anyone's hand.

Death. Grandfather's death back in Oria: a crust on a plate; a poem in a compact; clean white sheets; good last words. Death on top of the Carving: black burned marks; wide open eyes. Death down in the canyon: blue lines drawn; rain on a girl's face.

And in the cave, rows and rows of sparkling tubes.

It would never be *us,* not again. Even if they pulled our bodies from the water and the earth and made us work and walk again, it would never be like the first time. Something would be missing. The Society cannot do this for us. We cannot do this for ourselves. There is something special, irreplaceable, about the first time living.

Ky puts one book down and picks up another. Is he the one I loved first?

Or was it the boy who gave me my first real kiss? Every scrap Xander has given me has a solid memory underneath, one so distinct I can almost touch and taste and smell it. I can almost hear it, calling me back.

I always thought Xander was the lucky one to have been born in the Borough, but now I am not so sure. Ky has lost so much, but what he has is not a small thing. He can create. He can write his own words. Everything Xander has written in his life—tapped out on a port or a scribe—has not been his own. Others have always had access to his thoughts.

When I meet Ky's gaze the doubt I had a moment ago when he and Indie exchanged glances disappears. There is nothing uncertain in the way he looks at me. "What did you find?" he asks.

"A poem," I say. "I need to focus better."

"So do I," Ky says. He smiles "The first rule of sorting. It shouldn't be so hard to remember."

"Can you sort, too?" I ask, surprised. He's never mentioned this before. It's a specialized skill, not one that most people have.

"Patrick taught me," he says softly.

Patrick? The shock must register on my face.

"They thought Matthew would be a sorter someday," Ky says. "Patrick wanted me to know how, too. He knew I'd never have a good work assignment. He wanted a way for me to be able to use my mind once I couldn't go to school anymore."

"But how did he teach you? The ports would have registered it if he showed you there."

Ky nods. "He figured out another way." He swallows,

glances across the cave at Indie. "Your father told Patrick what you'd done for Bram—how you made it so he could play games on the scribe. It gave Patrick an idea. He did something along the same lines."

"And the Officials never noticed?"

"He didn't have me use my own scribe," Ky says. "He traded for one—from the Archivists. He gave it to me the day I got my work assignment at the nutrition disposal center. That's how I learned about the Archivists in Oria."

Ky's face stills; his voice grows far away. I know this look. It's the way he looks when he says something that he hasn't talked about in a long time, or ever before. "We knew the assignment wouldn't be a good one. I wasn't surprised. But after the Official left, I—" He pauses. "I went in my room and got out the compass. I sat there holding on to it for a while."

I want to touch him, to hold him, to put that compass back in his hand. Tears start in my eyes and I listen as he speaks, even more softly now.

"Then I got up and put on my new blue plainclothes and went to work. Aida and Patrick didn't say a word. Neither did I."

He glances at me and I reach for his hand, hoping he'll want my touch. He does. His fingers tighten around mine and I feel myself taking in another part of his story. This happened to him, while I sat in my house on the very same street, eating my premade food and listening to the port and daydreaming about the perfect life that was about to be delivered to me, the way everything always was.

"That night, Patrick came back into the house with a black market scribe. It was old. Heavy. With a screen so archaic it was laughable. At first I told him to take it back. I thought he'd risked too much. But Patrick told me not to worry about it. He told me that my father had sent him a page of old writing after Matthew died. Patrick said he'd used that page for the trade. He told me that he'd always planned to use it on something for me.

"We went to the kitchen. Patrick thought the rumble of the incinerator would cover any sounds we made. We stood where the port couldn't see us. So. That's how he taught me how to sort—mostly without speaking—just by showing me. I hid the scribe with the compass in my room."

"But that day the Officials came to take away all our artifacts," I say. "How did you hide it then?"

"I'd already traded the scribe when they came," he says. "For the poem I gave you for your birthday." He smiles at me, his eyes back with me now. Back with me here in the Outer Provinces. We have come so far.

"*Ky,*" I whisper. "That was too dangerous. What if they had caught you with the poem?"

Ky smiles. "Even then, you were saving me. If you hadn't told me the Thomas poem on the little hill, I would never have gone to the Archivists to exchange the scribe for your birthday poem. Patrick and I would have been caught. It was much easier to hide a single paper than it would have been to hide the scribe." He brushes his hand along my cheek.

"Because of you, there was nothing for them to take when they came to the house. I'd already given you the compass."

I put my arms around him. There was nothing for them to take because he had traded, given it all away, for me. Neither of us speaks for a moment.

Then he shifts a little and points to a page in an open book before us. "There," he says. "*River*. That's one of the words we need," and the way he says it, the way his mouth looks and his voice sounds, makes me want to leave these papers alone and spend my days in this cave or in one of the little houses or down by the water, trying only to solve the mystery of him.

CHAPTER 35
KY

As I turn the pages of the farmers' histories my own history flashes back to me. It comes in glimpses like the lightning outside the cave. Bright. Fast. I can't tell if I'm seeing more or being blinded. The rain pours down and I picture the river outside pushing everything before it. Running over the name carved on Sarah's little stone and leaving her bones bare.

Panic rises in me. I can't be trapped here. I can't come so close to breaking free and fail.

I find a notebook filled with lined paper covered in a childish scrawl. *S. S. S.* A hard letter to learn for the first one. Was it Hunter's daughter who wrote this?

"I think you're old enough now," my father said, handing me a piece of cottonwood he'd brought out of the canyon with him. He had one, too, and he made a mark in the mud left over from the rain the night before. "It's something I learned in the canyons. Look. *K.* That's how your name starts. They say you should always teach a person's name first. That way, even if they never learn to write anything else, they'll always have something."

Later, he told me he was going to teach the other children too.

"Why?" I asked. I was five. I didn't want him to teach the others.

He knew what I was thinking. "It's not knowing how to write that makes you interesting," he said. "It's *what* you write."

"But if everyone can write, I won't be special," I said.

"That isn't the only thing that matters," he said.

"You want to be special," I said. Even then I knew. "You want to be the Pilot."

"I want to be the Pilot so I can help people," he told me.

Back then I nodded. I believed him. I think he might have believed himself, too.

Another memory flashes to mind: a time when I took a note around the village for my father, running it from place to place so the others could have a turn reading it. The paper said the time and place of the next meeting and my father burned it as soon as I came home.

"What's this meeting about?" I asked my father.

"The farmers have refused again to join the Rising," he said.

"What will you do?" my mother asked.

He loved the farmers. They, not the Rising, were the ones who taught him to write. But the Rising had approached him first back before we were Reclassified. They planned to fight and he loved to fight. "I'll stay loyal to the Rising," he said. "But I'll still trade with the farmers."

Indie leans forward and catches my eye. She gives me a slight smile and her hand rests on her pack, as though she's just slipped something inside. What did she find?

I look at her until she turns away. Whatever it is, she's not showing Cassia either. I'll have to find out later.

A few months before the last firing, my father taught me to wire. That was his job—to repair the wiring on everything that fell apart in the village. Things broke often there and we were used to it. All our equipment was the leftovers from Society, just like us. The food-warming mechanisms in particular were always breaking. We even heard rumors that the meals the Society shipped us were mass-produced and contained standardized vitamins, nothing like the individually calibrated meals given to people back in the other Provinces.

"If you can do my jobs here," he said, "like fixing the food machines and the heaters in the houses, I can keep traveling into the canyon. No one will tell the Society that it's you working instead of me."

I nodded.

"Not everyone is good with their hands," my father said, sitting back. "You are. You come by it from both of us."

I glanced over to where my mother painted and then looked back to the wires I held.

"I always knew what I wanted to do," my father said. "I knew how low to score to get assigned to mechanical repair."

"That was risky," I said.

"It was," he said, "but I always come out where I should." He smiled at me and around him at the Outer Provinces, which he loved and where he belonged. Then he became serious. "Now. Let's see if you can do what I did."

I arranged the wires, the plastic tabs, and the timer the way he showed me, with one small alteration.

"Good," my father said, sounding pleased. "You have intuition, too. The Society says it doesn't really exist, but it does."

The next book I pick up is heavy, engraved with the word LEDGER. I turn the pages carefully, beginning at the end and working my way backward.

Though I half expected it, it still hurts when I see his trades in there. I know them by his signature on the lines and by the dates mentioned. He was one of the last to keep trading with the farmers, even when life in the Outer Provinces became more and more dangerous. He thought that quitting would seem like a sign of weakness.

Like it says in the pamphlets, there's always a Pilot, and others being groomed to take his or her place if the Pilot falls. My father was never the Pilot, but he was one of the people standing in line.

"Do what the Society tells you," I said to him when I got older and could see how many risks he took. "Then we won't get in trouble."

But he couldn't help himself. He was smart and cunning, but he was all action, no subtlety, and he never knew when to stop. I could see that even when I was a child. It wasn't enough to go into the canyons to trade—he had to bring writing out. It wasn't enough to teach me—he had to teach *all* the children and then their parents. It wasn't enough to know of the Rising—he had to move it forward.

It was his fault we died. He pushed too hard and took too many risks. The people wouldn't have been gathered together for a meeting if it weren't for him.

And after that final firing, who came to get the survivors?

The Society. Not the Rising. I've seen how they leave you when they don't need you anymore. I'm afraid of the Rising. Even more than that, I'm afraid of who I'd be in the Rising.

I walk over to where Indie stood when she slipped something into her pack. On the table in front of me sits a waterproof box full of maps.

I glance over at Indie. She's moved on. Her fingers turn the pages of a book and her bent head reminds me of the bell of a yucca flower tipped down toward the ground.

"We're running low on time," I say, picking up the box. "I'm going to find a map for each of us to use in case we get separated."

Cassia nods. She's found something else interesting. I

can't see what it is, but I can see the joy in her face and the way her body tenses with excitement. The very idea of the Rising makes her come alive. It's what she wants. Maybe it's even what her grandfather wanted her to find.

I know you came into the Carving for me, Cassia. But the Rising is the one place I don't know if I can go for you.

CHAPTER 36
CASSIA

Ky puts a map down on the table and reaches for a little black charcoal pencil. "I found another one we can use," he says to me as he begins marking the page. "I'll have to update it. It's a little old."

I pick up another book and flip the pages, looking for something to help us, but somehow I end up composing a poem in my mind instead. It's *about* Ky, not *for* him, and I find myself copying the mystery author's style:

> *I marked a map for every death*
> *For every ache and blow*
> *My world was all a page of black*
> *With nothing left of snow.*

I look over at Ky. His hands move as quick and careful with marking the map as they do with writing, as sure as they move over me.

He doesn't look up and I find myself wanting. I want him. And I want to know what he thinks and how he feels.

Why does Ky have to be able to sit so silent, hold so still, see so much?

How can he both draw me in and keep me out?

"I need to go outside," I say later, exhaling in frustration. We haven't found anything concrete—only pages and pages of history and propaganda about the Rising and the Society and the farmers themselves. At first it was fascinating, but now I'm aware of the river outside rising higher and higher. My back aches, my head hurts, and I feel a small flutter of panic beginning in my chest. Am I losing my ability to sort? First the wrong decision about the blue tablets, now this. "Has the lightning stopped?"

"I think it has," Ky says. "Let's go see."

In the cave full of food, Eli has curled up to sleep, packs filled with apples surrounding him.

Ky and I step outside. The rain comes down but the electricity has left the air. "We can move when it's light," he says.

I look over at him, at his dark profile lit faintly by the flashlight he carries. The Society would never know how to put this on a microcard. *Belongs to the land. Knows how to run.* They would never be able to write what he is.

"We still haven't found anything." I try to laugh. "If I ever go back, the Society will have to change my microcard. *Exhibits exceptional promise in sorting* would have to be deleted."

"What you're doing is more than sorting," Ky says simply. "We should rest soon, if we can."

He's not as driven as I am to find the Rising, I realize. *He's trying to help me, but if I weren't here, he wouldn't care at all about looking for a way to join with them.*

I think suddenly of the words of that poem. *I did not reach Thee.*

I push the words away. I'm tired, that's all, feeling fragile. And, I realize, I haven't heard Ky's complete story yet. He has reasons for feeling the way he does, but I don't know all of them.

I think of all the things he can do—write, carve, paint—and suddenly, watching him stand in the dark at the edge of the empty settlement, something sorrowful washes over me. *There is no place for someone like him in the Society,* I think, *for someone who can create. He can do so many things of incomparable value, things no one else can do, and the Society doesn't care about that at all.*

I wonder if, when Ky looks at this empty township, he sees a place where he could have belonged. Where he could have written with the others, where the beautiful girls in the paintings would have known how to dance.

"Ky," I say, "I want to hear the rest of your story."

"All of it?" he asks, his voice serious.

"Anything you want to tell me," I say.

He looks at me. I lift his hand to my lips and kiss his knuckles, the scraped places on his palm. He closes his eyes.

"My mother painted with water," he says. "And my father played with fire."

CHAPTER 37
KY

As the rain comes down I let myself imagine a story for us. The one I would write if I could.

The two of them forgot about the Rising and stayed alone in the township. They walked through the empty buildings. They planted seeds in the spring and harvested in the fall. They put their feet in the stream. They had their fill of poetry. They whispered words to each other that echoed off the empty canyon walls. Their lips and hands touched whenever they wanted for as long as they wanted.

But even in my version of what should happen I can't change who we are and the fact that there are others we love.

It didn't take long for other people to appear in their minds. Bram watched them with sad, waiting eyes. Eli appeared. Their parents walked past, turning their heads for a glimpse of the children they loved.

And Xander was there, too.

Back inside the cave, Eli is awake and searching through the papers with Indie. "We can't look forever," he says. His voice sounds panicked. "The Society's going to find us."

"Just a little longer," Cassia says. "I'm certain there's something here."

Indie puts down the book she held and lifts her pack to her shoulder. "I'm going down," she says. "I'll look in the houses again, see if there's anything we missed." Her eyes meet mine on her way out of the cave and I know Cassia notices.

"Do you think they've caught Hunter?" Eli asks.

"No," I say. "I think Hunter will finish things on his terms somehow."

Eli shivers. "That Cavern—it felt all wrong."

"I know," I say. Eli rubs his eyes with the heels of his hand and reaches for another book. "You should rest more, Eli," I tell him. "We'll keep looking."

Eli stares up at the walls around us. "I wonder why they didn't paint anything in here," he says.

"Eli," I say more firmly. *"Rest."*

He rolls himself back up in a blanket, this time in the corner of the library cave to be near us. Cassia is careful to keep the light of the flashlight away from him. She has twisted her hair back out of her way and her eyes look shadowed with exhaustion.

"You should rest too," I say.

"Something is here," she says. "I have to find it." She smiles at me. "I felt the same way when I was looking for you. Sometimes I think I'm strongest when I'm searching."

It's true. She is. I love that about her.

It's why I had to lie to her about Xander's secret. If I

hadn't, she wouldn't have stopped trying to find out what it was.

I stand up. "I'm going to help Indie," I tell Cassia. It's time to find out what Indie is hiding.

"All right," Cassia says. She lifts her hand from the book and lets the page she was reading become lost and unmarked. "Be careful."

"I will," I say. "I'll be back soon."

Indie's not hard to find. A flickering light in one of the houses below gives her away, as she knew it would. I make my way down the cliff path, which has grown slippery with the rain.

When I get to the house I look in the window first. The glass pane is wavy with age and water, but I can see Indie inside. The flashlight sits next to her and in her hands she holds something else that gives off light.

A miniport.

She hears me coming. I knock the port out of her hand but my fingers don't close around it in time. The port hits the ground but doesn't break. Indie sighs in relief. "Go ahead," she says. "Look at it if you want."

She keeps her voice low. In it I hear the sound of wanting something very much. Underneath it I hear the sound of the river in the canyon. Indie reaches out and puts her hand on my arm. It is the first time I have ever seen her willingly touch someone, and it stops me from smashing the miniport against the floorboards.

I look at the screen and a familiar face looks back.

"*Xander*," I say in surprise. "You have a picture of Xander. But how—" It only takes me a moment to realize what happened. "You stole Cassia's microcard."

"That's what she helped me hide on the air ship," Indie says, without a trace of guilt. "She didn't know. I hid it in with her tablets, and I kept it until I had a way to see what was on it." She reaches over and switches the port back off.

"Is this what you found in the library cave?" I ask her. "The miniport?"

She shakes her head. "I stole this before we came into the canyons."

"How?"

"I took it from the leader of the boys in the village the night before we ran. He should have been more careful. All Aberrations know how to steal."

Not all, Indie, I think. *Only some of us.*

"Do they know where we are?" I ask. "Does it transmit location?" Vick and I were never sure what the miniports could do.

She shrugs. "I don't think so. The Society's coming anyway, after what happened in the Cavern. But the miniport isn't what I wanted to show you. I was only passing time until you came." I start to say something about how she shouldn't have stolen from Cassia, but then Indie reaches into her pack and pulls out a folded square of a thick fabric. Canvas.

"*This* is what you need to see." She unfolds the material. It's a map. "I think it's the way to the Rising," she says. "Look."

The words on the map are encoded, but the landscape is familiar: the edge of the Carving and the plain beyond. Instead of showing the mountains where the farmers went, it shows more of the stream where Vick died, which runs across the plain and down the map. The stream ends in a black inky darkness that has white coded words written across it. "I think that's the ocean," Indie says, touching the black space on the map. "And those words mark an island."

"Why didn't you give it to Cassia?" I ask. "She's a sorter."

"I wanted to give it to *you*," Indie says. "Because of who you are."

"What do you mean?" I ask.

She shakes her head impatiently. "I know you can break the code. I know you can sort."

Indie's right. I *can* sort. Already I've figured out what the white words say: *Turn Again Home.*

It's from the Tennyson poem. It's Rising territory. *Home*, they've called it. And the way to get to it is by following the stream where the Society dropped poison and Vick died.

"How do you know I can sort?" I ask Indie, putting down the map and pretending I haven't decoded it yet.

"I've been listening," she says. And then she leans forward. With the two of us sitting in the glow of the flashlight, it seems like the rest of the world has gone black and I'm left alone with her and what she thinks of me. "I know who you are." She leans even closer. "And who you're supposed to be."

"Who am I supposed to be?" I ask her. I don't lean away. She smiles.

"The Pilot," she says.

I laugh and sit back. "No. What about that poem you told Cassia? That talks about a woman being the Pilot."

"It's not a poem," Indie says fiercely.

"A song," I say, realizing. "The words used to have music behind them." I should have known.

Indie exhales in frustration. "It doesn't matter *how* the Pilot comes or if it's a woman or a man. The idea is the same. I understand that now."

"I'm still not the Pilot."

"You *are*," she says. "You don't want to be, so you're running away from the Rising. Someone needs to bring you back to the rebellion. That's what I'm trying to do."

"The Rising isn't what you imagine," I say. "It's not Aberrations and Anomalies and rebels and rogues running free. It's a structure. A system."

She shrugs. "Whatever it is, I want to be part of it. I've been thinking about it my whole life."

"If you think this will take us to the Rising, why give it to me?" I ask Indie, holding up the map. "Why not give it right to Cassia?"

"We're the same," she whispers. "You and me. We're more alike than you and Cassia. We could leave right now."

She's right. I do see myself in Indie. I feel a pity so deep for her that it might be something else entirely. Empathy. You have to believe in something to survive. She's picked the Rising. I chose Cassia.

Indie's been quiet for a long time. Hiding. Running. On the move. I put my hand next to hers. I don't touch her fingers. But she can see the marks on them. I have scars from living here the first time that no Citizen of the Society would have.

She looks at my hand. "How long?" she asks.

"How long what?"

"How long have you been an Aberration?"

"Since I was a child," I say. "I was three years old when they Reclassified us."

"And who caused it?"

I don't want to answer but I can tell we're on the edge. It's as though she holds to the walls of a canyon. If I move wrong she will look over her shoulder, let go, and take her chances with the fall. I have to give her a little piece of my story.

"My father," I answer. "We were Citizens in the Society. We lived in one of the Border Provinces. Then the Society accused him of having ties with a rebellion and sent us all out to the Outer Provinces."

"*Was* he a rebel?" she asks.

"Yes," I say. "And then when we moved to the Outer Provinces he convinced our village to join with him. Almost everyone died."

"You still love him, though," she says.

I'm on the edge with her now. She knows it. I have to tell the truth if I'm going to keep her hanging on.

I take a deep breath. "Of course I do."

I said it.

Her hand rests on the ground next to me against the splintered floorboards. The rain outside the window falls in gold and silver dashes in the beam from my flashlight. Without thinking I touch her fingers gently.

"Indie," I tell her, "I'm not the Pilot."

She shakes her head. She doesn't believe me. "Just read the map," she tells me. "Then you'll know everything."

"No," I say. "I won't know everything. I won't know *your* story." This is a cruel thing to do because when someone knows your story they know you. And they can hurt you. It's why I give mine away in pieces, even to Cassia. "If I'm going to go with you, I have to know about you." I'm lying. I won't go with her to the Rising, no matter what. Does she know that?

"It all started when you ran," I say, encouraging her.

She looks at me, deciding. Suddenly—even though she is so sharp-edged—I want to reach out and hold her close. Not the way I hold Cassia. Just as someone who also knows what it means to be an Aberration.

"It all started when I ran," she says.

I lean closer to listen. Indie speaks more softly than usual as she remembers. "I wanted to escape the work camp. When they dragged me back to the air ship I thought I'd lost my last chance to get away. I knew we'd die in the Outer Provinces.

Then I saw Cassia on the ship. She didn't belong there, or in the camp either. I'd been through her things and I knew that she wasn't an Aberration.

"So why did she sneak on board the ship? What did she think she could find?" Indie looks straight into my eyes while she talks, and I can see she tells the truth. For the first time she's completely open. She's beautiful when she's not holding back.

"Later, in the village, I heard Cassia talking with that boy about the Pilot, and about you. She wanted to follow you, and that's when I first thought you might be the Pilot. I thought Cassia *knew* that you were the Pilot, but that she was keeping it a secret from me."

Indie laughs. "Later I realized that she wasn't lying to me. She hadn't told me that you were the Pilot because she hadn't realized it herself."

"She's right." I say it again. "I'm not."

Indie shakes her head dismissively. "Fine. But what about the red tablet?"

"What do you mean?"

"It doesn't work on you, does it?" she asks.

I don't answer but she knows.

"It doesn't work on me, either," she says. "And I bet it doesn't work on Xander." She doesn't wait for me to confirm or deny. "I think some of us are special. The Rising has chosen us somehow. Why else would we be immune?" Her voice is eager and again I know how she feels. To go from discarded to chosen—it's what all Aberrations want.

"If we are, the Rising didn't do anything to save us when the Society sent us out here," I remind her.

Indie looks at me scornfully. "Why should they?" she says. "If we can't find our way to them on our own, we shouldn't be part of the rebellion." She lifts her chin. "I can't tell exactly what the map says, but I know it tells us how to get to the Rising. It's like my mother said it would be. That black spot is the ocean. Where the words are—that's an island. We just have to get there. And *I* found the map. Not Cassia."

"You're jealous of her," I say. "Is that why you let her take the blue tablet?"

"No." Indie sounds surprised. "I didn't see her take it. I would have stopped her. I didn't want her to die."

"You're willing to leave her here. And Eli."

"It's not the same thing," Indie says. "The Society will find her and take her back where she belongs. She'll be fine. Eli too. He's so young. It must have been a mistake that he ended up out here."

"And what if it's not?" I ask.

She sends me a long, searching look. "You've left people and run away. Don't act like you don't understand."

"I'm not going to leave her," I say.

"I didn't think you would," Indie says. But she's not defeated. "That's partly why I gave you the scrap about Xander's secret. To remind you, if it came to this."

"Remind me of what?"

Indie smiles. "That you're going to be a part of the Rising

one way or another. You don't want to run and come with me. Fine. But you're still going to be part of the Rising no matter what." She reaches for the miniport and I let her take it. "You'll join because you want Cassia and it's what she wants to do."

I shake my head. No.

"Don't you think it would be better for you to be part of the Rising?" Indie says bluntly. "The leader, even? Otherwise, why would she choose you when she could have Xander?"

Why would Cassia choose me?

Predicted occupations: nutrition disposal worker, decoy villager.

Predicted chance of success: Not applicable to Aberrations.

Predicted life span: 17. Sent to die in the Outer Provinces.

Cassia would argue that she doesn't see me the way the Society sees me. She'd say their list didn't matter.

And to her it doesn't. That's part of why I love her.

But I don't think she *would* choose me if she knew Xander's secret. Indie gave me the scrap because she wanted to play on my insecurities about Cassia and Xander. But that paper—and the secret—mean even more than Indie guesses.

Something must show in my face—the truth of what Indie's said. Her eyes widen and I can almost see her thoughts settling into place: My reluctance to join the Rising. Xander's face on the microcard. Indie's own obsession with him and with finding the rebellion. In the whirling, determined kaleidoscope of Indie's bright, peculiar mind, these pieces make a picture that shows her the truth.

"That's it," she says, her voice certain. "You can't let her go to the Rising without you or you might lose her." She smiles. "Because that's the secret: Xander is part of the Rising."

It was the week before the Match Banquet.

They found me walking home and said, "Aren't you tired of losing, wouldn't you like to win, wouldn't you like to join us, with *us* you could win." I told them no. I said I'd seen how they lost and I'd rather lose my own way.

Xander found me the next evening. I was out in the front yard planting newroses in Patrick and Aida's flower bed. He stood next to me and smiled and acted as though we were talking about something common and everyday.

"Did you join?" he asked.

"Join what?" I asked Xander. I wiped the sweat from my face. Back then I liked digging. I had no idea how much I'd have to do later.

Xander bent down and pretended to help me. "The rebellion," he said quietly. "Against the Society. Someone approached me this week. You're part of it, too, aren't you?"

"No," I told Xander.

His eyes widened. "I thought you would be. I was sure of it."

I shook my head.

"I thought we'd both be in it," he said. His voice sounded strange, confused. I hadn't heard Xander sound that way

before. "I thought you'd probably known about it all along."
He paused. "Do you think they asked her, too?"

We both knew who he meant. Cassia. Of course.

"I don't know," I told Xander. "It seems probable. They
asked us. They must have had a list of people to approach in
the Borough."

"What happens to the people who say no?" Xander asked
me. "Did they give you a red tablet?"

"No," I said.

"Maybe they don't have access to red tablets," Xander
said. "I work at the medical center, and I don't even know
where the Society keeps the red ones. It's somewhere away
from the blue and the green."

"Or it might be that the rebellion only asks people to join
who won't turn them in," I said.

"How could they know that?"

"Some of them are still in the Society," I reminded him.
"They have our data. They can try to predict what we'll do."
I paused. "And they're right. You won't turn them in because
you joined. I won't turn them in because I didn't." *And
because I'm an Aberration,* I thought but didn't say. The last
thing I want to do is draw attention to myself. Especially with
a report about a rebellion.

"Why don't you join?" Xander asked. There wasn't any
mockery in his tone. He only wanted to know. For the first
time since I'd known him I saw something like fear in his eyes.

"Because I don't believe in it," I told him.

Xander and I were never sure if the rebellion had approached Cassia. And we didn't know if she'd taken a red tablet. We couldn't ask her either question without putting her in danger.

Later, when I saw her reading those two poems in the forest, I thought I'd made the wrong choice. I thought she had the Tennyson poem because it was a Rising poem, and I'd missed my chance to be in the rebellion with her. But then I found out that the poem she truly loved was the other one. She chose her own way. And I fell even more deeply in love with her.

"Do you really want to join the Rising?" I ask Indie.

"Yes," Indie says. *"Yes."*

"No," I tell her. "You want it now. You might be happy there for a few months, a few years, but it's not you."

"You don't know me," she says.

"Yes, I do," I say. I lean in fast and close and touch her hand again. She holds her breath. "Forget about all this," I say. "We don't need the Rising. The farmers are out there. We'll all go together, you and me and Cassia and Eli. Somewhere new. What happened to the girl who wanted to leave and lose sight of the shore?" I grab her hand tight and hold on.

Indie looks up, her face stunned. When Cassia told me Indie's story, I realized what had happened. Indie had told the version about her mother and the boat and the water so many times that she began to believe it too.

But now she remembers what she's trying to forget. That it wasn't about her mother. It was about her. After hearing her mother's song all her life, *Indie* built the boat and caused her own Reclassification. She failed to find the Rising. She never even lost sight of the shore. And, eventually, the Society sent her away from the ocean to die in the desert.

I know it happened that way because I know Indie. She's not the kind of person to watch someone else build a boat and set sail without her.

Indie wants to find the Rising so badly she can't see anything else. Certainly not me. I'm even worse than she thought I was.

"I'm sorry, Indie," I say, and I feel sorry. I ache all over with how sorry I am for what I'm about to do. "But the Rising can't save *any* of us. I've seen what happens when you join with them." I strike a match at the edge of the map. Indie cries out but I hold her off. The fire licks the edge of the fabric.

"No," Indie cries, trying to snatch the map again. I push her away. She looks around but we both left our canteens back in the cave. "No," Indie cries out again, and pushes past me out the door.

I don't try to stop her. Whatever she tries to do—catch the rain or go to the river for water—will take too long. The map is as good as gone. The air fills again with the scent of burning.

CHAPTER 38
CASSIA

It's hard to concentrate on the words before me when I wonder what is being said outside the cave in the night. I find myself reading poetry again, the next part of the *I did not reach Thee* poem:

> *The Sea comes last - Step merry, feet,*
> *So short we have to go -*
> *To play together we are prone,*
> *But we must labor now,*
> *The last shall be the lightest load*
> *That we have had to draw.*

The poem ends there, though I can tell other stanzas come after. The next page is missing from the book. But even in these few brief lines I hear the poet speaking to me. Though gone, but she or he still has a voice.

Why don't I?

Suddenly, I realize that this is why I'm so drawn to this author's poetry. Not only the words themselves, but a sense of *how* she could put them down and make them her own.

There's no time for this now, I remind myself. The next box is full of books that look similar to one another; they all have the word LEDGER carved into the leather of their covers. I pick up one and read some of the lines inside:

Thirteen pages of history, for five blue tablets. Trader fee: one blue tablet.

One poem, Rita Dove, original printing, for information regarding the movements of the Society. Trader fee: access to information exchanged.

One novel, Ray Bradbury, third printing, for one datapod and four panes of glass from a Restoration site. Trader fee: two panes of glass.

One page of the Book, for three vials medicine. Trader fee: nothing. Trader was executing a personal trade on his own behalf.

So this is how the trades were done and why so many of the books here are torn, the pages loose. The farmers put books back together, but they also had to take them apart, determine their worth, trade them away in bits and pieces. The thought makes me sad, though of course it was what they had to do.

It's like what the Archivists do, and what I did when I kept the tablets and traded the compass.

The tablets. Xander's notes. Did he hide something secret inside? I tear into the packet and put the contents out on the table in two rows: one of blue tablets, one of scraps.

None of the papers say anything about a secret.

Predicted occupations: Official.

Predicted chance of success: 99.9%.

Predicted life span: 80 years.

Line after line of information I already know or could have guessed.

I feel eyes on me. Someone stands in the door of the cave. I look up, shine my light across the sandy floor, begin to push the tablets and scraps into my bag. "Ky," I begin. "I was just—"

The figure is too tall to be Ky. Frightened, I move the light up to his face and he shields his eyes with his hands. Dried blood runs down his blue-marked arms.

"Hunter," I say. "You came back."

"I wanted to escape," Hunter says.

At first I think he means from the Cavern, and then I realize he's answering the question Indie asked before we climbed—*Which did you want?*

"But you couldn't go," I say, realizing. The papers left on the table in front of me flutter as he comes closer. "Because of Sarah."

"She was dying," Hunter said. "She couldn't be moved."

"The others wouldn't wait for you?" I ask, shocked.

"There wasn't time," Hunter says. "It could have compromised the whole escape. Others who weren't fast enough to cross decided to fight, but she was a child, and she was far too ill." A muscle in his cheek twitches and when he blinks tears run down his face. He ignores them. "I made an agreement with the others who stayed. I helped them rig their explosives up on the Carving, and they let me leave to be with Sarah instead of waiting for the fight." He shakes his head. "I don't know why it didn't work. The ships should have come down."

I don't know what to say. He's lost his daughter and everyone he knew. "You can still go find the others on the plain," I say. "It's not too late."

"I came back because there's something I promised to do," he says. "I forgot myself in the Cavern." He walks over to one of the long flat boxes on the table and lifts off the lid. "While I'm here, I can show you how to find the rebellion."

My fingers tingle in anticipation and I leave the poem behind on the table. *At last.* Someone who knows something real about the Rising. "Thank you," I say. "Will you come with us?" I can't bear to think of him alone.

Hunter looks up from the box. "There used to be a map here," he says. "Someone's taken it."

"Indie," I say. It must be. "She left a little while ago. I don't know where she went."

"There's a light in one of the houses," Hunter says.

"I'll come with you," I say, darting a glance over at where Eli sleeps in the corner of the cave.

"He'll be safe," Hunter says. "The Society isn't here yet."

I follow him out of the cave and down the rain-slicked

path, eager to find Indie and take back what she's hidden from us.

But when we open the door to the little lit house, it's Ky we see, firelight flickering on his face as he burns the map of where I wanted to go.

CHAPTER 39
KY

I see Cassia first, and then Hunter behind her, and I know I've lost. Even if the map burns, Hunter can tell her where to find the Rising.

She snatches the map from me and throws it to the ground, stomping on it to put out the flames. The edges crumple into fragments of black ash but most of the map is saved.

She's going to the Rising.

"You were going to keep this from me," Cassia says. "If Hunter hadn't come back, I would never have known how to find the rebellion."

I don't answer. There's nothing to say.

"What else are you hiding?" Cassia asks me, her voice breaking. She picks up the map and holds it in her hands. Carefully. The way she used to hold poetry on the Hill. "You lied about Xander's secret, didn't you? What is it?"

"I can't tell you."

"Why not?"

"It's not mine to tell," I say. "It's his." It's not just selfishness that keeps me from telling Cassia Xander's secret. I know he wanted to tell her himself. I owe him that. He knew *my* secret—my status as an Aberration—and he never told anyone. Not even Cassia.

This isn't a game. He's not my opponent and Cassia's not a prize.

"But this, on here," Cassia says, looking at the map, "is a choice. You were going to get rid of my—our—chance to *choose*."

The air in the house smells acrid and bitter from the burning cloth. I see with a chill that Cassia looks at me as a sorter would. Sifting facts. Calculating. Making a call. I know what she sees—the boy on the screen with the Society's list scrolling up next to him. Not the one who stood with her on the Hill or the one who held her in the dark of the canyon with the moon above.

"Where's Indie?" she asks.

"She went outside," I say.

"I'll find her," Hunter says, and he disappears through the door and Cassia and I are alone.

"Ky," she says, "this is the *Rising*." A trace of excitement comes into her voice. "Don't you want to be a part of something that could change everything?"

"*No,*" I say, and she steps back as if I've struck her physically.

"But we can't run forever," Cassia says.

"I've spent *years* holding still," I say. "What do you think I was doing back in the Society?" Then my words come out in a rush and I can't seem to stop. "You're in love with the *idea* of the Rising, Cassia. But you don't actually know what it is. You don't know what it's like to try to rebel and see everyone die around you. *You don't know.*"

"You hate the Society," Cassia says. Still trying to do the math, make the numbers add up. "But you don't want to be part of the Rising."

"I don't trust the Society, and I don't trust rebellions," I say. "I don't choose either of them. I've seen what they both can do."

"Then what else is there?" she asks.

"We could join the farmers," I say.

But I don't think she even hears me.

"Tell me *why*," she says. "Why would you want to lie to me? Why would you take a choice from me?"

Her gaze has softened and she's looking at me as Ky again—the person she loves—and somehow that's even worse. All the reasons I lied run through my head: *because I can't lose you, because I was jealous, because I don't trust anyone, because I can't even trust myself, because, because, because.*

"You know why," I say, anger flaring in me suddenly. At everything. Everyone. The Society, the Rising, my father, myself, Indie, Xander, Cassia.

"No, I don't," she begins, but I don't let her finish.

"Fear," I say, holding her gaze. "We were both afraid. I

was afraid of losing you. You were afraid, back in the Borough. When you took *my* choice away from me."

She steps back. I see it on her face that she knows what I'm talking about. She hasn't forgotten it either.

Suddenly I'm back in that hot, shiny room with red hands and a blue uniform. Sweat runs down my back. I'm humiliated. I don't want her to see me work. I wish that I could look up to catch a flash of her green eyes and let her know that I am still Ky. Not just another number.

"You sorted me," I say.

"What else could I do?" she whispers. "They were watching."

We've talked this through on the Hill but it seems different down in the canyons. It feels clear to me here that I will never reach her.

"I tried to fix it," she says. "I came all this way to find you."

"To find me, or to find the Rising?" I ask.

"Ky," she says. And stops.

"I'm sorry," I tell Cassia. "This is the one thing I can't do for you. I can't join the Rising."

I've said it.

Her face looks pale in the darkness of the abandoned house. Somewhere above us the sky seeps rain and I think of snow falling. Pictures painted with water. Poetry breathed between kisses. *Too beautiful to last.*

CHAPTER 40
CASSIA

Hunter pushes open the door behind us and walks in. Indie is with him. "We don't have time for this," he says. "There is a Rising. You can find it by following that map. Can you read the code?"

I nod.

"Then the map is yours for telling me what was in the cave."

"Thank you," I say. I roll it up carefully. The map is made of thick cloth and dark paints. You could use it in the rain and drop it in the water and it would last. But it can't hold up against fire. I look over at Ky, my heart aching, wishing we could bridge the river of what just happened as neatly as one could mark a crossing on a map.

"I'm leaving for the mountains to find the others," Hunter says. "Those of you who don't want to join the Rising can come with me."

"*I* want to find the Rising," Indie says.

"We can all go as far as the plain together, at least," I say. We can't come such a long way only to break apart so quickly.

"You should all start now," Hunter says. "I'll catch up to you when I'm finished blocking the cave."

"Blocking the cave?" Indie asks.

"We made a plan to seal off the cave and make it look like a landslide," Hunter says. "We don't want the Society to get our papers. I promised the other farmers I'd do it. But it will take me some time to prepare everything. You shouldn't wait."

"No," I say. "We can wait." We can't leave Hunter behind again. And though I know our group—our small, fragmented little group that has somehow come together—must splinter eventually, I don't want it to happen now.

"So *that's* why you saved some of the explosives," Ky says to Hunter. I can't read Ky's expression—his face is closed-off, remote. This is the Ky of the Society again and I feel a sudden ache of loss at the Ky of the Carving. "I can help you."

"You can wire?" Hunter says.

"Yes," Ky says. "In exchange for something I saw in one of the caves."

"A trade," Hunter agrees.

What is Ky trading for? What does he want? Why won't he look at me?

But no one argues anymore about splitting apart. We stay together.

For now.

~

While Ky and Hunter gather the wires, Indie and I hurry back to the caves to wake Eli and fill our packs with things we'll need for the journey. We ready the cave for the explosion by sealing the lids on the boxes in the library and stacking them back against the wall so they'll be protected. For some reason I'm drawn to the pages that have come loose from other books. I can't resist; I put some of these papers into my pack along with food, water, matches. Hunter showed us where we could find headlamps and other gear for the journey and gave us extra packs; we fill them, too.

Eli tucks paintbrushes and papers in alongside his food. I don't have the heart to tell him to throw them out and take more apples instead.

"I think we're ready," I say.

"Wait," Indie says. We haven't spoken much and I've been glad; I'm not sure what to say to her. I don't understand her—why did she take the map to Ky first? What else has she been hiding? Does she even think we are friends?

"I have to give you something." Indie reaches into her pack and takes out the delicate wasp nest. Even after everything, it's still miraculously intact. She holds it carefully in her hands and an image comes to my mind of her lifting a shell from the edge of the ocean.

"No," I say, touched. "You should keep it. You're the one who brought it all this way."

"That's not what I mean," Indie says, impatient. She reaches into the wasp nest and pulls something out.

A microcard.

It takes me a moment to understand.

"You stole this from me," I whisper. "Back in the work camp."

Indie nods. "It's what I hid on the air ship. I pretended later that I *hadn't* hidden anything, but I did. This." She holds it out. "Take it."

I do.

"And I took *this* from someone in the village." She reaches into her pack again and pulls out a miniport. "Now you can view the microcard," she says. "The only thing you're missing now is one of the scraps. But that's your own fault. You dropped it yourself when we were walking to the plain."

Bewildered, I take the miniport, too. "You found one of the papers?" I ask. "Did you read it?"

Of course she did. She doesn't even bother to answer the question. "That's how I knew that Xander had a secret," Indie says. "The scrap said he had one and that he'd tell you when he saw you again."

"Where is it?" I ask Indie. "Give it back."

"I can't. It's gone now. I gave it to Ky and he didn't keep it."

"Why?" I hold up the miniport, the microcard. "Why all of this?"

At first I think Indie won't say anything. She turns her face away. But then she looks back and answers after all. Her expression is fierce; her muscles tense. "You didn't belong," she says. "I knew it the minute I saw you in the work camp. So I wanted to see who you were. What you were doing. At first I thought you might be a spy for the Society. Later I thought you might be working for the Rising. And you had all those blue tablets. I wasn't sure what you planned with them."

"So you stole from me," I say. "Every step of the way, from the work camp into the Carving."

"How else was I supposed to find out anything?" She gestures to the miniport. "And you have it all back now. Better, even. Now you can look at the microcard whenever you want."

"I don't have everything," I say. "Remember? Part of Xander's message is gone."

"No it's not," Indie says. "I just told it to you."

I want to scream in frustration. "What about the silver box?" I ask. "You took that, too." It's not rational but suddenly I want it back, that memento of Xander. I want back *everything* that I've ever lost, whether it's been stolen or traded or taken. Ky's compass. Bram's watch. And, most of all, the compact from Grandfather with the poems snapped safely inside. If I had that back I'd never open it again. It would be enough to know that the poems were there.

I wish for the same thing with Ky, that I could tuck everything beautiful about our relationship inside and seal it up safe, shutting out all the mistakes we've both made.

"I left the box back at the work camp when I ran," Indie says. "I dropped it in the forest."

I remember how Indie always wanted to see the painting; how she threw it away when it disintegrated and I could tell that she cared; how she stood in the painted cave and stared at the girls in the dresses. Indie stole from me because she wanted what I had. I look at her and think that it's like looking at a reflection in a rippled place in the river. The image is not quite exact—it's distorted, churning—but so much the same. She's a rebel with a streak of safety and I am the opposite.

"How did you hide the microcard?" I ask.

"They didn't search me when they found me," Indie says. "Only on the air ship. And you and I figured out a way around that." She pushes her hair back from her face in a gesture that is perfectly Indie: abrupt but with an element of gracefulness about it somehow. I've never met anyone so direct and unashamed about trying to get what she wants. "Aren't you going to look?" she asks.

I can't help myself. I slide Xander's microcard into the miniport and wait for his face to come up.

I should have seen this information back in my home in the Borough with maple leaves rustling outside. Bram could have teased me and my parents could have smiled. I could have looked at Xander's face and seen nothing else.

But Ky's face came up, and everything changed.

"There he is," Indie says, almost involuntarily.

Xander.

I had forgotten how he looked, even though it's only been days since I've seen him. But it all comes back to me, and then his list of attributes begins to come up on the screen.

The list on the microcard is exactly the same as the one he concealed in the tablets; it's what Xander wanted me to see. *Look at me,* he seems to say. *As many times as it takes.*

I don't know how he added the extra line on the scrap Indie found. Could she be lying? I don't think so. And I wonder why he didn't just tell me his secret that day when we visited the Archivist. I thought we might not see each other again. Did he think differently?

But he didn't mean for someone *else* to read all about him. I click back through the records. The microcard wasn't only viewed last night; it was viewed the night before, the night before, the night before.

Indie's been looking at this all along. When? While I was sleeping?

"Do *you* know Xander's secret?" I ask her.

"I think so," she says.

"Tell me, then," I say.

"It's his secret to tell," she says, echoing Ky. Her voice sounds unrepentant, as always. But I notice something; a softening around her eyes as she looks at the picture on the screen.

And then I see. It's not Ky she loves after all.

"You're in love with Xander," I say, my voice too hard, too cruel.

Indie doesn't deny it. Xander is the kind of person an Aberration can never have. A golden boy, as close to perfect as they come in the Society.

He's not her Match, though. He's mine.

With Xander, I could have a family, a good job, be loved, be happy, live in a Borough with clean streets and neat lives. With Xander, I would be able to do the things I always thought I would.

But with Ky, I do things I never thought I could.

I want both.

But that's impossible. I look again at Xander's face. And, though he seems to tell me that he won't change, I know he will. I know there are parts of him I don't know, things happening in Camas that I don't see, secrets of his that I haven't learned that he will have to tell me himself. He makes mistakes, too—like giving me the blue tablets, a gift that was given with great risk and care but was not what he thought it would be. It didn't save me.

Being with Xander might be less complicated, but it would still be love. And I have found that love brings you to new places.

"What did you want with Ky?" I ask Indie. "What were you trying to do when you showed him that scrap and gave him that map?"

"I could tell he knew more about the Rising than he'd say," Indie says. "I wanted to make him tell me what it was."

"Why did you give this back to me?" I say, holding out the microcard. "Why now?"

"You need to choose," Indie says. "I don't think you see either of them clearly."

"And *you* do," I say. Anger wells up in me. She doesn't know Ky, not like I do. And she's never even met Xander.

"*I* figured out Xander's secret." Indie moves toward the entrance of the cave. "And it never occurred to *you* that Ky might be the Pilot."

She disappears through the door.

Someone touches my arm. Eli. His eyes are wide with worry and it shakes me out of my trance. We have to get Eli out of here. We have to hurry. This can all be sorted later.

I am tucking the microcard in my pack when I see it there among the blue.

My red tablet.

Indie and Ky and Xander are all immune.

But I don't know what I am.

I hesitate. I could put that red in my mouth and I wouldn't wait for it to dissolve. I would bite down, hard. Maybe even hard enough that my blood would mix with the red and it would truly be my choice, not the Society's.

If the tablet works, I will forget everything that happened in the last twelve hours. I won't remember what happened with Ky. I wouldn't have to forgive him for lying to me because

I wouldn't know that he had. And I wouldn't remember what he said about my sorting him.

If it doesn't work, I will finally know, once and for all, if I'm immune. If I'm special like Ky, and Xander, and Indie.

I lift the tablet to my mouth. And then I hear a voice from a place deep in my memory.

You are strong enough to go without.

Fine, Grandfather, I think to myself. *I will be strong enough to go without the tablet. But there are other things I'm not strong enough to go without, and I intend to fight for them.*

CHAPTER 41
KY

Carrying the boat is like carrying a body; it's heavy and bulky and awkward. "Only two can fit inside," Hunter warns me.

"That doesn't matter," I say. "It's still what I want."

He looks at me as if he's about to say something but then he decides against it.

We drop the boat in the little house at the edge of the township where Cassia, Indie, and Eli have gathered to wait for us. The boat hits the ground with a heavy thump.

"What is that?" Eli asks.

"A boat," Hunter says. He doesn't elaborate. Indie, Cassia, and Eli stare at the heavy roll of plastic in disbelief.

"I've never seen a boat like that," Indie says.

"I've never seen a boat," Cassia and Eli say at the same time, and then she smiles at him.

"It's for the stream," Indie realizes. "So some of us can get to the Rising fast."

"But the stream's all broken up," Eli says.

"It won't be anymore," I tell him. "A rain like this will have run it back together."

"So who's going in the boat?" Indie asks.

"We don't know yet," I say. I don't look over at Cassia. I haven't been able to meet her eyes since she found me burning the map.

Eli hands me a pack. "I brought this for you," he says. "Food, some things from the cave."

"Thanks, Eli," I say.

"There's something else," he whispers to me. "Can I show you?"

I nod. "Hurry."

Eli makes sure that the others can't see and then he holds out—

A tube from the blue-lit Cavern.

"Eli," I say in surprise. I take the tube from him and turn it over. Inside the liquid rolls and shifts. When I read the name engraved on the outside I draw in my breath sharply. "You shouldn't have taken this."

"I couldn't help it," Eli says.

I should break the tube against the ground or let it go in the river. Instead I put it in my pocket.

The rain has loosened rocks and turned the ground to mud. It won't take much to trigger a landslide and render the path to the caves impassable, but we also have to seal off the doors of the cave without destroying what's inside.

Hunter shows me the plan; a neatly organized diagram

of where and how and what to wire. It's impressive. "Did you make this?" I ask.

"No," he says. "Our leader did before she left. Anna."

Anna, I think. Did my father know her, too?

I don't ask. I follow her diagram and Hunter's adjustments. The rain pounds down above us and we do our best to keep the explosives dry.

"Go down and tell the others that I'm going to set the fuse," Hunter says.

"I'll do it," I say.

Hunter looks at me. "This was my assignment," he says. "Anna trusted me to get it right."

"You know this land better than I do," I say. "You know the farmers. If something goes wrong with the fuse, you're the one who can get everyone else out of here."

"This isn't some kind of self-punishment, is it?" Hunter asks me. "Because you were going to burn the map?"

"No," I say. "It's just the truth."

Hunter looks at me and then nods his head.

I set the timer on the fuse and run. It's instinct—I should have plenty of time. My feet hit the ground near the stream and I sprint toward the others. I haven't quite reached them when I hear the explosion go off.

I can't help myself—I turn and look.

The few small trees clinging to the cliff seem to come

away first; their roots tear away rocks and dirt with them. For a moment I see the dark distinct tangles of each life and then I realize the whole cliff beneath them slides too. The path severs into fragments and is turned under by water, mud, rock.

And the slide keeps going.

Too far, I realize, *it's coming too far and too close. It's going to reach the township.*

One of the houses groans and breaks and gives way to the mud.

Another.

The earth pushes through the township, splintering boards, shattering glass, snapping trees.

And then it goes into the river and stops.

The slide has cut a clean, slick, red-mud-and-rock swath through the township, and it's dammed part of the stream. The water will rise and the canyon might flood. Even as I think this, I see the others spilling out of the house and hurrying toward the path.

I run to help Hunter with the boat. It's for her. If what she wants is the Rising, I will help her reach it.

CHAPTER 42
CASSIA

The walk out is slow-going and miserable; we all slip and fall and get up again, over and over. We're painted in mud by the time we find a cave large enough for all of us to crowd inside. The boat won't fit. We have to leave it outside on the path and I hear the rain drumming on the boat's plastic hide. We haven't made it to the cave with the dancing girls; this cave is tiny and littered with rocks and refuse.

For a moment, no one can overcome exhaustion enough to speak. Our packs lie next to us. As we carried them and the weight became heavier and heavier with each muddy step, I imagined throwing out food, water, even papers. I glance over at Indie. The first time we climbed out to the plain, I was sick. She carried my pack most of the way.

"Thank you," I say to her now.

"For what?" She sounds surprised, wary.

"For carrying my things for me when we came through here the first time," I say.

Ky raises his head and looks at me. It's the first time he's really done so since the confrontation in the township. It feels good to see his eyes again. In the gloom of the cave, they are black.

"We should talk," Hunter says. He's right. What we all know, but have not said, is that everyone cannot fit in the boat. "What is everyone going to do?"

"I'm going to find the Rising," Indie says immediately.

Eli shakes his head. He doesn't know yet and I understand exactly how he feels. We both want the Rising, but Ky doesn't trust it. And, in spite of everything that happened with the map I know we both still trust Ky.

"I still intend to find the other farmers," Hunter says.

"You could go on without us," Indie says to Hunter. "But you're helping us. Why?"

"I'm the one who broke the tubes," Hunter says. "The Society might not have come for you so quickly if I hadn't done that." Though he's only a few years older than we are, he seems much wiser. Perhaps it is having a child; perhaps living in such a hard place; or maybe he would have been this way in the Society, too, in an easy comfortable life. "Besides," Hunter says, "while we carry the boat, you help with our packs. It is in our best interest to help each other out of the Carving. Then we can go our separate ways."

Ky doesn't say anything.

The rain comes down outside and I think of the piece of his story that he gave me back in the Borough that said, *When it rains, I remember.* I vowed to remember, too. And I recall how Ky told me to trade the poems. He didn't warn me away from the Tennyson one, even though he knew I had it too, and even though he knew it might help me discover the Rising. He left those choices—of what to trade and what to do with what I found—up to me.

"What is it you hate about the Rising, Ky?" I ask him softly. I don't want to do this in front of everyone else; but what other option do I have? "I need to decide where to go. So does Eli. It would help us if you explained *why* you hate it so much."

Ky looks down at his hands and I remember the picture he gave me back in the Society, the one that showed him holding the words *mother* and *father*. "They never came to help us," he says. "With the Rising, rebellion ends in death for you and the people you love. Anyone who survives is left behind to turn into someone else."

"But the *Enemy* killed your family," Indie says. "Not the Rising."

"I don't trust them," Ky says. "My father did. I don't."

"Do you?" Indie asks Hunter.

"I'm not certain," Hunter says. "The last time the Rising came into our canyon was years ago." We all, even Ky, lean forward to listen. "They told us they'd managed to infiltrate everywhere, even Central, and they tried again to convince us to join them." Hunter smiles a little. "Anna proved too stubborn. We lived for generations on our own and she thought that we should keep doing it."

"They're the ones who sent in those pamphlets," Ky says.

Hunter nods. "They sent the map we're using, too. They hoped we'd change our minds and come to find them."

"How did they know you could read the code on the map?" Indie asks.

"It's our own code," Hunter says. "We used it in the township sometimes when we didn't want an outsider to know what we were saying."

He reaches into his pack and pulls out one of the headlamps. Night has fully fallen outside the cave.

"They knew the code from some of our youth who left to join up with them." Hunter switches on the light and sets it on the ground for us to see each other by. "The farmers as a whole never joined, but now and then a few of our younger people did. I left to find the Rising myself, once."

"You did?" I ask in surprise.

"I never made it," Hunter says. "I got as far as the stream on the plain before I came back."

"Why?" I ask.

"Catherine." Hunter's voice is hoarse. "Sarah's mother. She wasn't Sarah's mother then, of course. But Catherine could never have left the township and I decided I couldn't leave her."

"Why couldn't she leave?"

"She was going to be the next leader," he says. "She was Anna's daughter, and she was exactly like Anna. When Anna died, there would have been a vote to accept or reject her oldest child as the leader, and we all would have accepted Catherine. Everyone loved her. But she died giving birth to Sarah."

The light inside the cave illuminates our muddy boots while our faces disappear into the darkness. I hear him taking something out of his pack.

"Anna left you," I say, stunned. "She left you, and she left her granddaughter—"

"She had to do it," Hunter says. "She had other children and grandchildren and a township to lead." He pauses. "You see why we're reluctant to judge the Rising too harshly. They want the greater good for their group. We cannot fault them when we do the same."

"It's different," Ky says. "You've been here since the beginning of the Society. Rebellions come and go."

"How did you escape all those years ago?" Indie asks eagerly.

"We didn't," Hunter says. "They let us leave." While he tells the story, he draws the lines of blue back on his arms with a piece of chalk he's taken from his bag.

"You have to remember that the people back then *chose* the Society and its controls as a way to prevent a future Warming event and as a way to help eliminate illness. We did not, so we left. We would not participate in the Society; so we would not receive its benefits or protection. We would farm and eat and keep to ourselves and they would leave us alone. For a long time, they did. And if any came, we cut them down."

Hunter continues. "Before all the original villagers in the Outer Provinces died, they used to come into our canyon for help. They told stories of being sent away for loving the wrong person or wanting a different occupation. Some came to join with us, and others came to trade with us. After the time of the Hundreds, our papers and books had become incredibly valuable." He sighs. "There have always been people like the Archivists. I'm sure there still are. But we were cut off when the villages died."

"What did you trade for?" Eli asks. "You had everything in the canyons."

"No," Hunter says, "we didn't. The Society's medicine was always better, and there were other things we needed."

"But if all your papers are so valuable," Eli asks, "how could you leave so many of them behind?"

"There's too much," Hunter says. "We couldn't carry it all across the plain. Many of the people tore out pages or brought books that they wanted. But it was impossible to bring every-thing. That's why I had to seal off the cave and hide the rest. We didn't want the Society to be able to destroy or take everything if they found it."

He finishes marking one of his arms with the lines and reaches to put the blue chalk back into his pack.

"What do those markings mean?" I ask, and he stops.

"What do they look like to you?"

"Rivers," I say. "Veins."

He nods, interested. "They look like both. You can think of them that way."

"But what are they to you?" I asked.

"Webs," he says.

I shake my head, confused.

"Anything that connects," he says. "When we draw them, we usually draw them together, like this." He puts his hand out so that our fingers touch. I almost jump back in surprise, but I hold myself still. He traces the chalk along his fingers and then crosses over onto mine and runs the line of blue gently up my arm.

He sits back. We look at each other. "Then you would continue the lines yourself," he says. "Along you, and then you would touch someone else and begin a line for them. And so on."

But what if the connection was broken? I want to ask. *Like when your daughter died?*

"If there is no one else for the lines," he says, "you do this." He stands up and pushes his hands against the sandstone wall of the overhang. I imagine a series of tiny cracks spreading from the point of pressure. "You connect to *something*."

"But the Carving doesn't care," I tell him. "The canyons don't care."

"No," Hunter agrees. "But we're still connected."

"I brought this," I say to Hunter, reaching into my pack and feeling shy. "I thought you might want it."

It's the poem with the line he used for Sarah's grave. The one about *across the June a wind with fingers goes.* I took it from the book.

Hunter takes it and reads it aloud:

"They dropped like Flakes -

They dropped like Stars -

Like Petals from a Rose -

When suddenly across the June

A wind with fingers - goes -"

He pauses.

"It sounds like what happened to us out in the villages," Eli says. "People died like that. They dropped like stars."

Ky puts his head in his hands.

Hunter reads on.

"They perished in the Seamless Grass -

No eye could find the place -

But God can summon every face

On his Repealless - List."

"Some of us believed in another life someday," he says. "Catherine did, and Sarah did, too."

"But you don't," Indie says.

"I didn't," Hunter says. "But I never told Sarah that. How could I take that away from her? She was everything to me."

He swallows. "I held her while she fell asleep every night, all those years of her life." Tears slip down his cheeks the way they did earlier in the library cave. He ignores them, as he did then.

"I had to move away little by little," Hunter says. "Lift my arm. Pull my face away from where I tucked it into her neck; draw back so that my breath no longer ruffled her hair. I did this gradually so that when I left she didn't know I was gone. I saw her into the night.

"In the Cavern, I thought I'd break all the tubes and then die in the dark," Hunter says. "But I couldn't do it."

He looks down at the page again and reads the line he carved for her. *"Suddenly across the June a wind with fingers goes,"* he says, almost sings, his voice sad and soft. He stands up and shoves the paper in his pack. "I will check the rain," he says, and goes to stand outside.

By the time Hunter comes back in, everyone has fallen asleep except for Ky and me. I can hear Ky breathing, on the other side of Eli. It's crowded in here, and it would be easy to reach out and touch Ky but I hold back. It is so strange to take this journey together when there is such distance between us. I can't forget what he did. I can't forget what *I* did, either. Why did I sort him?

I hear Hunter settle near the entrance of the cave and I wish I hadn't given him that poem. I didn't mean to bring him pain.

If I died here, and someone were to carve my epitaph on

the stone of this cave, I don't know what I would want them to write.

What would Grandfather have chosen for his epitaph?

Do not go gentle

Or

I hope to see my Pilot face to face

Grandfather, who knew me better than anyone else did, has become a mystery.

So has Ky.

I think suddenly of that time at the showing, when he had all that pain that none of us knew and we laughed while he cried.

I close my eyes. I love Ky. But I don't understand him. He won't let me reach him. I have made mistakes, too, I know it, but I am tired of chasing him through canyons and out onto plains and stretching out my hand only to have him take it some times and not others. Perhaps that's the real reason he's an Aberration. Perhaps even the Society couldn't predict what he would do.

Who put Ky into the Matching Pool in the first place? My Official pretended that she knew, but she didn't. I decided it didn't matter anymore—*I'd* chosen to love him, *I'd* chosen to find him—but the question comes to mind again.

Who could it have been? I've thought of Patrick. Aida.

And then I have another thought, the most striking, unlikely, believable one of all: *Could it have been Ky?*

I don't know how he could have done it, but I also don't

know how Xander could have managed to get the papers inside the tablet compartments. Love changes what is probable and makes unlikely things possible. I try to remember what Ky said back in the Borough when we talked about the Matching Pool and the mistake. Didn't he say that it didn't matter who put the name in, as long as I loved him?

I've never known his whole story.

Maybe only parts of our stories can keep us safe. The whole can feel like too much to bear, whether it's the story of Society or a rebellion or a single person.

Is this what Ky feels? That no one wants the whole? That his truth is too heavy to carry?

CHAPTER 43
KY

Everyone else sleeps.

If I wanted to run, now would be the time.

Cassia told me once that she wanted to write a poem for me. Did she ever get past the beginning? What words did she use for the end?

She cried before she slept. I reached out to touch the ends of her hair. She didn't notice. I didn't know what to do. Listening to her made me ache. I felt tears stream down my face too. And when I accidentally brushed Eli with my arm his face was wet where *his* tears ran down.

We have all been carved out by our sorrow. Cut deep like canyon walls.

I saw my parents kissing all the time. I remember one time when my father had been in the canyons and just come back. My mother stood painting. He came close. She laughed and drew a streak of water along his cheek. It glistened. When they kissed she wrapped her arms around him and let the paintbrush fall to the ground.

It was kind of my father to send that page to the Markhams.

If he'd never done that, Patrick might never have known about the Archivists and couldn't have told me the way to contact them in Oria. We would never have had the old scribe. I would never have known how to sort, or how to trade. I wouldn't have been able to give Cassia her birthday poem.

I cannot let my parents go unmarked any longer.

Careful not to step on anyone, I feel my way over to the back of the cave. It doesn't take long to find what I'm looking for within my pack—the paints Eli gathered for me. And a paintbrush. My hand closes around its bristles.

I open the jars of paint and set them in a row. Reach out again and make sure the wall is in front of me.

And then I dip the brush in and make a stroke above me on the wall of the cave. I feel some of the paint drip onto my face.

I paint the world, and then my parents in the middle of it, while I wait for the light to come. My mother. My father. A picture of her looking at a sunset. A picture of him teaching a boy to write. It might be me. In the dark I can't be sure.

I paint Vick's stream.

I paint Cassia last.

How much do we have to show the people we love?

What pieces of my life do I have to lay bare, carve out, and put before her? Is it enough that I have pointed the way to who I am?

Do I have to tell her how back in the Borough I was sometimes jealous and bitter about how different I was? How

I wished I were Xander, or any of the other boys who got to keep going to school and who would at least have a chance to be Matched with her?

Do I have to tell her about the night when I turned my back on all the other decoys and only took Vick and Eli? Vick, because I knew he'd help us survive, Eli to appease my guilt?

I have to tell her the truth, but I haven't even told it to myself.

My hands begin to shake.

The day my parents died I was alone on the plateau. I saw the fire come down. Afterwards, I ran to find them. That much is true.

When I saw the first bodies I was sick. I threw up. And then I saw that some things had survived. Not people, but objects. A shoe here. A perfect, unopened foilware meal there. A paintbrush with clean bristles. I picked it up.

Now I remember. What I've lied to myself about all along.

After I picked up the paintbrush and looked over and saw my parents dead on the ground, I didn't try to carry them. I didn't bury them.

I saw them and I ran.

CHAPTER 44
CASSIA

I am the first to wake. A beam of sunlight shines through the door of the cave and I glance over at the others in surprise, wondering how they haven't yet noticed the bright light and the absence of rain.

Looking at Ky and Eli and Hunter, I think of how many invisible injuries are possible. Ones scored on your heart, your brain, your bones. *How do we all stand?* I wonder. *What is it that keeps us moving?*

When I step out of the cave, the sky blinds me. I put my hand up the way Ky does to block the sun, and when I bring my hand back down, I think for a moment that I've left a thumbprint, a mark of wavy dark lines blotting the sky. Then the print moves and turns, and I see that it is not the whorls of my fingers but the whirls of a flock of birds, tiny, moving high in the distance. And I laugh at myself for thinking I could touch the sky.

When I turn back to wake the others I draw in my breath.

While we slept, he painted. With swift, light strokes; paint-dripped haste.

He covered the back of the cave with rivers of stars. He made the world rocks and trees and hills. He painted a stream, too, one dead and alive with footprints along its bank, and a grave marked with a stone fish whose scales cannot turn back the light.

At the center he painted his parents.

Painting in the dark, he couldn't see. The scenes blend and bleed into one another. Sometimes the colors are strange. A green sky, blue stones. And me, standing there in a dress.

He painted it red.

CHAPTER 45
KY

The sun beating down on the boat makes it hot to touch. My hands turn red and I hope she doesn't notice. I don't want to think anymore of the day she sorted me. What's done is done. We have to go forward.

I hope she feels the same way, but I don't ask her. At first it's because I can't—we all walk single file on the narrow path and everyone else could hear—and then it's because I'm too tired to frame the words. Cassia, Indie, and Eli help Hunter and me with our packs but my muscles still burn and ache.

The sun wears on and clouds gather on the horizon.

I don't know which would be better for us—dry or rain. Rain makes it hard to walk but it does cover our tracks. We're walking another fine line for survival. But I've done what I can to make sure Cassia comes out on the right side of this line. That's what the boat is for.

Once in a while it's useful on dry land—when the path is too muddy and torn up to walk on, we put the boat down, walk over it, and pick it up again. It leaves marks like long narrow footprints on the path. If I weren't so tired I might smile. What will the Society think when they see the prints? That something enormous came down and picked us up and walked with us right out of the Carving?

Tonight we'll camp. I'll talk to her then. By night I'll know what to say. Right now I'm too tired to think of anything that could make everything right.

We make up for the lost time from the day before. No one rests. We all push through, stealing sips of water and pieces of bread along the way. We have almost reached the edge of the Carving when the light becomes dusky with evening and rain begins to fall.

Hunter stops and eases his part of the boat to the ground. I do the same. He looks back at the Carving behind us. "We should all go now," he says.

"But it's almost dark," Eli says.

Hunter shakes his head. "We're running out of time," he says. "There's nothing to stop them climbing over from the Cavern once they find out what's happened. And what if they have miniports? They might call in people to cut us off at the plain."

"Where's *our* miniport?" I ask.

"I threw it in the river before we left the township," Cassia says. Indie draws in her breath.

"Good," Hunter says. "We don't want anything that could track us."

Eli shivers.

"Can you keep going?" Cassia asks him, sounding worried.

"I think so," Eli says, looking at me. "Do you think we should?"

"Yes," I say.

"We have the headlamps," Indie adds.

"Let's go." Cassia reaches to help us lift the boat.

We hurry to the the bank, moving as fast as we can. I feel stones under my feet, thrown from the river. I wonder which one is the fish that marks Vick's grave. In the dark it all looks different and I'm not sure I know where he lies.

But I know what Vick would have done if he were still living.

Whatever he thought would take him closest to Laney.

In the trees, in the light of a headlamp that we smother down low, Hunter and I snap the boat open and insert the pump. The boat takes shape quickly.

"Two can ride in it," Hunter says. "The others who want to make their way to the Rising will have to follow the stream on foot. That way will be much slower."

The air sighs into the boat.

For a moment I stand completely still.

The rain comes down again, stinging-cold and clean. It's different from the storm before—this is a shower, not an onslaught. It will end soon.

"Somewhere higher, this water is snow," my mother used to say, opening her palms to catch the drops.

I think of her paintings and how quickly they dried. "Somewhere," I say out loud and hope she hears, "this water is nothing at all. It is lighter than air."

Cassia turns to look at me.

I imagine these drops of rain hitting the scales of the sandstone fish I carved for Vick. *Every drop helps the poisoned stream,* I think, holding my hands out open wide. Not catching the drops or trying to hold them. I'm letting them leave their mark and then letting them go.

Let go. Of my parents, and the pain of what happened to them. Of what I failed to do. Of all the people I failed to save or bury. Of my jealousy of Xander. Of my guilt over what happened to Vick. Of worrying about what I can never be and who I never was in the first place.

Let go of it all.

I don't know if I can, but it feels good to try. So I let the rain hit my palms heavy. Run down my fingers to dirt. *Every drop helps me,* I think. I tip my head back and try to open myself back up to the sky.

My father might have been the reason all those people died. But he also helped make their lives bearable. He gave them hope. I used to think that didn't matter but it does.

Good and bad. Good in my father, bad in me. No fire raining on me can burn it away. I have to get rid of it myself.

"I'm sorry," I say to Cassia. "I should never have lied to you."

"I'm sorry, too," she says. "The sorting was all wrong."

We look at each other in the rain.

"It's your boat," Indie says to me. "Who's going in it?"

"I traded for it for you," I say to Cassia. "It's your choice who comes with you."

I feel the way I did before the Match Banquet. Waiting. Wondering if what I'd done would be enough for her to see me again.

CHAPTER 46
CASSIA

Ky," I say. "I can't sort people again." How could he ask this of me?

"Hurry," Indie says.

"You did it right last time," Ky says. "I belong out here."

It's true. He does. And even though trying to find him has been the hardest thing I've ever done, I am stronger because of it.

I close my eyes and think of the relevant factors.

Hunter wants to go to the mountains, not the river.

Eli is the youngest.

Indie can pilot.

I love Ky.

Who should go?

This time, it's easier, because there's only one choice—one configuration—that feels right to me.

"It's time," Hunter says. "Who do you choose?"

I look at Ky, hoping he'll understand. He will. He would do the same thing. "Eli," I say.

CHAPTER 47
KY

Eli blinks. "Me?" he asks. "What about Ky?"

"You," Cassia says. "And Indie. Not me."

Indie looks up, surprised.

"Someone has to get Eli down the river," Cassia says. "Hunter and Indie are the only ones who know anything about water like this, and Hunter's going to the mountains."

Hunter checks the boat. "It's almost ready."

"You can do it, can't you?" Cassia asks Indie. "You can get Eli there? It's the fastest way to take him someplace safe."

"I can do it," Indie says, without the slightest sound of doubt in her voice.

"A river is different from the sea," Hunter warns Indie.

"We had rivers that went to the sea," Indie says. She reaches for one of the oars that came wrapped inside in the boat and slots the pieces together. "I used to run them at night, for practice. The Society never saw me until I went to the ocean."

"Wait," Eli says. We all turn. He lifts his chin and looks at me with his solemn, serious eyes. "I want to cross the plain. That's what you wanted to do first."

Hunter glances over in surprise. Eli will slow him down. But Hunter is not the kind of person who leaves anyone behind.

"Can I come with you?" Eli asks. "I'll run as hard as I can."

"Yes," Hunter says. "But we have to go now."

I grab Eli and pull him into a hug. "We'll see each other again," he says. "I know it."

"We will," I say. I shouldn't promise a thing like this. My eyes meet Hunter's over Eli's head and I wonder if Hunter said the same thing to Sarah when he told her good-bye.

Eli tears away from me and throws his arms around Cassia and then Indie, who looks surprised. She hugs him back and he straightens up. "I'm ready," he says. "Let's go."

"I hope we meet again," Hunter says to us. He raises his hand in a kind of salute and in the light of the headlamp I see the blue marks all down his arm. We all stand for one last moment looking at each other. Then Hunter turns to run and Eli follows him. For a moment through the trees I see the lights from their lamps and then they're gone.

"Eli will be all right," Cassia says. "Won't he?"

"It was his choice," I say.

"I know," she says. Her voice is soft. "But it happened so quickly."

It did. Like that day I left the Borough. And the day my parents died, and when Vick crossed over. Good-byes are like this. You can't always mark them well at the moment of separation—no matter how deep they cut.

Indie pulls off her coat and, with a quick sure movement of her stone knife, slices out the disk inside. She throws it on the ground next to her with a flourish and turns toward me. "Eli's decided what to do," she says. "What about you?"

Cassia looks at me. She reaches up to brush the rain and tears from her face.

"I'll follow the river," I say. "I won't be as fast as you and Indie will be in the boat, but I'll catch up with you at the end."

"Are you sure?" she whispers.

I am. "You came a long way to look for me," I say. "I can come to the Rising with you."

CHAPTER 48
CASSIA

The rain turns lighter, turns to snow. And I have a sense that we have not yet arrived, that we are still reaching. For each other. For who we are meant to be. I look at him, knowing that I will never see everything, understanding that now, and I make the choice again.

"It's hard to cross over," I tell him, my voice breaking.

"Cross over where?" he asks.

"To who I need to be," I tell him.

And then we both move.

We have both been wrong; we will both try to make things right. That is all we can do.

Ky leans in to kiss me, but his hands stay down at his sides.

"Why won't you hold me?" I ask, drawing back a little.

He laughs a little, holds out his hands as if in explanation. They are covered in dirt and paint and blood.

I pull his hand to mine, put my palm against his. I can feel the grit of sand, the slick of paint, and the cuts and scrapes that speak of his own journey.

"It will all come clean," I tell him.

CHAPTER 49
KY

When I pull her to me she feels eager, warm and reaching, but then she flinches slightly and draws back. "I'm sorry," she says, "I forgot." She pulls a small tube from inside her shirt. She notices the shock on my face and rushes on. "I couldn't help it."

She holds the tube out for me to see, trying to explain. It glints in the light from our headlamps and it takes me a moment to read the name: REYES, SAMUEL. Her grandfather. "I took it when you were all looking at Hunter, after he broke the tube."

"Eli stole one too," I say. "He gave it to me."

"Who did he take?" Cassia asks.

I look over at Indie. She could push the boat away now and leave Cassia behind. But she doesn't. I knew she wouldn't. Not this time. If you want to go where Indie wants to go, you couldn't find a better pilot. She'll carry your pack and get you through the rough water. She turns her back to us and stands perfectly still under the trees next to the boat.

"Vick," I tell Cassia.

It surprised me at first that Eli didn't choose his parents, and then I remembered that they wouldn't have been there.

Eli and his family had been Aberrations for years. Vick must have been Reclassified recently enough that the Society hadn't had time to remove his tube.

"Eli trusts you," she says.

"I know," I say.

"I do, too," she says. "What are you going to do?"

"Hide it," I say. "Until I know who was storing the tubes and why. Until I know we can trust the Rising."

"And the books you brought from the farmers' cave?" she asks.

"Those too," I say. "I'm going to look for the right place while I'm following the river." I pause. "If you want me to hide your things, I can. I'll make sure they get to you somehow."

"Won't they be too heavy to carry?" she asks.

"No," I say.

She hands me the tube and reaches into her pack for the collection of loose papers that she took from the cave. "I didn't write any of those pages," she says, an ache in her voice. "Someday I will." Then she puts her hand against my cheek. "The rest of your story," she says. "Will you tell it to me now? Or when I see you again?"

"My mother," I begin. "My father." I close my eyes, trying to explain. What I say makes no sense. It's a string of words—

When my parents died I did nothing

So I wanted to do

I wanted to do

I wanted to do

"Something," she says gently. She takes my hand again and turns it over, looking at the mangled mess of scrapes and paint and dirt that the rain hasn't yet washed away. "You're right. We can't do *nothing* all our lives. And, Ky, you did something when your parents died. I remember the picture you drew for me back in Oria. You tried to carry them."

"No," I say, my voice breaking. "I left them on the ground and ran."

She wraps her arms around me and speaks in my ear. Words just for me—the poetry of *I love you*—to keep me warm in the cold. With them she turns me back from ash and nothing into flesh and blood.

CHAPTER 50
CASSIA

Do not go gentle," I tell him, one last time, for now.

Ky smiles then, a smile I've never seen before. It's the kind of daring, reckless smile that could make people follow him straight into a firing, a flood. "There's no danger of that," he says.

I put my hands on him, run my fingers over his eyelids, find his lips, meet them with mine. I kiss the plane of his cheekbones. The salt of his tears tastes like the sea and I don't see the shore.

He's gone, in the trees, and I'm in the river, and there's no time left.

"Do what I say," Indie tells me, shoving an oar into my hands and yelling over the sound of the water rushing near us. "If I say left, paddle on your left. If I say right, paddle right. If I tell you to lean, do it." The beam of her headlamp glares in my eyes and I'm relieved when she turns to face forward. Tears stream down my cheeks from the farewell and the light.

"Now," Indie says, and we both push the boat away from

the bank. We sit suspended for a moment and then the stream finds us, pushes us along.

"Right," Indie calls.

Scattered snowflakes star our faces as we ride, little white dashes in the light from our headlamps.

"If we ever flip over, stay with the boat," Indie yells back to me.

She can only see far enough ahead to have time for one fast call, one quick decision; she's sorting in a way I never could, with spray in her face and water shining silver and black branches tearing at us from the banks, broken trees looming at us from the center of the stream.

I copy her, follow her, shadow her strokes. And I wonder how the Society ever caught her that day on the ocean. She *is* a Pilot, on this river, tonight.

Hours or minutes, they don't matter, it's only changes in the water and turns in the stream, shouts from Indie and oars flicking water as we move them from side to side.

I glance up, once, aware that something is happening above me; night lifting, the earliest part of morning that is still black, but black that feels like it's rubbing off around the edges, and I miss the moment Indie screams at me to paddle right and then we're over, over in the stream.

Cold dark water, poisoned from the Society's spheres, rushes over me. I see nothing and feel everything, freezing water, driftwood battering me. It's the moment of my own death, and then something else hits my arm.

Stay with the boat.

My fingers scrabble along the edge, and I find one of the grips and hold on, pulling myself to the surface. The water tastes bitter; I spit it out and cling tight. I'm inside the boat, under it, trapped and saved in a bubble of air. Something tears my leg. My headlamp is gone.

It's like the Cavern, I'm caught but alive.

"You *will*," Ky said then, but he's not here now.

Suddenly I remember the day I met him, that day at the clear blue pool, when he and Xander both went under but came back up.

Where's Indie?

The boat shoots to the side and the water goes still.

A light shines in. Indie, pushing the boat up. She held on to the outside and somehow she still has her headlamp. "We're in a smooth spot," Indie says fiercely. "It won't last. Get out here with me and *push*."

I swim out under the side. The water is black and glassy, puddled for a moment in a wide place in the stream, dammed somehow from below. "Did you hold on to your oar?" Indie asks, and to my surprise, I did. "On three," Indie says, and she counts, and we flip the boat back over and grab again for the sides. She flops, fast, like a fish, into the boat and grabs my oar to pull me over, too.

"You held on," she says, "I thought I was finally done with you," and she laughs, and so do I, both of us laughing until we hit the next wave of river and Indie screams, wild and triumphant. I join in.

"The real danger begins now," Indie says when the sun comes up, and I know she's right. The river is still fast; we can see better, but we can be seen, and we are exhausted. The heavier cottonwoods here have been choked out by thinner, less concealing trees that grow spindly, grayish-green, and snarled with thorns. "We have to stay close to the trees for cover," Indie says, "but if we're going too fast and we hit those thorns, they'll finish our boat."

We pass a huge dead cottonwood with scaly brownish bark that has fallen over, tired and done after years of holding on to the bank. *I hope Hunter and Eli are in the mountains*, I think, *and that Ky has cover in the trees.*

Then we hear it. Something overhead.

Without saying a word, we both pull closer to the bank. Indie reaches with her oar into the thorny branches but it slips and doesn't hold. We start to drift and I stab my oar into the water, pushing us back.

The ship overhead flies closer.

Indie reaches out and grabs hold of the thorny branches with her bare hand. I gasp. She hangs on and I jump out and pull the boat over to the side, hearing the rasp of the thorny bushes along the plastic. *Please don't break*, I think. Indie lets go, her hand bleeding, and the two of us hold our breath.

They pass over. They haven't seen us.

"I'd like a green tablet right now," Indie says, and I start laughing in relief. But the tablets are gone, along with everything else we had, swept away when we flipped in the water. Indie had tied our packs to one of the boat's handles but the water tore them away in spite of her careful knots; some branch or tree cut right through the rope and I should be grateful it wasn't our flesh or the plastic of the boat.

Once I'm back inside, we keep close to the bank. The sun climbs high. No one else flies over.

I think of my second lost compass sinking to the bottom of the river, like the stone it was before Ky changed it.

Evening. The reeds at the edge of the stream whisper and hush in the breeze, and in the traces of the sunset in a high and lovely sky, I see the first star of the evening.

Then I see it shining on the ground, too. Or not the ground, but in water that stretches out dark in front of us.

"This," Indie says, "is not the ocean."

The star flickers out. Something has passed over it, either in the sky or in the water.

"But it's so huge," I say. "What else could it be?"

"A lake," Indie says.

A strange hum comes across the water.

It's a boat, coming fast for us. There is no way to outrun it and we are both so tired we don't even try. We sit there together, hungry and aching and adrift.

"I hope it's the Rising," Indie says.

"It has to be," I say.

Suddenly, as the humming draws closer, Indie grabs my arm. "I would have chosen blue for my dress," she tells me. "I would have looked right into his eyes, whoever he was. I wouldn't have been afraid."

"I know," I say.

Indie nods and turns back to face what's coming. She sits tall. I picture the blue silk—the exact color of my mother's dress—blowing around Indie. I picture her standing by the sea.

She is beautiful.

Everyone has something of beauty about them. In the beginning for me, it was Ky's eyes I noticed, and I love them still. But loving lets you look, and look, and look again. You notice the back of a hand, the turn of a head, the way of a walk. When you first love, you look blind and you see it all as the glorious, beloved whole, or a beautiful sum of beautiful parts. But when you see the one you love as pieces, as whys— *why he walks like this, why he closes his eyes like that*—you can love those parts, too, and it's a love at once more complicated and more complete.

The other boat comes closer and I see that the people on board wear waterproof gear. Is it to avoid getting wet? Or do they know the river is poisoned? I wrap my arms around myself, suddenly feeling contaminated, though the skin hasn't burned from our bones and we've resisted the temptation of drinking the water down.

"Put your hands up," Indie says. "Then they can see we don't have anything." She puts her oar down across her lap and raises her hands in the air. The gesture is so vulnerable, so uncharacteristic of her, that it takes me a moment to follow her lead.

She doesn't wait for them to speak first. "We've escaped," she calls out. "We've come to join you."

Their boat draws closer. I look at them, taking in their slick black clothes and their number: nine of them. Two of us. They stare back. Do they note our Society coats, our battered boat, our empty hands?

"Come to join whom?" one asks.

Indie doesn't hesitate. "The Rising," she says.

CHAPTER 51
KY

I run. Sleep. Eat a little. Drink from one of the canteens. When it empties I throw it to the side. No point in filling it with poisoned water.

I run again. On and on along the bank of the river, keeping to the trees when I can.

I run for her. For them. For me.

The sun shines down on the stream. The rain has stopped, but the broken pools are connected again.

My father taught me to swim one summer when we had more rain than usual and some of the holes in the land became pools for a week or two. He taught me how to hold my breath, stay afloat, and open my eyes underneath the blue-green water.

The pool in Oria was different. Made of white cement instead of red rock. You could see all the way to the bottom in most places, unless the angle of the sun blinded you. The water and the edges met in neat lines. Kids jumped off the diving board. It seemed that the whole Borough came to swim that day, but it was Cassia at the side of the water who caught my eye.

It was the way she sat, so still. She seemed almost suspended while everyone else called and screamed and ran. For a moment—the first time since I'd come to the Society—I felt clear. I felt rested. When I saw her there, something in me felt right again.

Then she stood up and I could tell from the tightness in her back that she was worried. She stared at a spot in the pool where a boy swam deep underwater. I walked over to her as fast as I could and asked, "Is he drowning?"

"I can't tell," she said.

So I went under to try to help Xander.

The chemicals in the pool burned my eyes and I had to close them for a moment. At first the pain and the way the bright light made it seem red behind my eyelids made me think that I was bleeding and going blind. I put my hands up to check but I only felt water, not blood. My panic embarrassed me. Fighting the pain, I pulled my hands away and opened up my eyes again to look around.

I saw legs and bodies and people swimming and then I stopped looking for someone drowning. All I could think was—

—there's nothing here.

I'd known the pool was clean and neat but seeing it from below was so strange. Even in the rain pools that only lasted for a little while life took hold. Moss grew. Water bugs skittered in the sun along the surface until the pools dried up. But there was nothing along the bottom of this place but cement.

I forgot where I was and tried to breathe.

When I came up choking I could tell that she saw the differences in me. Her eyes rested on the scrape on my face from the Outer Provinces. But it was as though she was a little like me. She noticed the differences and then she decided what mattered and what didn't. She laughed with me then, and I loved the way the laugh reached her green eyes and crinkled the skin around them.

I was a kid. I knew I loved her but I didn't know what it meant. Over the years everything changed. She did. I did.

I hide the tubes and the papers in two different places. It's impossible to know if the tubes are still viable outside of their cases in the Cavern—but Eli and Cassia trusted me. In case of flood, I put the tubes up high in the knot of an old cottonwood tree.

The papers won't have to stay hidden for long so I bury them low in the ground and mark the place with a rock I carve. I'm pleased with the pattern. It could be waves in the sea. Currents in a river. Ripples in the sand.

Scales on a fish.

I close my eyes for a moment and let myself remember the people who are gone.

Rainbows glimmered in the stream. Golden grass tangled along the bank where Vick ran and thought about the girl he loved. His boots left unnotched prints in the earth.

The sun set over a land that my mother found beautiful.

Her son painted next to her with his hands dipped in water. Her husband kissed her neck.

My father came out of a canyon. While he was inside, he'd seen people growing and harvesting crops of their own. They knew how to write. He wanted to bring all of that to the people he loved.

The lake is only a few hundred yards away. I leave the cover of the trees.

CHAPTER 52
CASSIA

After coming across so many dead in the Carving, so many still, silent tubes in the cave, the scene of life in the camp before me makes my heart pound with joy. All these people living, moving. In the Carving I could almost believe we were the last people in the world. As the people in the other boat tow ours to the shore of the lake, I glance over at Indie and she smiles, too. Our hair streams out behind us and our oars lie across our laps. *We've made it,* I think. *At last.*

"Two more," one of the men in the boat in front of us calls out, and in spite of my happiness at finding the Rising I wish that he had been able to call out *three.* Soon, I tell myself. Ky will be here soon.

Our boat scrapes along the shore and I realize that it's not *our* boat any longer; it belongs to the Rising now. "You've reached us just in time," says one of the people who towed us in. He holds out his black-gloved hand to help us. "We're about to move. It's not safe here anymore. The Society knows where we are."

Ky. Will he make it in time? "When?" I ask.

"As soon as we can," the man says. "Come with me." He

leads the way to a small cinder-block building near the edge of the water. The metal door is closed tight but he knocks loudly and it opens immediately.

"We found two on the lake," he says, and the three people inside stand up, the metal of their old Society-issue chairs scraping as they push back from a table full of maps and miniports. They wear green plainclothes and their faces are covered but I can see their eyes.

"Get them sorted," one of them says, a female Officer. "You've been in the river?" she asks us.

We nod.

"We'll have to have you decontaminated," she says. "Take them there first." Then she smiles at us. "Welcome to the Rising."

As we leave the tiny building the three Officers watch us. Two have brown eyes, one has blue. One female. Two males. All with fatigue lines around their eyes. From working too long? Doubling as Society and Rising?

They're going to sort me, but I can do the same.

After we've washed, a young woman swabs our arms and checks for contamination. "You're clean," she tells us. "It's a good thing it rained and diluted the poison." Then she leads us through the camp. I try to take in what I can while we walk but don't see much more besides other cinder-block structures, little tents, and one enormous building that must house something huge.

Once we're inside another small building, the woman

opens one of the doors that line the hallway. "You'll be in here," she says to Indie, "and you, in here." She opens a second door for me.

They're going to split us up. And we were so intent on survival, we didn't even think about what we should say.

I remember the prisoner's dilemma. This is where they catch you; how they tell if your story is true. I should have assumed the Rising might use it, too.

There's no time to decide. Indie looks at me and gives me a little smile, and I remember when she helped me hide the tablets on the air ship. We managed to keep things hidden before. We can do it again. I smile back at her.

I just hope we both think the same things should stay secret.

"State your full name, please," a pleasant-voiced man says.

"Cassia Maria Reyes."

Nothing. No flicker. No sign of recognition at the name, no mention of Grandfather or the Pilot. I knew better than to expect it, but I still feel a tiny chill of disappointment.

"Society status."

Decide, quickly, how much to tell. "Citizen, as far as I know."

"How did you come to be in the Outer Provinces?"

I will keep Grandfather and his poems out of it; the Archivists, too. "I was sent here by mistake," I lie. "An Officer in my work camp told me to board the air ship with the other girls and wouldn't listen to me when I told him I was a Citizen."

"And then?" the man says.

"Then we ran to the Carving. A boy came with us but he died." I swallow. "We came to a settlement but it was empty."

"What did you do there?"

"We found a boat," I say. "And a map. I read the code. It told us how to find you."

"How did you learn about the Rising?"

"In a poem. Then again in the settlement."

"Did anyone else come with you out of the Carving?"

The questions come too fast to think. Is it better to let them know about Ky? Or not? My hesitation, small enough, has given it away, and I answer honestly because I'm preparing to lie about something else. "Another boy," I say. "He was from the villages, too. We couldn't all fit in the boat, so he's coming on foot."

"His name?"

"Ky," I say.

"The name of your other companion, the girl who is here now?"

"Indie."

"Last names?"

"I don't know." It's true of Indie and partly true of Ky. What *was* his last name when he first lived out here?

"Did you find any indication as to where the people in the canyon might have gone?"

"No."

"What made you decide to join the Rising?"

"I don't believe in the Society anymore after what I've seen."

"That's enough for now," the man says kindly, shutting off the miniport. "We'll access your Society data and find out more about where we should put you."

"You have the Society's data?" I ask in surprise. "Out here?"

He smiles. "Yes. We've found that while our interpretations differ, the data itself is often sound. Please wait here."

In the little cement room with walls completely devoid of life, I think back to the Cavern. It had Society all over it—in the tubes, the organization, the camouflaged doors. Even the crack in its shell, the secret way in that Hunter knew, was like the cracks in the Society. I remember other things. Dust in the corners of the Cavern. A tiny blue light on the floor burned out and unreplaced. Did the Society become overwhelmed by everything they have tried to control and hold?

I picture a hand letting go, drawing back, severing a connection, and the Rising coming in instead.

In the end, the Society decided that I wasn't worth saving. My Official thought I was an interesting experiment; she let me skip taking the red tablet and she watched to see what I would do. I mistook her individual interest for Societal interest—I thought they might think I was special—but it seems I was never anything more to them than an excellent sorter, an interesting research project that could be dropped at any time because I would ultimately do what they predicted.

What will the Rising think of me? Will they view my data differently? They must. They have more of it. They know about my dash into the Carving and my rush down the river. I've taken so many risks. I have changed. I feel it, *know* it.

The door opens.

"Cassia," the man says. "We've analyzed your information."

"Yes?" *Where will they send me?*

"We've decided that you would best serve the Rising from within the Society."

CHAPTER 53
KY

Please state your full name."

Which one should I use? "Ky Markham," I say.

"Society status?"

"Aberration."

"How did you learn about the Rising?"

"My father was a member of it a long time ago," I say.

"How did you find us?"

"From a map we found in the Carving."

I hope the answers I'm giving are the same ones she did. As always, we didn't have enough time. But I trust my instincts and I trust hers too.

"Was there anyone traveling with you other than the two girls who came earlier on the boat?"

"No," I say. This one is easy. I knew Cassia will never give Eli and Hunter away, no matter how much she wants to believe in the Rising.

The man leans back. His voice is even. "Now," he says. "Ky Markham. Tell us more about why you came to join us."

After I finish talking, the man thanks me and leaves me alone for a few moments. When he comes back, he stands in the doorway. "Ky Markham."

"Yes?"

"Congratulations," he says. "You've been assigned to work as an air-ship pilot and sent to Camas Province to train. You'll be of great service to the Rising."

"Thank you," I say.

"You'll leave late tonight," he says, pushing open the door. "Eat and sleep in the main hall with the others." He points to one of the larger tents. "We've been using this camp to gather escapees like yourself. In fact, one of the girls you came with should still be here."

I thank him again and make my way to the hall as quickly as I can. When I push open the flap of the tent, she is the first person I see.

Indie.

I'm not surprised—I thought this might happen—but my heart sinks anyway. I'd hoped to see Cassia again here. Now.

I *will* see her again.

Indie sits alone. When she sees me she moves down the table so there's room at the end for me. I walk past the others eating and talking about their assignments. There are a few girls but most are boys and all of us are young and wearing black plainclothes. A line for the food has formed at the opposite end of the tent, but I want to talk to Indie. I sit next to her and ask the first, most important thing. "Where's Cassia?"

"They sent her back to the Society," Indie says. "Central. Where Xander's going." She spears a piece of meat with her fork. "Cassia still doesn't know his secret, does she?"

"She will soon enough," I say. "He'll tell her."

"I know," Indie says.

"How did they send her back?" I ask.

"By air ship," Indie says. "They sent her to a work camp where someone in the Rising can filter people back into Society on the long-distance train. She's likely all the way to Central by now." Indie leans forward. "She'll be fine. The Rising checked her data. The Society hadn't even Reclassified her yet."

I nod, leaning back. Cassia must be disappointed. I know she hoped to stay in the Rising.

"How was the run?" Indie asks.

"Long," I say. "How about the river?"

"Poisoned," she says.

I start laughing then, relieved to have confirmation that Cassia is all right from someone who—in spite of everything—I trust. Indie joins in too. "We made it," I say. "None of us died."

"Cassia and I fell in the river," Indie says, "but we seem to be fine."

"Thanks to the rain," I say.

"And my piloting," she says.

"They'll notice you, Indie," I say. "You're going to matter to them. Be careful."

She nods.

"I still think you're going to run," I tell her.

"I might surprise you," she says.

"You have before," I say. "What's your work assignment?"

"They haven't told me yet," she says, "but we leave tonight. Do you know your assignment? Where are you going?"

"Camas." If I had to go someplace away from Cassia, Camas is where I'd pick. Vick's home. I might be able to find out what happened to Laney. "Apparently my data indicates that I would be a good pilot, too."

Indie's eyes widen.

"Of an air ship," I clarify. "Nothing more."

Indie looks at me for a moment. "Well," she says, and I think I hear a teasing note in her voice. "*Anyone* can fly an air ship. You point them in the right direction and push a button. It's not like running a river. Even someone as young as Eli could—" She stops, the playful tone in her voice gone, and she puts down her fork.

"I miss him too," I say quietly. I put my hand on top of hers and hold tight for a moment.

"I never told them about him," Indie whispers. "Or Hunter."

"Neither did I," I say.

I stand up. I'm hungry, but there's something else I have to do. "Do you know when you leave tonight?" I ask Indie.

She shakes her head.

"I'll try to come back in time to say good-bye," I tell her.

"Cassia didn't want to leave here without saying good-bye to you," Indie says. "You know that."

I nod.

"She told me to tell you she knows she'll see you again," Indie says. "And that she loves you."

"Thank you," I say to Indie.

I keep waiting for the Society to fly in low and black over the lake but they haven't yet. Though I know it wasn't what Cassia wanted, part of me can't help but be glad that she is out of the thick of the Rising.

To blend in here, it's all right to show urgency and purpose. Others walk to board air ships and pack tents. I don't have to keep my eyes down. I nod to others as we pass.

One thing I can't show, however, is despair. So even as the night comes and I still haven't found what I want, I don't allow any of the worry to show on my face.

And then at last I see someone who looks right.

Cassia doesn't like to sort people. I'm all too good at it and I worry I'll grow to like it too much. It's a talent I share with my father. And all it takes is a misstep or two for that talent to become a liability instead of an asset.

Still, I have to chance it. I want Cassia to have those papers to trade back in the Society. She might need them.

"Hello," I say. The man isn't packed yet—someone who has to stay to the end, but low-ranking enough that he's not in attendance at the late-night meetings with those deciding strategy. Someone who manages to be useful and under the radar and competent but not excellent. It's the perfect position for someone who is—or used to be—an Archivist.

"Hello," he answers, his expression blank and polite, his voice pleasant.

"I'd like to hear the Glorious History of the Rising," I say.

He's quick to hide his surprise, but not quick enough. And he's smart. He knows that I saw. "I'm no longer an Archivist," he says. "I'm with the Rising. I don't trade anymore."

"You do now," I say.

He's not quite strong enough to resist. "What do you have?" he asks, glancing around almost imperceptibly.

"Papers from within the Carving," I tell him. I think I see a gleam in his eyes. "They're near here. I'll tell you how to find them, and then I need you to get them to a girl named Cassia Reyes who was just sent to Central."

"And my fee?"

"You choose," I say. It's the payment no real trader or Archivist can resist. "Any selection you want is yours. But I know what's there and I'll find out if you take more than one. I'll turn you in to the Rising."

"Archivists are honest in trade," he says. "It's part of our code."

"I know," I say. "But you told me you weren't an Archivist anymore."

He smiles then. "It never leaves you."

Meeting with the Archivist made me late, and I don't get to say good-bye to Indie. The air ship she's on begins to pull away in the last of the sun's light and as it does, I see that it's been burned and damaged along the bottom. As though it tried to land somewhere that people didn't want it to be and was fired upon. The decoys' guns couldn't do this.

I think I'm looking at one of the air ships the farmers tried to take down.

"What happened to that ship?" I ask someone standing next to me.

"I don't know," he says. "It went out a few nights ago and came back like that." He shrugs. "You're new, aren't you? You'll learn that you only know your own assignments. It's safer that way if we get caught."

That's true enough. And even if I'm right about how that ship got burned, it could be something other than what I think. Maybe the Rising came down to try to help the farmers, but they thought the ships were Society.

Maybe not.

The only way I can figure out how this works is by living on the inside.

The Archivist finds me a few hours later, just as I'm about to leave. I step away from my group to talk to him for a moment. "It's confirmed," he says. "She's back in Central. I'll effect the trade immediately."

"Good," I say. She's safe. They said they'd take her back and they did. One point for the Rising. "Did you have any trouble?"

"None at all," he says. Then he hands me the stone I carved with scales. "It seemed like a pity to leave this behind, even though I know you can't take it with you," he says. The Rising has similar rules to the Society: No unnecessary possessions. "It's a beautiful piece of work."

"Thank you," I say.

"Not many people know how to make letters like this," he says.

"Letters?' I ask. Then I see what he means. I thought I carved ripples. Or waves. Or scales. But what it really looks like is the letter C, over and over again. I put the rock on the ground to mark another place where we've both been.

"Do you ever teach anyone?" he asks.

"Only once," I say.

CHAPTER 54
CASSIA

It's early spring now, and the ice at the edge of the lake in Central has begun to melt. Sometimes, while I walk to work, I look out over the railing at the air-train stop to see the gray water in the distance and the red branches of bushes along the shore. I like stopping here. Seeing the wind wave the water and brush the branches reminds me that, before I returned to the Society, I crossed over rivers and canyons.

But the view isn't the only reason I pause. The Archivist I deal with sends someone to watch me and to see how long I wait. It's how she knows whether or not I've agreed to the terms for our next trade. If I stop here until the next train comes in—a few more seconds now—it means that I accept. Over the past few months, the Archivists have come to know me as someone who doesn't trade often, but who does have items of value.

I turn from the lake and see the city, its white buildings and masses of dark-clothed people moving through. It reminds me of going into the Carving, and again I remember that time long ago in the Borough when I saw the diagram of my body, those rivers of blood and those strong white bones.

Just before the next train slides in, I start down the steps. The price is too low. I don't accept. Yet.

I didn't know I had this inside of me.

I didn't know all that was inside of him, either. I thought I did, but people run deep and complicated like rivers, hold their shape and are carved upon like stone.

He sent me a message. Such a thing is difficult to do, but he is in the Rising, and he has managed the impossible before. The message tells me where I can meet him. After I've finished work, I will go to see him.

Tonight. I will see him tonight.

A pattern of frost blooms along the cement wall at the bottom of the stairs. It looks, I imagine, as if someone painted stars or flowers at exactly the right time; a momentary capture of beauty that will too soon vanish.

ACKNOWLEDGMENTS

This book would not exist without the kindness and support of:

Scott, my husband, and our three wonderful boys (Cal, E, and True);

my parents, Robert and Arlene Braithwaite; my brother, Nic; my sisters, Elaine and Hope; and my grandmother Alice Todd Braithwaite;

my cousins Caitlin Jolley, Lizzie Jolley, Andrea Hatch, and my aunt Elaine Jolley;

writer and reader friends Ann Dee Ellis, Josie Lee, Lisa Mangum, Rob Wells, Becca Wilhite, Brook Andreoli, Emily Dunford, Jana Hay, Lindsay and Justin Hepworth, Brooke Hoopes, Kayla Nelson, Abby Parcell, Libby Parr, and Heather Smith;

Jodi Reamer and the wonderful team at Writers House— Alec Shane, Cecilia de la Campa, and Chelsey Heller;

Julie Strauss-Gabel and the fantastic group at Dutton/ Penguin—Theresa Evangelista, Anna Jarzab, Liza Kaplan, Rosanne Lauer, Casey McIntyre, Shanta Newlin, Irene Vandervoort, and Don Weisberg;

and all the readers, always.

WILL

CASSIA AND KY

BE *REUNITED?*

Don't miss the incredible
final installment of their story

COMING 2012

NOW IT'S TIME TO HEAR FROM THE AUTHOR OF

MATCHED AND CROSSED

HERSELF, ALLY CONDIE

Q WHERE DID THE IDEA FOR THE MATCHED SERIES COME FROM?
A *Matched* was inspired by several events – specific ones, like a conversation with my husband and chaperoning a high-school prom – and general ones, like falling in love and becoming a parent.

Q HOW LONG DID IT TAKE YOU TO WRITE IT?
A It took me about nine months to write *Matched* and another nine months to write *Crossed*.

Q WHAT IS YOUR WRITING PROCESS?
A I write every day except Sunday. I can't write when my kids are awake – I'm the worst multitasker in the world! – so I usually put in the time during their naps or after they have gone to bed. I write fairly slowly – about 1,000 words a day when I'm drafting, and I write terrible first drafts. Once I've finished a first full draft, I'll go over it literally dozens of times to finesse it and smooth out the plot.

Q WHO IS YOUR FAVORITE CHARACTER IN THE MATCHED SERIES AND WHY?
A My favorite character in the series is Cassia, because she experiences the most growth. I always think that is the most interesting part of the novel to write – the character's evolution.

Q HOW DID YOU COME UP WITH THE NAMES CASSIA, XANDER AND KY?

A I went through several names to get the right name for Cassia. I had some rather specific criteria for the name: I wanted something classical, unusual, and botanical. I also love names that start with 'C'. My sister was the one who drew my attention to the name Cassia, which fits all of these criteria and also just seemed to fit the girl on the page. Xander and Ky were easier. Their names came to mind almost immediately – I wanted names that sounded familiar but also looked a little different and unusual.

Q WHY DID YOU CHOOSE TO WRITE FOR A TEENAGE AUDIENCE?

A I used to teach high school, so when I started writing, I automatically began writing for young adults. I think teenagers are interesting, honest, passionate – I loved working with them and I love writing for them.

Q WHICH BOOKS DID YOU LOVE TO READ WHEN YOU WERE A TEENAGER?

A I read a lot of Agatha Christie, Anne Tyler, and Wallace Stegner. I must have read Tyler's *Saint Maybe* fifteen times in high school. Really, I loved to read anything I could get my hands on!

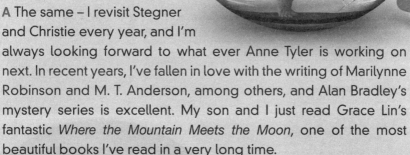

Q WHEN YOU TAKE A
BREAK FROM WRITING
NOW, WHAT DO YOU LIKE
TO READ?
A The same – I revisit Stegner
and Christie every year, and I'm
always looking forward to what ever Anne Tyler is working on
next. In recent years, I've fallen in love with the writing of Marilynne
Robinson and M. T. Anderson, among others, and Alan Bradley's
mystery series is excellent. My son and I just read Grace Lin's
fantastic *Where the Mountain Meets the Moon*, one of the most
beautiful books I've read in a very long time.

Q SPEAKING OF WRITING, WHEN CAN WE LOOK FORWARD TO
MEETING CASSIA AGAIN?
A We're hoping to have the third book out about one year after the
release of the second. So, if all goes well, it won't be too long!

Q LASTLY – HOW DID YOU FEEL WHEN YOU HEARD *MATCHED* WAS
GOING TO BE PUBLISHED, AND HOW DID YOU CELEBRATE?
A To be honest, I cried. Just sat there and cried, and then I called
my husband, who has been incredibly supportive and lovely, and
then we both cried. Later that night, after we got our three little boys
to sleep, we got takeout for dinner from our favorite restaurant.
That's when the hysterical laughter began – the 'Can you believe this
might really be happening?!?' laughter. It was a very fun, very
emotional day.

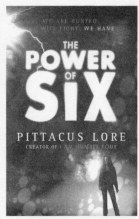
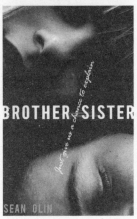

THE SOCIETY CHOOSES EVERYTHING.

THE BOOKS YOU READ.
THE MUSIC YOU LISTEN TO.
THE PERSON YOU LOVE.

Yet for Cassia the rules have changed. Ky has been taken
and she will sacrifice everything to find him.

And when Cassia discovers Ky has escaped to the wild frontiers
beyond the Society there is hope.

But on the edge of society nothing is as it seems . . .

A REBELLION IS RISING.

And a tangled web of lies and double-crosses
could destroy everything.

Critical acclaim for MATCHED:

'Unmissable' – *Marie Claire*
'**** Utterly thrilling' – *Closer*
'Don't miss this gripping page turner' – *She*
'A must read' – *Sun*

www.matched-book.com   U.K. £9.99

WATCHED BY SOCIETY

TRAPPED BY RULES

FREED BY LOVE?

MATCHED

ALLY CONDIE